Hard

Also by Emma Gold

Easy

Emma Gold

Hard

FLAME
Hodder & Stoughton

First published in Great Britain in 2001 by Hodder and Stoughton
This edition published in 2002
A division of Hodder Headline

A Flame paperback

2 4 6 8 10 9 7 5 3 1

A CIP catalogue record for this title is
available from the British Library

ISBN 0 340 76697 2

Typeset by Palimpsest Book Production Limited,
Polmont, Stirlingshire
Printed and bound in Great Britain by
Mackays of Chatham plc, Chatham, Kent

Hodder and Stoughton
A division of Hodder Headline
338 Euston Road
London NW1 3BH

For my darling sister Louise
With all my love to Sarah, Marketa and Ros.
And thank you to Kirsty and Annette

The Primal Curse

The moment when God tells Adam he has to work for a living.

And unto Adam he said, Because thou hast hearkened unto the voice of thy wife, and hast eaten of the tree, of which I commanded thee, saying, Thou shalt not eat of it: cursed is the ground for thy sake; in sorrow shalt thou eat of it all the days of thy life;

Thorns also and thistles shall it bring forth to thee; and thou shalt eat the herb of the field;

In the sweat of thy face shalt thou eat bread, till thou return unto the ground; for out of it wast thou taken; for dust thou art, and unto dust shalt thou return.

Genesis 3:17–19

Part One

The Colleague

I'm a pimp. I send girls out to work while I sit on my arse all day, chatting on the phone. I get part of their earnings and, obviously, the harder they work, the more money I get. But I am not unreasonable. I won't send girls out to clients they don't like (unless I am desperate) and I don't pressurise them too much if they are not feeling well enough to go out on a job (unless I am *really* desperate). I just hate letting the clients down, especially as there are loads of other agencies that are only too happy to send out a temporary secretary at the last minute. That's why I don't like the girls letting *me* down.

Anyway, I shouldn't be calling them girls. As I keep telling Bert, our short-arsed, crusty old book-keeper, they are not girls, they are women. Last week, he even referred to a woman in her late fifties as a girl. 'Look, Bert,' I said, 'I think once a girl has started menstruating, she is entitled to be called a woman.' He looked horrified when I mentioned the word 'menstruating'; even more so when I continued: 'And I think they are certainly entitled to be called women by the time they have *stopped* menstruating.' Bert scurried off, looking forlorn and harassed but not daring to utter his usual 'silly girl' to me in case I mentioned women bleeding again.

I used to be a temp so I know what it's like to have to go out to work. But then again I used to be a lot of things: lawyer, drug dealer, estate agent, candlestick-maker, baker, TV researcher, party organiser, waitress, dental nurse, conference organiser, painter and decorator, shop assistant – to name but a few.

As far as I am concerned, it doesn't really matter what you do. You work for someone else through the best eight hours of your day (daylight), during the best years of your life (most of your adult life), five days a week, forty-eight weeks a year, when you could be lying in bed, lying in the sun, lying in front of the fire, going to the cinema, reading a book, walking in the countryside, making a beautiful meal, hanging out with your friends, spending time with your loved ones, thinking, daydreaming, fishing, sculpting, painting, planting flowers, meditating. Or having sex.

It's a shame that I can't combine sex and money, but prostitution is the only thing from which I have not been able to make any money. I did once ask a guy to pay me for a night in the sack. We'd met each other several times through friends and got on really well. One Saturday night on the town during the Christmas holiday season we got on particularly well and he ended up back at my place. In the morning we lay in bed chatting quite amicably until he told me his plans for the day. 'Yeah,' he said casually, 'today I'm taking this girl I'm really after to an art gallery and then out for lunch.' Having seen from his face that I was not the girl in question (he wasn't smiling or even looking at me – in fact, he was looking for his pants), I started getting dressed. 'That sounds lovely,' I told him. 'By the way, that will be one hundred pounds.' 'What are you talking about?' he said, looking confused. 'Well, you treated me like a prostitute, now you can pay me,' I said. 'I want some money.' He started laughing nervously, refused to pay once he realised I was being serious, and then dashed for the door. He didn't even bother to haggle.

Still, like most people, I have rent to pay, clothes to buy, drugs to smoke and videos to rent. Therefore, I need to work. Now I know that some people enjoy working – they may even look forward to going in to work – but I have never been one of them. The best I can say is that, in the case of my present job, I *don't mind* going to work. There are always other things that I would rather be doing, but as jobs go it's not too bad. As I said, I send secretaries out to temporary assignments and *they* do the work. Meanwhile, I sit on the phone, chatting to the girls (sorry, women) and the clients, who are mostly women too. It is all rather nice.

I also get on well with my co-worker, Tina, who deals with finding permanent work for secretaries. Tina is in her early fifties but looks like she's in her late thirties (if you screw up your eyes), and I'm not sure that I mean that as a compliment. Her hair has been dyed yellow blonde and is pulled straight every morning with the help of a mega-wattage professional hairdryer and a variety of hair products that are applied at every stage of the daily ritual (during washing, after washing, before drying, during drying and after drying). I know about these products as Tina often slips out at lunchtime to invest in a new miracle shampoo/lotion that she swears will change her life. I am not the sort of person who likes to quell excitement so I coo over each new purchase (despite the fact that I believe she is wasting her time and money. Tina could have beautiful, curly, rich brown hair and her life would then be so much easier, but for some weird reason a lot of women seem to want the exact opposite of what they have in the hair department, hence, I suppose, the cruel invention of the perm. My six-year-old niece's greatest wish on her birthday was to have her lovely curly ringlets pulled straight). I have even become quite creative at making fresh and constructive comments on the product's smell, texture, predicted efficacy and informative literature.

Tina's eyebrows have been plucked and redrawn. The eyebrow on the right side has been drawn into an arched line giving her a perpetual 'How about it, you and me?' expression. I think this is deliberate. Her nails are long, tipped, square and painted. I am fascinated by her ability to type at eighty words a minute with these talons. To be honest, I don't know how she even manages to hold a pencil, let alone write anything legible, but she seems to have integrated the nails into her repertoire of daily tasks.

She also manages to totter around quite effortlessly on four-inch heels every day. I've even seen her run for the bus a few times and it is an impressive sight. I know high heels make one look taller, slimmer and more elegant whilst making wondrous transformations to the shape of one's calf, but I personally feel very strongly about high-heeled shoes. They throw your spine out of alignment and fuck up your knees (hence the high proportion of women who require knee replacements as they get older) and, unless you are a real pro, walking any further than from a car to a dinner table is a distinctly uncomfortable activity. At lunchtime I want to be able to nip out, run up to the bank then down to the shops; with heels I can just about make it to the photocopier in the next room.

Tina and I disagree vehemently on the subject of high heels. She thinks I am making a fuss about nothing and claims to find them more comfortable than flat shoes, but I then pointed out that since she has been wearing high heels since she was about four years old – when it was still fashionable to smoke – she doesn't know any better. The way I look at it is that I don't mind wearing make-up (although it is a pain trying to remove mascara every night) and I don't mind doing the emotional housework in relationships (I did mind but I have come to terms with it); I don't mind strapping my tits up every day in a bra and I don't *really* mind doing the washing up at family occasions while my male relatives remain seated. But I do draw the line at footwear that (a) rearranges the alignment of the bones housing my central nervous system, (b) results in plastic knees, and (c) turns the basic human function of walking upright into a crippled limp after only a few feet.

However, high heels do look great on Tina, whose slim but muscley legs are often out on show, one way or another. She still wears very short skirts and I can't make up my mind whether I approve or not. In theory I suppose I do, but on a good day Tina looks like she is trying far too hard and on a bad day, she can look like a man in drag. She separated from her husband eight years ago when she discovered that he had remortgaged their beautiful home in Maida Vale to repay his gambling debts, and divorced him a year later when the said beautiful house was repossessed. Despite still feeling a little bitter about her change in lifestyle (she now lives in a maisonette in Hendon and works for a living instead of shopping and lunching), she is delighted that she is no longer obligated to fake pleasure during love-making with her tubby husband.

During one quiet afternoon at work when the phones actually stopped ringing for a couple of hours, when the boss was out and Bert, the dozy book-keeper, was playing Solitaire again in the back office, she described her husband's sexual technique to me. Apparently, she would be lying in bed and he would emerge from the bathroom looking hopeful. As he walked towards her, a leg would be lifted and cocked to one side and his expression would temporarily change from desire to grimace as he farted. There would be an obligatory sniff of each armpit while kneeling on the bed looking at her, a rough grope of her breasts, and within minutes he would be on top of her, pumping away furiously. This lasted approximately two and a half minutes and she didn't know whether to feel pleased or angry that it was all over so quickly. He would then belch, fart again, roll over, and she would soon be serenaded to bitter insomnia by the sound of him snoring like a bear.

Since the divorce Tina has been busy discovering, for the first time, that sex can be pleasurable. Hence the hair and skirts. She reckons that long blonde hair, short skirts and high heels guarantee a shag every night of the week. No matter how old, how young, how ugly, how beautiful, how fascinating, how thick, how clever. Every night. A shag. Guaranteed. Not that she does, she assures me, although she continually jokes about having carpet burns from being on all fours the night before. She is just making up for lost time. All those years when she was young, beautiful and supple, wasted on a stodgy little gambler whose love-making lasted less time than it takes to make a cup of tea. Having been brought up as a strict Catholic by her Italian parents, sex was not something that was debated at dinner time, or, in fact, at any time. Women were, she tells me, demure virgins until marriage when they became uncomplaining sperm depositories.

Her rebellion started the day her divorce became final when she ended up seducing her solicitor, a mild-mannered, softly spoken young Scottish man with strawberry blond hair, who by all accounts, turned out to be a right animal in the sack. And she hasn't looked back. There is no-one special in her life at the moment. She has two or three regulars who take her out for dinner and take her away for the weekend. Occasionally the names of the men change, depending on who is in or out of favour. Sometimes, she tells me, she yearns for one man to settle down with, but after her husband's gambling exploits she doesn't want to put her life in the hands of another. And then she laughs and tells me that, anyway, she likes variety.

I admire Tina. I know worse things happen to people than losing your home and a luxurious lifestyle, but she doesn't sit there like a victim moaning about it. Yes, she complains about her dishonest dickhead of a husband, but it is in the manner of someone who has moved on rather than someone who is stuck in the past and irreversibly angry. She is so relieved to be independent and in control of her life that she rarely complains about the fact that, say, she rather than Jerome at Daniel Galvin now straightens her hair. What I admire is Tina's resourcefulness. She allowed herself about three months to wail and fall apart on discovering that they were going to have to sell the family home. She then set about rebuilding her life, and from what I can see she is doing a bloody good job. There isn't much spare cash floating around, but she still seems to enjoy herself. Tina doesn't love working either, but she always turns up in a good mood with a ready sense of humour, and is certainly going to try and enjoy herself while making as much money as she can.

Tina is, however, very pious when it comes to her two sons who she clearly adores. Adores. Worships. Spoils. I can't believe all the things she does for them. She still buys them clothes, and whereas she economises on her own wardrobe, she splashes out on designer labels for them. The younger one, Mario, who is twenty-five, still lives at home, and I can't imagine him being in a hurry to move out given the extensive domestic services on offer. He rings each day and tells her what he fancies for dinner in the evening so that she can go out at lunchtime and buy the appropriate ingredients. She makes his bed, does his ironing and tidies his room. She even told me once that she cleans his shoes. Meanwhile, at weekends she takes five cooked meals round to Luca, the older one, so that he can have a home-made meal every night the following week. He's nearly thirty and Mum's still making his dinner.

Tina was devastated when Luca didn't move back home after university. She just couldn't understand it.

'Why would he want to waste money on rent when he can live with me for free and have everything done for him?' she asked me.

'Maybe he wants his independence,' I suggested, privately irritated by the question.

'But he used to come and go as he pleased anyway. He was always out and about doing what the hell he liked for as long as I can remember. The sort of kid who had an active social life at ten!'

'But it's not the same,' I said. 'Say he wanted to bring a woman back for the night?'

That stopped her.

'He's not the sort to have a serious relationship,' she said.

'Precisely why he needs his own pad,' I said. 'For all the one night stands that he doesn't want you to know about.'

'*Dio mio*! You mean he prefers meaningless sex with some cheap tart to living in a warm, happy, clean environment with his family, having his suits dry-cleaned, his shirts ironed, his shoes polished, his sheets washed and pressed every week?' she asked incredulously.

'Looks like you've got a normal son,' I congratulated her, while privately noting the classic sexual hypocrisy: that women who have one night stands are 'cheap tarts'. There's no point in saying anything – you are wasting your time with the over-forties.

Tina says that no-one else will ever do all that she does for Luca and Mario, and I get the feeling that this is intentional. If no-one else will ever do all these things for the boys, she will never lose them. They will always need their good old mama. Meanwhile, I tell her, she has set impossible standards for other women. No wonder that even at the beginning of the twenty-first century some men are still helpless, lazy slobs (I don't know many personally, but I hear about them sometimes). She has no right to complain about men when she is helping to create a new generation whose expectations are that women are there to serve them, I tell her.

She listens but she does not hear. Her boys mean everything to her. She remained with their father through all his gambling highs and lows for the sake of the boys. That, and the Catholic belief system that, if I've understood it right, says it's better to be unhappy with the wrong person for the rest of your days than try to be happy by making a fresh start elsewhere. To give the boys credit, they do ring Tina every day and appear to be as devoted to her as she is to them.

Unfortunately, I've never met the sons, despite my intense curiosity; I have seen photos and they both have that delicious, dark, glossy, Italian look. You see, the thing is that although Tina and I have become close – we talk openly to each other about our hopes, fears, problems and triumphs – we never mix outside work. This is not my rule, by the way. I just follow

Tina's lead. When she leaves the office, she leaves us all behind and she doesn't look back. Actually, it's rather bizarre. I once bumped into her out shopping one weekend and, although she was charming and polite, there was a detached coolness about her that is completely absent at work. It is hard not to be offended, although apparently I should not take it personally. My predecessor, Lisa, told me that she once rang Tina at home to see how she was after she had been off work sick for a few days. Lisa said Tina could not get off the phone quick enough. She immediately thanked Lisa for ringing and said she would see her back at work as soon as she was better. It's as if she compartmentalises her life: her boys (sacred), her sex life (busy), and her work life (100 per cent committed while she's there, switches off when she leaves).

So despite being intrigued about her boys, I have yet to meet them. I'm too shy to chat to them on the phone, especially as Tina is usually sitting opposite me and it would be inappropriate to flirt. I am not holding my breath for an invitation to dinner. It is weird, but as there are so many other things that I appreciate about her, I decide not to torment myself over this. I just accept that these are her boundaries and pride prevents me from pushing myself where I am clearly not wanted.

The Boss

Six months ago we swapped bosses. The previous owner, Mr Fox, was a classic control freak. Over-diligent potty training had left him stuck in the anal stage of development, with a need to control everything around him rather than just his own bowel movements. Everything had to be done the right way, i.e. *his* way. The most annoying thing he could do was interrupt you in the middle of something with the innocent-sounding 'May I make a suggestion?'. Before waiting for a response (which in my case would be '*No*, please don't'), he would quickly take over the task you were completing quite happily and efficiently. In one week alone he taught me how to photocopy an A4 piece of paper ('Make sure you line up the paper in the corners of the glass pane on the machine.' 'Really!' I say), how to staple two pieces of paper together ('The staple should be diagonally placed a half-inch equidistant from the top left-hand corner.' 'Have you got a ruler?' I ask), and how to write the date on phone messages ('Always write the month in full rather than in numbers – people get confused.' 'Yeah, idiots like you,' I think). There was even an instruction in the loo on how to flush the goddam toilet.

I liked him, though. He was fair. Annoying but fair. I knew where I was with him. But his interfering ways and lack of enthusiasm for the business meant that when, eight months ago, he told Tina and I that he was selling the business to our current boss, Wayne, I was delighted. Apart from which, I love change, and Wayne seemed like a good laugh when I chatted to him before he actually bought the business, and that was one thing Mr Fox definitely was not. (If you can't have a laugh at work, then you really might as well pack up and sign/move on.)

Initially, Tina did not embrace the news with the same amount of zeal. She was quiet when Mr Fox left the room after his dramatic announcement that he was selling Search.

'What's up darlin'?' I asked.

'Wayne will probably want to get rid of a golden oldie like me,' she said, suddenly looking lined and tired.

'But Foxy just told us that Wayne will keep us both on,' I reassured her.

'Of course that's what he's going to say in the beginning, but he won't want an old dolly bird on the front desk.'

'Isn't it illegal to get rid of someone because of their age?' I wondered aloud. 'Anyway, I'm sure he won't. You are brilliant at your job,' I lied.

She *was* good at her job, but not brilliant. You know the saying which goes something like 'If you fling enough mud, some of it will stick'? Well, that basically summarises Tina's approach to filling permanent positions: send off loads of both suitable and unsuitable applicants for a job and you never know your luck, one of them might just get the damn job. Sometimes, I am pleasantly surprised. Like the time a local import/export agency in Highgate pointedly specified typing skills of fifty words per minute plus fluency in French, and then took Versha, an inexperienced twenty-year-old with a typing speed of twenty-five words per minute who was fluent in Urdu. 'She's cheap and she's cute so they took her,' Tina explained to me when I expressed disbelief at how dramatically the client had compromised their firmly stated requirements.

At other times I simply cringe at how badly wrong she gets it. Last week, for example, a beautiful, firm-bodied, long, lustrous blonde-haired graduate with accompanying belly button ring, cropped top, platform boots, stunning exam results and a solid sense of self-belief, came to register at Search. This girl was looking for a temp job while also seeking a permanent job in – surprise, surprise – the media. I liked her. She was smart and full of hope and vitality, not yet having been burned by the world of work. Tina was also taken with her and asked for her CV, alluding to some promising jobs that might interest her. I knew for a fact that we didn't have anything remotely glamorous enough for this babe, unless you'd call estate agent junior, charity administrator or legal secretary in the property department of a law firm in Barnet hot and sexy positions. This girl was going straight to the top, or at least wherever the hell she wanted to go. She wasn't going to wilt in suburbia. Not yet, anyway.

The next day I listened in horror as Tina telephoned the girl to tell her about a new job that had just come in – customer services for an IT company in Colindale ('Really exciting young company, great opportunities, lovely dynamic boss, why don't you just go and meet them, seriously, not exactly what you're looking for, I know, but they'd love you, would really suit you . . . Really? Well, if you change your mind, you're missing a great opportunity, etc.').

'Not at all surprised,' I said to Tina when she put the phone down. Quite subtle for me. I could just as easily have said, 'Are you completely clueless? Why the hell would she want to work for some computer twats in Colindale?', but I kept it mild. We do have to work together.

'Robert at Kudos would have loved her,' she said, sighing.

'I'm sure he would have done. And she may have loved him and they may have been very happy together, but I think that is highly unlikely. She's had work experience on *TV-AM* and *TFI Friday* – I really don't think she's going to settle for customer service in the IT industry in Colindale!'

While Tina wasn't brilliant at finding the right person for the right job, she did excel at selling the agency's services to prospective clients. She was fantastic at the canvassing calls. She was Classy, Professional, Sensible Older Woman on the phone to women and Husky, Flirty, I'll Do Whatever I Can To

Please You Woman to men. I reminded her of this to reassure her that Wayne would keep her on.

'Say he does decide to offload me,' Tina said. 'I'm on the scrap heap. I've seen how hard it is to place women of my age. Everybody asks for somebody young. God, it makes me sick.'

I couldn't argue with her over that. On joining the agency, I was totally shocked when I realised how ageist the world of work is. Nearly every employer specifically requests someone young. It really annoys me that youth is valued every time over experience, wisdom and maturity, and I just don't understand it.

'You're such a polished, impressive person, Tina. You'd get in anywhere. They'd just have to meet you and I'm sure you'd win them over,' I said.

This time I meant it. Tina is a powerful, competent woman and everyone loves self-sufficient people.

'And you look fabulous. At least ten years younger than you are,' I added. 'Anyway, it's not going to happen. You are Search. Wayne will want continuity. All the clients know and love you.'

And that was true, too. She'd been with the agency for seven years. Mr Fox was so taken with her when she registered for a permanent job a year after her divorce that he recruited her for the permanent side immediately.

'I've still got a mortgage to pay every month. I can't afford to lose this job.'

So, after twenty-five years in the recruitment game, Mr Fox finally decided that he'd had enough. Well, he actually decided he'd had enough about five years ago but it took him that long to (a) come to terms with the fact that he'd had enough, and (b) find someone prepared to pay him more than a thousand pounds for the business. Mr Fox's ennui with Search shows in the décor of our office, which hasn't been touched since it was painted grey and pink in the early Eighties. Whichever interior designer dreamed up the combo should be sent back to prison, which is presumably where they came up with the sick and miserable idea of choosing the colour grey. Try and get your head round the fact that the walls of the office where I spend at least eight hours of my day are prison grey and the paintwork is pastel pink. Although I'm well over my feng shui phase (an entreaty to the Angel of Love in the relationships corner of my flat hasn't produced anything juicy so far and anyway, spirituality is *so* end of last century), I do think that the colour of a room does impact on your frame of mind. Surely a grey office doesn't inspire one to great heights of personal achievement. I mentioned this to Mr Fox several times and while he did admit that it looked dreary, his loss of interest in the business prevented him from actually doing anything about it.

The furniture was probably secondhand when Mr Fox got hold of it twenty-five years ago and was therefore battered as well as dated. Shelves with files containing client details, job sheets and applicant details surrounded three out of the four walls in the front office where Tina and I worked. When I first arrived at Search, a whole shelf stretching across the wall behind my desk contained a row of files marked 'Dead Ladies A–F, G–L . . .' etc. These files contained details of all those ladies who had worked for us in the past but who were now no longer on the books. By the end of my first week I had renamed all the files on the basis that it looked as though we had an unfeasibly high mortality rate among our temps.

Despite the rather glum décor, the office nonetheless has a faded, relaxed charm and we often have trouble getting rid of applicants who seem quite happy to sit with Tina and me, drinking tea and chatting about life. Perhaps this is because the agency is so unimposing, and people usually associate job-hunting with formality and stress rather than having a laugh in the shabby but clean surroundings of a first floor flat in a Victorian house.

There are three other rooms in the agency's offices: Wayne's office, the accounts room at the back, and a room where everything from the fax and photocopier to the fridge and kettle is kept. Wayne's room is next to ours and despite constant colour consultations, it is still in its grey period. Nearly six months after buying the business his 'Good Luck' cards are still up on the filing cabinet. At the end of Wayne's first day at Search, after he'd roared off in the little red sports car, Tina and I crept into his room to investigate. Not much had changed apart from the presence of what I believed to be an Aboriginal dream-catcher wind chime dangling from the window. However, even more disconcerting than the flaky implications of this were the messages in the cards on the filing cabinet. The first one I picked up was ostensibly innocuous but open to interpretation by the cynical: 'Wayne, Hope your new business is a great success, Love Auntie Carol'.

'Your new business,' I said to Tina, passing the card to her. 'What happened to the last one?'

'I don't know,' she said, handing me another card, 'but read this.'

I opened the card. 'Wayne, Congratulations on your new business, Hope it works out this time, Love Mum & Dad'. All six cards contained a similar theme, hinting at previous failures and wishing him success in what was clearly seen as yet another of his hare-brained schemes. Tina and I were mildly concerned at the omens we had seen, not least the wind chimes, but knew that we could run the business with or without him.

Having worked with Wayne for six months now, I believe he bought a secretarial agency because he thought that as he was getting a divorce, it would be a good opportunity to surround himself with women, although I don't know if *he* realises that that was the reason he bought Search. Could anyone be that scheming? All I know is that he is a dreadful flirt and can't help himself when it comes to women (actually, make that girls). Within five minutes of a member of the female sex coming into the agency, he will suddenly appear in the front office to check a file, or to make a cup of coffee or to fiddle with one of the computers. Having given the aforementioned female a surreptitious once-over and decided that she falls within the correct age limit (i.e. the younger the better), he will invite her into his office for a 'psychometric personality test'. Of course, everyone loves an opportunity to talk about themselves in depth, so the girl is only too happy to trot into Wayne's office for a chat about who they really are and what they really want. They emerge an hour, sometimes two, later, looking flushed at all the undivided and flattering attention they have received. Invariably, they are clutching pieces of paper containing three key statements, known as positive affirmations, such as I AM WONDERFUL, I DESERVE A SATISFYING NEW JOB and I NOW FANCY UGLY LECHEROUS MEN.

In my opinion, Wayne has a tiny cock. All the signs are there: the penis-mobile (a passé red sports car with a long bonnet and the number plate W4YNE 69), the failed marriage (who wants to be lumbered with a small cock for the rest of their lives?), the thin, short fingers, the small, shell-like ears and the constant flirting. Tina agrees, while also wondering whether he may suffer from premature ejaculation. Apparently, he fits the personality profile of a classic prem-ejac man (I bet the psychometric test doesn't reveal that), namely immaturity and an inability to concentrate on any one thing for more than five minutes (apart from attractive, young women). We don't discuss his sexual attributes very often, however, and especially not at lunchtime. He's our boss and we find him sexually repugnant.

Tina is safe from his attention. As I've said, he's the kind of guy that attaches a sell-by date to women. I'm not as safe, despite the fact that I am over twenty-five years of age, the reason being that, although I am thirty-two, I have been told that I can pass for early-twenties. It's probably because I'm not married. Have you noticed that unattached women always look five years younger than the attached ones? So I do get some unwanted attention from Wayne. But nothing I can't handle. Sometimes I tell myself that he is just a physically demonstrative person: when his dad came to visit him in the office soon after he bought the business, I noticed that they kissed each other on the cheek. Other times, I just know that it is an excuse to squeeze against me. He's basically harmless, and if the worst of it is having to suffer the odd hug and kiss on the cheek in return for a quiet and happy work life, I am, if not happy, then willing to play the game. Isn't work one big pay-off? Isn't it a careful compromise between what you are willing to endure and how much you are paid?

The rules are fairly simple. Don't mention the word 'hard'. As in 'hard disk', 'hard drive', 'hard work', 'hard luck' – you get the drift – as Wayne starts giggling and making pathetic innuendoes. He'll reinterpret hard to mean erect, and it can be difficult to remain po-faced when the desire to tell your boss to grow up and get a life is combined with an assertive, no bullshit personality. Somehow, so far, I have managed not to say anything too offensive. Having Tina sitting there pulling faces behind his back helps.

Does Wayne sound awful? Because the thing is, apart from the above, he really is a wonderful boss.

'Wayne, I'm moving house tomorrow. Can I book a day off?'

'Sure, no problem.'

'Wayne, it is so dead here this afternoon. No-one's coming in and the phones haven't rung all day.'

'Let's close early. You've all worked hard this week.'

He often buys us lunch or brings us treats in the afternoon. He is very encouraging of our successes and commiserates when we (very occasionally) lose clients, rather than having a go at us. OK, so we have to put up with him calling a

floppy disk a 'stiffy', but in general, he lets us get on with
our work.

Actually, part of the reason why he leaves us alone is that,
like a lot of little boys with new toys, he is already bored with
the business. For the first few months, he rushed into the office
each morning, enthusiastically gabbling on about his ideas for
the new Search. He was going to completely redecorate the
office. In fact, he was going to feng shui the office. There
was talk of plants, fish tanks, crystals and chimes. He was
going to chuck out all the old 1970s furniture and replace
it with cherry wood desks and sofas. There was going to
be a chill-out waiting area for applicants, with motivational
literature on the coffee table. The spare office with the fridge
and kettle was going to be turned into a proper little kitchen,
with microwave and coffee machine. The whole recruitment
procedure was going to be computerised. Out with the little
pink index cards and dirty plastic containers and in with
a state-of-the-art, custom-made computer system containing
details of all the women on the books, including their bra size.
He told us of the new telephone system he was going to install
whereby when a client rang, before we had even picked up
the phone all their details would appear magically on a screen
before us. There would be self-esteem courses in the evening,
free computer training and hospitality events for clients. Oh,
the wonderful things we discussed! Such excitement! There
were plans for branches to be opened all over North London
– we were going to take over the world, or at least corner the
market in secretarial recruitment.

Six months down the line, despite incessant visits from
sales people from telecommunication, feng shui and computer
companies, precisely nothing has changed. Well, maybe that's
not fair. We do have two new posters in the front office:
one with two polar bears and the words 'The Customer
Always Comes First' and another with a penguin and the
profound message 'Believe In Yourself. And we have a new

printer in the front office. Only it doesn't work. Wayne, who fancies himself as a computer wizard, changed the old printer (which worked perfectly well) to a new colour printer which prints 100 pages a minute, has exciting graphic facilities and a mammoth memory, but which prints only half of the letter you have sent to print. I think it was a 'fell off the back of a lorry unmissable bargain' that should have been missed. These are the only 'improvements' that have been implemented thus far.

Wayne has moved on from the recruitment business. He now has a new toy. He is deeply immersed in a network marketing cult. It used to be called pyramid selling until pyramid selling was exposed as a particularly clever way of getting lots and lots of invariably thick people to work very hard, earning next to nothing themselves while amassing a large personal fortune for the people at the very top of the pyramid. Pyramid selling was also very effective at ensuring that the worker ants in the remaining rows of the pyramid fell out with all their friends, family and casual acquaintances due to their rhinoceros-skin insistence that you (a) buy one of their alarms, water filters, magic dishcloths, jewellery, etc, (b) come to a sales meeting at the Luton Hilton on Sunday, and (c) promise to harass *everyone* you know or with whom you come into contact to do the same.

So now it's called network marketing and nothing has changed. The company to which Wayne has affiliated himself sells vitamin supplements – all the vitamins you need in a day in tablet form. I am sceptical of anything that allows you to eat crap all day as long as you swallow a couple of pills in the afternoon. Apart from which, haven't they proved that your body can't absorb these vitamins, most of which are expelled when you shit?

The word that I would use to describe Wayne's attitude to the wonder product, however, is evangelical. He comes in to the office the morning after a sales meeting at the Elstree

Moathouse eyes glazed over and ranting about the number of desperate saddos that have signed up. He actually says things like 'It's a chance of a lifetime. I will never have another opportunity like this.' I look at him in wonderment, lost for words. Obviously, it would be pointless and counterproductive, perhaps even dangerous, to take the piss out of him or the organisation. Instead, I enquire sweetly, 'But Wayne, how do you know what the rest of your life holds? How do you know something better might not turn up?' He looks at me pityingly. After all, I am missing out on the chance of a lifetime. He thrusts a folder at me which contains fifty or so receipts for vitamins. At first sight it all looks terribly impressive – until you look at the receipts more closely and see that they are all for piffling amounts. And this is what he spends ten hours a day, seven days a week, devoting himself to. I give it another couple of months.

I know pervy bosses aren't always ugly but Wayne, I am afraid to say, is rather repulsive to look at. I met him before Tina, who was on annual leave when he first came to the office to enter into discussions with Mr Fox. Wayne and I chatted while he sat waiting for Foxy in reception, sussing each other out.

When Tina returned to work she demanded to know everything about the new man in our lives. As Wayne was rumoured to be on the verge of divorce, she was keen to pump me for information. 'How old would you say he was?' she asked.

'Early forties I'd guess.'

'And when is he taking over?'

'In three weeks' time. Old Foxy and him are still ironing out the details of the deal. Last time I heard, they were bickering over whether the contract for the water cooler was included in the purchase price.'

'Oh well, if they're talking about minor things like that, the deal must be near to completion, although that wanker Fox argues about everything. God, I am *so* pleased that arsehole is leaving. This new guy has to be better. What does he look like? Fuckability status report required please.'

'Unless you are turned on by men that disgust you, I don't think you'll be interested,' I informed her.

'Is he really that bad? Are you sure you're not being fussy again?'

You see, Tina thinks that the reason I am single is that I am too fussy, and having seen photos of some of her conquests, I think she may have a point. I don't necessarily go for looks but I do draw the line at grotesque.

'I bet he's quite nice really,' she went on. 'Are you sure you're not trying to put me off 'cause you are secretly interested?'

'Look, if I give you a full description you can make up your own mind,' I offered.

'Go from head to foot,' Tina demanded.

'Well, he's going bald,' I started, strictly following her instructions.

'Bald is good,' she said. 'The balder the better. Bald means plenty of testosterone which means lots of energy in the sack which should mean passion and satisfaction.'

'Yes – *should*, I will give you that,' I said, 'but he's one of those bald guys who over-compensates with the rest of the hairdo. It's all long and curly at the back, possibly even styled with a hairdryer and round bristle brush. He doesn't actually comb the long bits over the bald bit, but it is definitely over-fussy at the back and sides.'

'I'll take your word for it. What about the face?' She was in a bad mood now.

'His face is a bit crusty, a bit flaky, like he's got some sort of skin condition.'

'Lord forgive you! Listen, it could be stress,' Tina commented. 'Mr Fox told me that the divorce is very acrimonious.'

'Yeah, well. I'm not saying it's his fault that he's got dandruff on his face, but you did ask. He wears glasses, by the way.

Tinted ones with gold-plated rims. Not very cool. What else? Oh yes, he's got a double chin. Body-wise, we're talking short legs, extended belly and no arse,' I added truthfully. 'What do you reckon? Am I being too fussy again?'

'Well, I suppose it's a good thing,' she sighed. 'Work and sex don't mix, or as my husband used to say, you don't shit where you eat. It all ends in tears and then you have to face the person every day of the week or leave your job. I just thought it might be nice to have an object of fantasy at work to juice me up for the evening.'

'We've got Bert,' I joked. 'Piss off,' said Tina.

Bert, the book-keeper, is only sixty but looks and acts like a very old man. He's also bald, and it seems that all the hair that was previously on his head has been forced to resprout elsewhere. His eyebrows are so long they look like a reverse fringe. His ears are throughly coated as are his hands – you can just about make out the fingernails. He is also racist, sexist and inversely ageist (he hates the young), and if he calls me a 'silly little girl' once more I'll tell Wayne that he spends most of the day playing computer games. Wages never get paid on time, account queries are never responded to, new bank details are given and lost, and different charging rates are painfully negotiated with clients only for Bert to forget and invoice the old, lower rates. In fact, I think he is the most incompetent person I have ever come across in a work environment. And like most thoroughly incompetent people, they fool themselves that it is everyone else who is at fault. Occasionally, when someone else does make a mistake, he comes into the front office to sniff out the error and then bangs on about it for weeks. He really is infuriating. He also smells unpleasant. Should you wander blindfold into the accounts office, you would swear you were in a dog kennel. Wearing three layers of clothing (vest, shirt and cardigan) in all weathers probably doesn't help the situation, although a Dettol bath and a wire brush might.

So that's us, the team: Tina, Wayne, Bert and myself. All working for the Search employment agency for secretarial staff, based on the first floor of a Victorian house in West Hampstead. We pride ourselves on being a small but exclusive agency.

Oh, I haven't introduced myself. My name is Emma, I'm thirty-two and the heroine of this story.

The Job

I really quite like my job – as jobs go. It is sociable, chatting to people all day. We get lots of people dropping in, looking for work, and no-one stays long enough to really irritate me. The bitching potential of different people coming into the office every day is phenomenal. We can't help it, Tina and myself. Tina, the lapsed Catholic, always prefaces her bitching with the words 'Lord forgive me . . .'. As in 'Lord forgive me, but that girl was seriously thick.' Or 'Lord forgive me, but that woman was so boring.' Or 'Lord forgive me, but that woman smelt like dog shit.'

I don't ask the Lord for his forgiveness as I see bitching as my God-given right. Especially when it comes to women who are, as Tina puts it, 'full of themselves'. Our pet hate is women who think they are the absolute dog's bollocks. Not that there is anything wrong with that in itself; it is just that the women who rate themselves are invariably the least entitled to do so. When these women come to register at Search, one is, at first, impressed by their self-assurance when they start telling you about their vast experience and phenomenal talents. Then, while they are doing a typing test, you look through the results of the spelling and grammar tests. You note with alarm that in the multiple choice section they have ticked the 'sheeps' option as the correct answer to the plural of 'sheep'. You work out that their score in each of the tests is about 25 per cent, whereas the average score is around 75 per cent. They bash the keyboard to bits during the typing test and then ask to do the test again, blaming the keyboard for being slow. The result tends to reveal a below average typing speed but is accompanied by bleats that they are usually much, much faster. 'Please come and sit over here,' I say, pointing to a chair by my desk, 'and let me know what kind of work you are looking for,' ready to suggest an administrative role. A filing clerk, perhaps. But before I have time to suggest anything, they are off. 'Well, I'd like a senior PA role. Something really meaty that will stimulate me. Salary wise, something in the region of thirty thousand. Perhaps with a car.'

As well as their skills being in inverse proportion to their belief in themselves, they also seem to share another characteristic. They are very fussy. 'Well, I won't go into town. And I will not get the tube under any circumstances. I'll only go to a place where I can drive and park. And I need to leave early on Mondays as I have a regular chiropody appointment. I won't work with accountants – too boring. Or estate agents – too hectic. Please don't send me to any lawyers either – they tend to be very fussy about accuracy. I like big offices with lots going on. I won't work for a small company, I had a bad experience working in a small office. Perhaps working in television or film. And I won't do any audio typing – I don't like the feel of those earpieces in my ears.'

'Any other requirements?' I enquire sweetly, knowing that the only place I will be sending her is home. Tina glances at me from behind their back, right eyebrow arched.

'No, that's it. I'm really very open to your suggestions,' and before I can stop her she has launched into a long, boring story about how under-appreciated she was in her last job as (unsurprisingly) nobody seemed to recognise her formidable talents.

We're nice about people, too. For every big-headed moron that comes into the office, we get down-to-earth, competent, capable women who just happened to be born a generation too early. They are legal secretaries instead of lawyers and medical secretaries instead of doctors. Sometimes I feel sad about this. It must be very frustrating to take the subservient role when, deep down, you know that you could do the boss's job better than them.

We get plenty of women looking for temporary work who normally do other things. Actresses, stunt women, students, musicians, singers. We also get the 'in-between jobbers' – it's hard to tell who has been sacked, who has been made redundant and who has resigned. Very few people tell the truth about why they leave their jobs, me included. I don't really care why people leave their jobs; if I like someone and think they are bright and competent, I will send them out to a client. And I don't get it wrong very often.

Monday

Work, paradoxically enough, is a comfort. One wakes up wanting to cut one's throat; one goes to work and in fifteen minutes one wants to cut someone else's – complete cure!
                                                    Philip Larkin

The reason I am so enthusiastic about my job at the moment is that the rest of my life is so boring. Work distracts me from the fact that I fear that my life is going nowhere. I wake up in the morning wondering what the hell it's all about. I traipse around the flat, making tea, finding something to wear, eating a bowl of cereal, putting on my make-up. Depending on what time I get up, whether we have any milk in the flat and, more importantly, whether I have any clean, matching clothes, I am out of the flat within anything from fifteen to forty-five minutes of waking up. As I either scurry or meander (depending on the above) down West End Lane to the office in West Hampstead, I am already beginning to forget that I am restless, dissatisfied, single and ageing.

Today I am feeling particularly morbid after another week-end of inactivity. My flatmate, Simon, once said to me that the difference between me and him was that when we went out for the evening, he was just looking for a good night out while I was looking for a new experience to change my life. Well, I'd just had another Saturday night which had not changed my life. It was a pleasant enough evening, meeting up with a couple of girlfriends and going to a party where I didn't fancy anyone, then back to Claudia's for a spliff or five and a half-hearted laugh. To be honest, sometimes I think the best part of an evening is getting dressed up to go out. Listening to music, making yourself look the best you've looked all week and all that hopeful anticipation that something really rather wonderful will happen to brighten up your existence. I spent Sunday lounging around reading the papers, chatting on the phone, then went to the cinema in the evening. That may sound like a good weekend to some people, but after eight months of similar uneventful weekends, I am bored to tears. I need some excitement. I need some romance. I need some sex.

At least I feel reasonably rested and ready for work. I arrive at ten minutes to nine to the usual array of excuses on the answer phone from the temps letting us down. Sandra is supposed to be going to Greenberg & Co., the accountants down the road. Instead, she's left a message saying that she has found a better paid temporary job from another agency and she hopes I understand. I curse her with venom. She let me down last week and I am annoyed with myself for trusting her again. At least she gave me a few days' notice last time.

There's also a message from Cynthia saying that she can't go to the estate agents in Hampstead until tomorrow as her daughter is unwell and she needs to take her to the doctor. Which is fine, *if* she is telling the truth, which I have a nasty feeling she isn't. Either that or her daughter is extremely sickly as I've heard this one from Cynthia many times before, and one thing this job does to you is make you cynical about work excuses. So I curse Cynthia with venom, too. And then I curse her daughter.

Lara is supposed to be on reception at the doctor's surgery in Cricklewood, but I can hear her on the phone to Tina explaining that she has been offered a permanent job and won't be able to make the booking after all. Tina is polite and charming on the phone.

'Congratulations, Lara. That's wonderful,' she enthuses. 'Don't you worry. We'll find someone else for the surgery. We wish you all the best in your new job.'

As she puts the phone down, she says to me, 'Stupid cow.' I agree with her. She could have told them that she was committed elsewhere this week. Now I am totally screwed. How can she let me down like this at the last minute? Especially as we've really helped her out in the past. Ungrateful minx. 'Shit, Tina. I don't have anyone else on the books with medical experience.'

'What about Roberta?' Tina suggests. 'Didn't she work in a hospital once?'

'Yes, about five years ago for a two-week booking. Well, I could give her a try. She always asks for loads of money, but I suppose I am desperate.' I ring Roberta and get the answer phone. I leave a pleading message for her to call as soon as poss. I ring five other women. I catch two on their mobiles. They have taken jobs from other agencies. One is on her way to work, the other is already there. Another woman starts haggling with me over rates of pay and demands more than the client is paying us. I try to flatter her by telling her that we can't afford her but won't she do it anyway? She starts whining so I tell her to forget it – we are not in business simply to fund her lifestyle. Another of the women is not prepared to travel to Cricklewood and I don't blame her: she lives in Islington and doesn't have a car. I don't even bother to beg.

Finally, I get hold of Tanya who agrees to go. I feel a bit nervous about sending Tanya as clients always tell me that she spends hours on the phone making personal calls. How do I tell her this without pissing her off and losing her co-operation? She is notoriously touchy and can get stroppy very quickly if she senses any hint of criticism. I decide to turn it round. 'Listen Tanya,' I say, confidingly. 'They are really hot on personal calls at the surgery. They were really pissed off with the last person we sent as she made a couple of calls.'

Tanya acts outraged. 'Oh, no. I would *never* do that. I always use my mobile at lunchtime.'

'Of course you do. That's really professional of you. Thank you. Anyway, I just thought I would warn you.' *Cool.* Next problem is that it takes Tanya about two hours to get ready.

'Can you get there as soon as possible?' I plead.

'I'll try my best, Emma. But I've just got up and I haven't

33

had my bath yet. I need at least an hour to get ready.'
Shit.

'Well, can you make a real effort to speed it up this morning.'
This is a mistake. She's touchy, remember.

'Emma, you have just called me. I called you for work on
Friday and you told me there wasn't anything. Now you ring
me up first thing Monday morning and I am prepared to go
to Cricklewood, but please don't pressurise me. If you need
someone there any sooner you had better call someone else.
I like to make an effort with my appearance. This takes some
time. You don't want me turning up looking a mess do you?'
Fuck off.

'No, of course not. Look, I'll ring the client now and tell
them that you will be with them in about an hour, OK?'

Tanya softens. 'I'll do my best. By the way, thanks for the
booking.' I quickly ring the client to let them know that the
wonderful Lara who I raved about last week is not going to
help them out this week, after all. Instead, I tell them, Tanya
is coming. 'Does she have GP surgery experience?' *Shit. I forgot
to check.* 'I think so. She's temped for us for years and she's a
very experienced receptionist.' At least that bit is true. 'She'll
be with you in an hour maximum,' I add hopefully.

I'm in the middle of describing Tanya's superb message-
taking skills when another call comes in for me. Tina is
mouthing that Jackie, is on the phone. Jackie was due at
a law firm in Kilburn half an hour ago. I gather from the
half of the conversation that I can hear that Jackie is on
her mobile and can't find anywhere to park. I finish the
call to the doctor's surgery in Cricklewood and speak to
Jackie.

'What's the problem?' I ask her, trying to keep the annoyance out of my voice.

'I've been driving around the back streets of Kilburn for half
an hour and I can't find anywhere to park. I am getting really
pissed off. If I can't find anywhere in the next five minutes, I

am going home. You didn't tell me it was this difficult to park around here,' she says accusingly.

'It's not. You just have to be prepared for a ten-minute walk once you've parked.'

'Ten minutes!' Jackie says scornfully. 'I can't park for miles.' *Oh, fuck off.*

'You poor thing. Keep trying,' I urge her, my attempt at sympathy sounding rather weak.

Yet another call comes through for me. It's Mr Greenberg from the accountants down the road, asking where his temp is. *Shit, fuck, bugger.* 'I was just about to call you, Mr Greenberg.' I decide to come clean and tell him the truth. 'Sandra has let us down. I am really sorry. Give me half an hour and I'll find you someone really good.'

He sounds harassed. 'We are pretty desperate here. Emma, please get back to me as soon as you can.'

Mr Greenberg's call reminds me that I haven't rung the estate agents to let them know that Cynthia won't be with them until tomorrow. I am friendly with the woman who orders the temps and she is understanding. Despite the fact that I have other pressing calls to make, I decide it would be politic to have a quick schmoozy chat with the client to compensate for the fact that she will be doing two people's jobs for the day due to Cynthia not being there. I am just praying that Cynthia will turn up tomorrow. I need to call her to elicit a cast-iron guarantee that she will be there.

While I'm on the phone to the estate agents, Roberta calls back. I mouth to Tina to keep her on hold for a minute. I rush off the phone and take the call from Roberta.

'Hi, Roberta, how are you? Can you work this week?' Turns out she is free and is prepared to go to the accountants. Only problem is that she is not experienced at using Excel, which Mr Greenberg uses occasionally. I ring Mr Greenberg to find out how much of the work is going to be done on Excel.

'Most of it,' he says. 'When is the temp coming?' he wants to know.

'Soon. I'll call you back.' I ring Roberta and tell her to come into our office for some quick training on Excel before going to the client.

'Oh, no,' she says, 'I wouldn't feel comfortable. I am not a quick learner. I can't pick things up that easily.' *You pathetic cow, help me out!*

'OK,' I say, reluctantly, 'I understand. I'll find someone else.'

Apparently, while I've been on the phone to Roberta, Tina has taken a call from Jackie, who has had enough of looking for somewhere to park and has gone home. I ring Roberta back. 'Can you get to Kilburn? Have you worked for lawyers before?' Once I have assured here there is no Excel and we have haggled over rates and I have agreed to pay her far more than I would normally pay a legal temp, she is practically out of the door and on her way to Kilburn. I ring the lawyers and give them the bad and good news (no Jackie, but excellent Roberta on her way). I start chatting with Tara, the woman on reception at the lawyers with whom I normally have a laugh. After ten minutes of swapping news, I suddenly remember that Mr Greenberg is still waiting for a temp. Tara is in the middle of a long, rambling story about a barbecue party she attended at the weekend. I try and wind the call up. Tara takes no notice and is beginning to describe the plot of the video she watched on Saturday night. Tina can see I am struggling and rings in on the other line. Tara can hear the phone ringing and I now have the perfect excuse to go without pissing her off.

I search through the index cards on my desk of all the women looking for work. Suddenly, a miracle. Nicola, one of our best temps who had gone AWOL for a couple of weeks, rings. 'Is there any work?'

I am practically crying by now. 'You use Excel, don't you?'

'Sure.'

Details given: client's address and telephone number, directions, work type, client's funny habits, etc. We are cool. I ring Mr Greenberg who is grateful that I have found someone so quickly.

I put down the phone and look at my watch. It is half past nine.

The Book-keeper

Tina brings me a cup of tea and a Danish.

'How was your weekend?' she asks, soothingly. We haven't even had a chance to say hello.

'Uninspring. And yours?'

'Very nice, actually. Roger took me to see *Chicago* which was fabulous. Then he took me home and we made mad, passionate love for about three hours. Which ain't bad for a forty-six year old man.'

I am impressed.

'How are the boys?' I always like to hear about Luca and Mario, particularly Luca, who sounds like a dude.

'The boys are fine. Luca said he felt like a Chinese, so instead of Sunday lunch, I made aromatic crispy duck with the pancakes and plum sauce. It took hours to prepare that and the chicken cashew dish. I also made some satay, which I know they love. I spent most of Saturday shopping for the ingredients and then I got up early Sunday morning to make everything. It was worth it, even though I felt bloody exhausted for the rest of the day. Anyway, they both loved it. Luca doesn't like Roger, though. He thinks he's slimy. He's nice to him for my sake but I can tell that Roger irritates him. I can't exactly tell Luca that part of the reason I like Roger so much is that he can fuck all night long. The boys prefer Donald, who they think is more genuine. Donald is OK, but he doesn't have any money and I'm not bailing anyone out any more. By the way, remind me that I need to take Luca's watch to the jewellers at lunchtime. It needs a new battery.'

I look at her like she's mad. Why does she do everything

for these boys? Why can't Luca get his own battery? At the same time, something in me envies them this kind of maternal devotion and care.

Despite my disdain for Luca's dependence on his mother, I do daydream about meeting this man. Is it because you rarely hear so much about someone, while knowing that you will never meet them? Or because the photos I have seen of him show that he is just my type? Or is it his sense of humour, reported vicariously by Tina? Normally when people repeat funny remarks that their loved ones make, I find I have to force a smile and fake a few laughs. Either way, I am intrigued. Luca sounds genuinely amusing and good-natured. From what I can gather, he takes the piss out of everyone and has the nerve to do so to their faces. Tina tells me that when Luca rings up and Wayne answers, he enjoys asking him if he has any more plans for the business. This morning, I can hear Wayne telling him about his radical website plans. Tina and I make faces to each other. We've heard all about the website that Wayne has been designing for the past six months.

Bert turns up late, cursing useless women drivers.

'God, you even blame women for the fact that you over-sleep! By the way, Mr Greenberg wants you to ring him to discuss invoice queries and can you send Sandra her P45 please.'

'Slow down,' he whines. 'You'll need to write all this down.' And he trundles off to the accounts office at the back to make a smell and play Solitaire.

Tina gets up to go to the kitchen to make Bert a cup of coffee.

'Why do you always make his coffee?' I ask her. 'We all make coffee for each other except him. He only makes it for himself, and he doesn't have to do that very often as you make it for him.'

'I don't mind,' she says, filling the kettle with water.

I don't push it. Tina and I will never agree over women's

roles in relation to men. She thinks I am an uncompromising militant feminist. I think I am an enlightened modern woman who understands the importance of making a stand, however small. I think she is a slave to men. She thinks she is a warm, kind-hearted generous person who likes making people happy. To be fair to her, she does make me tea, too, but then I make drinks for her and Bert does not. She claims to feel sorry for Bert who she reckons is badly browbeaten at home. Bert's wife makes his lunch for him and the sad, soggy sandwiches do not look like they are made with love. He is given the same thing every day – a cheese sandwich and an orange. Apparently, he told Tina that he's not allowed biscuits and sweets, and as he has to account for even the loose change in his pocket, he daren't go out and buy any, either. It all sounds rather grim and may explain why (a) he hates women, and (b) he hangs round whenever a box of chocolates appears in the office, scrounging as many as he can before I put my foot down and tell him that he is being greedy.

The rest of the day proceeds relatively smoothly. A couple of intelligent, good-humoured women come into the office. No prima donnas, thank God. A couple of cranky but gorgeous old guys call in with freelance typing work. A rather delicate and elegant lady who must be in her seventies comes in fuming. She has just had an argument with an ex-boyfriend from many years ago with whom she has recently become reacquainted. She tells me that she is so angry she can't write legibly and will I type a letter for her if she dictates it to me? Every sentence is interrupted with a shake of the head and the mutter, 'He hasn't changed at all.' The letter express her disappointment and dismay that, even after *sixty* years, he is still selfish, thoughtless, unreliable and, it seems, only after one thing. We don't make much money from these odd little typing jobs, but I like the involvement with people's lives. And I like being helpful and polite and a nice young lady. It's the brainwashing.

We also provide a CV service. Having had so many jobs myself, I have become an expert at lying through my teeth when applying for new jobs. I can produce highly 'creative' curriculum vitae and as I have enormous sympathy for fellow misfits in the world of employment, I like to share this gift with others. With some delicate probing into candidates' achievements, I can convincingly convert the junior level into the managerial, if required, and if appropriate. I can also make long spells on the dole miraculously disappear.

People come into the agency expecting me to type up their scruffy hand-written and pathetically inadequate CV. Instead, they leave an hour later, fifty quid poorer, but with a knock-your-socks-off resumé, substantially increased confidence and a whole new outlook on their chosen career. We start chrono-logically and quickly skip over anything which makes the job-seeker feel ever so slightly uncomfortable. Poor exam results? Put in the exams, leave out the results! Too many jobs in too short a space of time? Skip a few! Merge some! Got the sack? The company dissolved! No use asking anyone for a reference – Pratt & Co. no longer exist. Worked somewhere wonderful for six weeks? Whoops! We typed six months by mistake.

My favourite bit is the personal profile at the beginning of the CV. After spending an hour in someone's company, I can usually find at least five positive characteristics, even if I don't particularly like them (although preparing a CV with someone is usually a bonding experience; all those revealed vulnerabilities can make anyone seem adorable). If they've had twenty jobs, they are 'flexible' rather than unreliable. If they have stayed in the same job for ten years, they are 'loyal' rather than timid. If they are slow and stolid, they are 'reliable, punctual and have great attention to detail'. If they are unstable and weird, they are 'creative and work well on their own initiative'. You get the picture.

Do I sound unscrupulous? Because I do have two fundamen-tal rules. Rule number one: I don't actually make anything up.

I may bend the truth a little, I may omit, I may exaggerate, but there are no outright lies. Rule number two: I am not phoney. I do actually believe the flexible, loyal, reliable, punctual, etc., bit. It just depends how you choose to view people, and when I prepare CVs the compassionate and sympathetic side of my nature prevails. As far as I am concerned, my job is to get the job-seeker an interview. After that, they are on their own.

In the afternoon someone comes into the agency wanting a career change. A man in his early-thirties from Northern Ireland who has an extremely heavy accent. God, I think, this is going to be an uphill struggle, I can barely make out a word he is saying. He looks a bit scruffy and dishevelled. He tells me that he is working in the depot of a tinned food factory, loading and unloading deliveries. We start with education. Turns out he has a degree in electrical engineering from Belfast's Queens University. An upper second as well. However, due to the chronic unemployment in his part of Northern Ireland, he had never found appropriate work. After lengthy and frustrating spells on the dole, interspersed with some manual labour for his uncle's company (to be described on his CV as 'involved in running the family construction business'), he decided to try his luck in England. When he moved to London, he needed to take something straightaway in order to fund his living expenses. He began work in the depot and has languished there for the last three years, a victim of low self-esteem, an occasionally unintelligible accent and employers' prejudices against the Irish. I am determined to provide him with a fuck-off, top-quality, high-profile CV. It is a challenge. However, once I manage to decipher what he is saying, I am able to turn his menial, manual job into a position of impressive authority and responsibility. After the glowing personality profile, we both feel quite emotional. He leaves happy and motivated.

Wayne rolls up after lunch, looking facially flaky. The flakier the face, the messier the divorce proceedings. He's in a bad mood and goes straight to his office. Tina gives it five minutes then gently disappears into his office with a cup of tea and one of her home-made chocolate brownies (as requested by Mario at the weekend). She emerges a few minutes later and pulls a face.

'His parents have telephoned his wife and apparently offered her their support,' she tells me. 'He's furious.'

'I'm not surprised. I think parents should stick by their kids whatever happens.'

'Not necessarily. My ex-husband's parents still ring me every week and his mother offered her support to me constantly throughout the divorce, especially when she heard what had gone on.'

'Well, she'd got to know and love you and maybe that is the case here, too. I just think during this delicate stage of the divorce proceedings, they should be on Wayne's side, or at least neutral. I'd be really hurt if my parents sided with someone else against me, no matter what I'd done.'

'Maybe they know things that we don't,' she says.

'Like what?' I ask.

The phone rings. Someone wants a quote for temporary work. I tell them our (reasonable) rates, hear a sharp intake of breath and know not to waste too much time on the call, especially as Tina and I are in the middle of a conversation. I take an address to which to send details and put the phone down.

'Like maybe he cheated on her and they know. I don't know, Emma. We don't know the whole story. With me, some people looked on and thought that Victor was having financial difficulties and that I just walked out on him. They didn't know his difficulties were self-inflicted from late-night poker games. I was criticised a lot by people because I chose not to explain what had really happened. I didn't want everyone to know what a loser I was for sticking by a man with a self-destructive gambling addiction for seventeen years. I'd rather people think I was a bitch than a loser.'

'OK, so I don't know what went on. I just get the feeling that Wayne is the black sheep of the family, and in his parents' eyes everything he does is wrong. He's probably been labelled the baddie and has had a lifetime of his parents siding with everyone against him, starting with teachers and now, finally, his wife. Maybe they are being nice to her as they feel it's their fault somehow, you know, for creating such an insecure son.'

'I hear you but I don't agree. They did their best but they're probably disappointed with the results. Look, why is he not working in the family business and the brother and sister are?'

'Parents get the children they deserve. Same with everything. The more you put in, the more you get out. And don't tell me that you wouldn't stick by your sons, whatever they did.'

'I'll always love them, no matter what they do, but if I thought they had done something wrong, I'd be the first to tell them. There's this girl who rings Mario all the time. He saw her for a month or so, then decided she wasn't for him and he hasn't had the decency to call her back and tell her it's over. I told him that I am not going to lie for him. If she rings up and he's there then I'm bloody well going to put him on the phone. It's not nice to leave her hanging on.'

'Yes, it is a bit wimpish, but there's a difference between telling him to speak to her and telling her that you think your son is in the wrong. And that's what I'm saying with—'

Wayne's door opens and out he comes looking a little happier.

'How are you darling?' he asks me, one hand in his pocket rearranging his testicles.

'Very well thanks. We've got loads of temp bookings this week,' I quickly add, feeling guilty for having spent most of the afternoon gossiping with Tina, even though I haven't had a proper lunch break.

'Let's have a look at the bookings sheet,' he says, which is hanging on the wall behind me. And before I have time to pass it to him, he leans over me to get to the sheet of paper, his body momentarily touching mine and his hand brushing against the side of my breast. I quickly bend to the side to avoid further physical contact and, despite feeling slightly flustered, we carry on our conversation as normal. The space invasion has only taken two or three seconds. If you'd blinked, you might have missed it. He might have leaned over a man in that way; another woman with personal space issues might have leaned over me in that way. It could have happened to anyone. My breast was in the way. He's having a bad day. He's stressed. His parents don't think much of him. He likes me. He's a good boss. He's basically harmless. Maybe he needs some physical contact. It just doesn't seem appropriate to tell him to back off.

Let's face it, it's easier not to say anything at all. So we talk about temps and how busy we are and how rich I am going to make him.

Bert trundles into the front office with a sheaf of papers under his arm. He's wearing a checked shirt, navy blue jumper, brown chunky-knit cardigan, grey polyester trousers and black leather Hush Puppy shoes that are curled up at the toes. He smells of fried fish and urine.

Bert has clearly been waiting for Wayne's presence in the office before running through his list of queries based on the weekly timesheets and my proposed invoicing. He likes Wayne to be aware of all the invoicing mistakes I make.

'You've really confused me this week Emma,' he says, with a loud, disgruntled sigh.

'That's not difficult,' I say, smiling outwardly while grimacing inwardly at the thought of spending thirty minutes explaining the bleedin' obvious to Bert.

'You are still not making things clear. I've got my usual list of queries for you. Why haven't you invoiced Greenbergs for last week? Didn't Sandra Miller go there?'

Wayne raises his eyebrows at me. I have forgotten to invoice them. This is the first time I have ever forgotten to invoice a client. Decision time: do I bullshit in front of Wayne and pretend that no-one went to Greenbergs, or do I admit my mistake? I quickly calculate the cost to the company of keeping face: £350. Ten per cent for me. Is it worth lying for £35? No.

'Shit. You're right, but it wasn't Sandra. Cynthia was there for three days and she must have forgotten to fax me her timesheet. I'll prepare an invoice for you,' I say, hoping that that will be the end of it and that we can move on to the next query.

'Well, fancy forgetting to invoice a client,' Bert says, triumphantly. 'If I hadn't remembered, we'd have lost that money, you know. This isn't the Girl Guides – we're not here to lend a helping hand for free. If we don't charge the clients, you don't get your cut either, you daft girl. You really need to keep a proper note of who goes where. It's no good relying on your memory to invoice clients. Luckily, I also work here and I remembered that we have an ongoing arrangement with them this month. We can't afford to make mistakes like that, Emma.'

'It was a mistake, for God's sake. Of course I keep a note of the bookings. I made a mistake, OK?'

'Have you heard this, Wayne?' Bert shouts to Wayne who is now in the photocopier room.

'So send them an invoice. What are you making such a fuss about? That's why you both do the invoicing, so we don't miss anything,' says Wayne.

It's so easy to forgive your boss the odd sneaky grope when he backs you up with the likes of Bert.

After the third query, I am hyperventilating with annoyance at Bert's sluggish grasp of our invoicing procedure. Admittedly, the first mistake was mine, and he has tried his hardest to milk it for everything it's worth. The rest of his queries are a repeat of his weekly gripes.

'You haven't put the charging rate for the West Hampstead Medical Centre,' he complains.

'But we've had the same temp there for the last three weeks and the rate hasn't changed,' I moan.

'Well, write it down. Doesn't hurt anyone to clarify these things,' he whines.

'It does. It hurts me. It's obvious you should charge them the same. They always pay twelve-fifty an hour. They have done for the last year. Why should it be different this week?' I bleat.

'I am just checking with you. But if you wrote it down, I wouldn't have to check with you. I could save your time and mine.'

'OK, OK. I'll always write down the charge rate. Now, what's next?'

'Don't rush me. When you rush, mistakes get made. No doubt that is exactly what happened with the invoice for Greenberg. Now just slow down please, young lady.'

So I wait for him to painstakingly write the charging rate in red on the invoice sheet, circle it several times and underline it twice. He then makes a separate note on the pad of paper with his list of queries and carefully puts a tick against number two which says 'Greenberg's charging rate', while my blood pressure soars and the beginning of an ulcer named Bert gestates in my stomach.

'Now, what's next?' he asks himself, shuffling through the many sheets of paper he has brought with him and consulting his pad.

But something outside distracts him. A car is having difficulties parking in a small space opposite. He goes to the window, stands and stares for a while and then shouts jubilantly, 'I knew it! It's a woman!'

Tina laughs but I can't. He just annoys me too much. I wish I didn't rise to the bait but I always do, partly because I am forced to spend time with him every Monday going through the damn invoicing, whereas her contact with him is minimal.

All in all, it is a busy and demanding day and I am the last one in the office.

At half past six there is an unexpected buzz on the intercom. I lean over to pick up the phone and find out who the hell wants what now.

'We're closed, I'm afraid,' is my sociable, helpful opener.

'Sorry to bother you. This is Luca Moretti. Is my mum there? I'm supposed to be picking up my watch.'

'Luca, your mum's gone. Maybe she's left the watch up here. Do you want to come up?'

I buzz him in.

The Man

Shit, shit, shit. Where is my lipstick? Too late, I can hear Luca bounding up the stairs and he's soon knocking on the door. I open it to find a medium height, toned but stocky, tanned, deep brown-eyed, thick eye-lashed, big-nosed, lustrously dark-haired man with the cheekiest smile in the world leaning against the door post. He's out of breath.

'Come in,' I say, as calmly as possible. 'I'm Emma, we've spoken on the phone a few times.' We shake hands. It's all rather formal.

'Sorry to bother you,' he says. 'I was supposed to pick up mum downstairs fifteen minutes ago. I thought I might have missed her so I've just run all the way to the tube. She wasn't there so I thought she might have come back here.'

'No. She must have forgotten. Maybe she left the watch in her drawer.'

I hunt for the key (knowing that the watch ain't going to be in the drawer, but determined to keep this gorgeous guy in my company as long as possible). I find the key to Tina's desk drawer and – surprise, surprise – there's no watch.

'You don't look how you sound,' he comments, as I rustle through the drawers.

'Better or worse?' I want to know.

'Well, Mum said you were very attractive,' he says, smiling, his eyes following me around the office.

'And?'

'And you are.'

'Did she say anything else?'

'Mum never mentions work. She just said you were lovely.'

I am a bit flustered and don't know what to say. I have a tendency to babble crap in these circumstances, but now even this ability fails me. I just stand there looking at him. He seems unperturbed by my silence. I get the feeling he is used to people listening to him.

He continues, 'You sound very businesslike on the phone. Very formal. Not exactly unfriendly but verging on it. I think the word might be prissy.'

He doesn't know that I am too embarrassed to flirt with him in front of his mother. 'So you thought I'd be wearing a navy blue Marks & Spencer's suit and sensible court shoes. I haven't even got a bun,' I say, pointing to my short blonde crop.

'Well, maybe not M&S, but certainly not the Millennium outfit you *are* wearing.' He is referring to my metallic silver wraparound mini-skirt and knee-length silver boots. 'Very stylish. I love it.'

'Thank you. You look different, too,' I say.

'What did you expect?' he asks.

'Well, I wasn't sure if you had arms and legs.'

'Why? You got a thing for paraplegics?' he asks. 'Anyway, why shouldn't I have?'

'Well, it's just that as I know your mum does everything for you, I thought you might not be fully functioning,' I reply.

He laughs. 'Two arms and two legs, both fully functioning.' He holds out his arms and I resist the urge to throw myself into them. 'You think I am spoilt by Mum, but you know she derives enormous pleasure from spoiling me and my kid brother. I wouldn't want to deny her that. Would you?'

'No, of course not. I'm not that mean.'

'But you are *quite* mean?' he wants to know.

'Yeah. Quite. But not spiteful, and I'm only mean to people who are mean to me. I don't start off by being mean.'

'Fair enough. I'm not mean at all. Even if someone is mean to me, I don't generally respond by being mean back,' he says.

'Does that mean you're a sucker?'

'More a licker than a sucker,' he says, smiling.

I'm embarrassed. Once again, and this is a rare occurrence, I am lost for words and have zero to answer back with. There are a few minutes of awkward silence, then he asks if he can use the loo. While he's in there, I find my make-up but then decide it will be too obvious if I am suddenly wearing lipstick when he returns, not that men necessarily notice such things. I flap around the office aimlessly. When he returns from the loo, I tell him that I am going to lock up. He offers me a lift home. I tell him that I only live up the road.

'How about a quick drink across the road?' he persists. 'I finally get to meet you and I want to talk to you more.'

'Just a quickie then.'

'I was only offering you a drink,' he says, smiling.

'God, you're really saucy. I'm going to tell your mum.'

'Where do you think I got it from?'

We head over the road to the pub. Although I may look calm and self-assured on the outside, my heart is pumping fast and there are shooting sensations in my knickers. Thankfully, he takes the conversational lead and tells me again that his mum doesn't discuss anything to do with work and that he actually knows nothing about me. I remark that I had noticed that she did switch off when she left the office.

'I thought it was only men who compartmentalised.' Luca says. 'I just can't believe she didn't tell me about you – you're great! But then she's like that with her boyfriends as well. We only get to meet them very rarely, although that suits me. She's got the worst taste in men. Have you met any of them?'

'No, but I've seen the photos.'

A quick drink turns into a few long drinks and we are soon chatting about all sorts of harmless, impersonal things, like Wayne's network marketing, Bert's body odour and Luca's thick as shit colleague who vehemently agrees with everything their boss says so that his naïve employer thinks she's bright, switched on and going to go far. I decide to ask him whether I should mention to Tina that we were in the pub tonight.

'Why not?' he wants to know.

'I don't know. It feels a bit awkward,' I say, suddenly feeling foolish for making a big deal out of something which is simply a pleasant but unmemorable encounter for him.

'Well, I suppose she might tell my girlfriend,' he says, after a while.

The smile leaves my face without permission from my pride. I didn't know he had a girlfriend. Why the hell had he asked me out for a drink?

'I'd better go,' I say, reaching for my jacket.

'If I had one,' he says, grabbing my jacket from me.

'One what?'

'You know what.'

'Are you the tormenting type?'

'Only if I'm allowed to get away with it.'

'Oh, so you are the type of guy you can never relax with. The minute I think I can chill out, let down my guard and be nice, you're wondering how to take the piss and/or sleep with my best friend.'

Now the smile leaves his face. He takes a long drink, lights a cigarette and plays with the packet without looking up.

'Have I said something wrong?' I ask, concerned. He looks really upset.

'What you just described – that pretty much happened to me. Last year.' He's quiet again.

'Do you want another drink?' I ask.

'I'd prefer something to eat? Do you like pizza?'

'Love it, but I only eat the equivalent of a bird's leftovers in one sitting. If you promise not to judge me for leaving half, I'd love to come.'

The mood lightens as we topple along to the restaurant.

Over dinner, Luca tells me last year's story. He'd been single for six months and, contrary to the gigolo image portrayed by his mother, he only goes out with women if he really likes them. He says he's fussy. Some of his mates always like to have a girlfriend – 'serial boyfriends' he calls them – but he's not really interested in being with someone just for the sake of it. Then, last year he met this girl at work who, although not initially his type, he fell for nonetheless. She was so relentless in her pursuit of him that he was flattered, and he soon became used to her devoted attention. Her attractiveness was heightened by the fact that all the men at work fancied her, too.

I want to know why she wasn't his type. Turns out she was very materialistic and genuinely impressed by cars, watches, designer labels, postcodes and crap like that. But against his better judgement, he fell for her. It was nice having someone so involved in his life, someone he could talk to, open up to, who seemed fascinated by the minutiae of his existence. Once he was hooked and had made the appropriate declarations of love, however, she told him that he wasn't the man she thought he was. Luca thinks she lost respect for him because he fell for her and allowed himself to be vulnerable in front of her. A week after she dumped him, he found out that she was already sleeping with one of his work colleagues, a friend of his, despite her tears and protestations that she was devastated that it hadn't worked out with Luca.

'She sounds like one of those women who judge their worth by whether they can get men to fall in love with them, but whose fundamental self-dislike means that when men *do* actually fall for them, they despise them for their lack of judgement. Your big mistake was to fall for her. If you'd have held back, more or less permanently, she'd still be with you.'

'It was a mistake and it wasn't. I found out what she was like, but in a way I knew all along, and that's why I didn't go for it for a while. She is the most professional flirt I've ever met. The kind that actually gazes into your eyes over dinner and swoons over everything you say and do. It's addictive and

I can't believe I fell for it. I also felt humiliated in front of people at work. Eventually, everyone knew we were together and then, suddenly, she's all over someone else.'

'Shit.'

'Yeah, it was.'

'So do you hate women now?'

'No, but I don't like her much. She ended up dumping my friend as well after a month and is now seeing one of the senior managers.'

'Is he married?'

'How did you know?'

'Just a classic case.'

'I'm impressed.'

'So am I.'

'What about?'

'About the fact you've been so honest and open with me. I appreciate it.'

He smiles, looking rather pleased with himself. 'Have I done well?'

'Yes, we are all very pleased with you!'

He walks me back to my flat. I have already decided it would be extremely unwise to invite him in, especially as I know my flatmate, Simon, is around and he is so unbearably horny at the moment that I am worried the mad glint in his eyes will send Luca running. Simon's a gay Italophile who hasn't had sex for quite a while.

As we stand outside the flat, Luca asks me for a kiss.

'I don't think my boyfriend would like it,' I say.

His smile disappears again. 'Are you joking now?' he asks earnestly.

'What do you think?' I say, challengingly.

'Yeah . . .'

And I invite him in.

The Day After

We never did decide whether I was going to tell Tina. I can't look her in the face the next day. In fact, I don't even want to go into work. I want to lie in bed daydreaming about Luca's hairy chest, which is a little sad, really. Don't you think I want to be one of those girls that is so casual and confident about the availability of eligible men that they don't give a second thought to the man who kissed them (or more) the night before? Sure, I wish I was one of those girls with a bottomless pit of suitable dates who only remember that they had a man in their bed when someone asks them what they did last night and they suddenly recall that a man made mad passionate love to them a mere five hours ago. Even more admirable are the women who are so together and so busy forging ahead with the rest of their lives that they simply have neither the time nor the inclination to dwell on the male species from a romantic perspective.

If I like the look of someone, I can obsess about happy futures after a mere glance in their direction. If, however, I like the sound of someone, I am much more cautious on the basis that looks are inversely proportional to telephone charisma (i.e. the more ubelievably sexy the voice, the plainer the man; same principles apply to women, by the way).

I am crap at being balanced. I can rarely manage to sustain a good working life and a good love life. Not that I have a good love life yet, you understand. Luca stayed until I kicked him out at about three o'clock in the morning. He kept asking me whether he was staying the night and I kept informing him that he was going home. In fact, I insisted that whatever happened between us at my flat, his shoes needed to remain on his feet at all times. That's my rule. Shoes stay on on the first night. The rule is open to negotiation, but my negotiating powers were just that bit more convincing than Luca's. As we lay on my bed (shoes hanging over the edge of the mattress), mooching and smooching, we looked at each other and smiled. 'In case I forget to tell you later, thanks for a lovely evening,' I said. He grabbed me towards him and started kissing me again, his eyes shutting and the bulge in his trousers hardening to steel. Although we were still kissing, I could feel him smile as he slyly tried to kick off his shoes. I heard a clunk as one fell to the floor.

'Time to go now,' I said, sitting up. His smile vanished and he slowly stood up, a resigned look on his face.

'You know we could have a fabulous night together,' he said, doing up his shirt and reaching for his keys.

'Yeah, I know,' I replied. 'But would we have a fabulous morning together too?' Silence.

Then, 'I reckon we would be still smiling at each other,' he said, smiling again.

I smiled back. And he left.

I keep yawning in the office and Tina asks me what I got up to the night before. As she knows I have been leading a nun-like existence, she is understandably curious as to why I have the louche movements of someone whose body has been adored the night before. What do I tell her? Before I have time to decide how to respond, the phones start ringing. I pick up one line. 'Search, good morning, can you hold?' I then pick up another line. 'Search, good morning, can you hold?'

'Depends on what I am being asked to hold.' It's Luca. I panic and immediately press the hold button and take the first caller, while mouthing to Tina that her son is on the phone. Although I can hear Tanya moaning about her job at the surgery, I wouldn't be able to tell you the specifics of her complaint. This is because I am listening to Tina chatting to Luca and asking him what he did last night. She comments that he sounds tired. He is speaking and she is looking serious. She puts down the phone and looks at me. I spin out the call to Tanya while I am basically shitting it. As I end the call, Tina asks me to ring Luca. I start to get flustered and look for paper clips under my desk.

'He needs a temporary secretary and I said he should deal with you.'

'Oh, right,' I say, emerging from under my desk. 'Did he give you any details?' I ask casually.

'He was a bit offhand with me actually, which is not like him at all. When I asked him what he did last night he got all touchy and told me that I ask too many personal questions.' Tina shakes her head, looking hurt. I decide not to ring him back until she makes another call. When I do ring Luca's number I decide to keep it as professional as possible.

'Hi, is that Luca? This is Emma from Search.'

'Cut the crap. When can I see you again?'

'I hear from your mother that you need a temporary secretary? Can I take the details?'

'Yes. I want someone medium height with short blonde hair who wears silver boots and looks like she's about to board a lunar aircraft. Do you have anyone who fits that description? I have urgent needs.'

'I'm afraid we don't have many women on our books who can do that.' I can see Tina looking at me, questioningly. 'It's quite difficult to find someone with shorthand at such short notice.'

'I don't remember specifying the size of her hands. Listen, I want to see you later. I know it's difficult to speak in front of Mum.'

'Yes, you're right.'

'Just give me a one-word answer. Do you want to see me again?'

'Yes.'

'Are you free tonight?'

'I'll try and find someone with shorthand, but I may not be able to ring you until later.'

'Don't ring me. Just see me. I'll be at your flat at eight tonight.'

'OK. Thanks for using Search.'

'I haven't even started.'

Yikes.

I feel awful lying to Tina. I have the distinct feeling that she would not be happy that her son and I could be about to embark on a romantic escapade. While she's at lunch, I try to figure out exactly why I think she would be opposed to the match. Apart from anything else, it would be incredibly embarrassing for me to come into work having shagged her baby boy the night before. She is very possessive about her sons and this is the first time I've had more than a two-minute conversation with one of them, let alone put my hand down one of their trousers.

I start to wonder what Tina really thinks of me. I know we get on well. And I think she cares about me. She bought me a birthday present, she comforted me when my last boyfriend dumped me, she said she missed me like crazy when I was off sick, she says she looks forward to the patter of my tiny feet in the morning. So why do I think she would be pissed off if she thought her son was my boyfriend? I think she does approve of me as a human being. I just sense that perhaps I am not quite good enough for one of her sons. Now that may be paranoid low self-esteem at work. But it has happened before.

I think back to Elliott Rayner, the first guy to whom I completely lost my heart. I was mad, mad, *mad* about Elliott. And I mean mad in the sense of insane, psychotic, listless, melancholic, manic and delirious. I actually used to count the hours before I was due to see him, and as I only used to see him once or twice a week, there were a lot of hours to be ticked off. I suppose, in fairness, the rest of my life was pretty empty. I was sixteen and there was fuck all else going on except exams and the accompanying revision.

There was nothing that I did not adore about Elliott – his wit, his charm, his intelligence, his looks. In fact, I adored him almost as much as he adored himself, but not quite as much as his mother adored him. My God. Trying to get past his bitch of a mother was a test of such wily resistance and cunning, I'd all but given up ringing him.

Things didn't go too well the first time I met her. She was due to drop her precious son round at my home one Saturday night. I gave him my address over the phone: 38 Greenfield Road. He asked me what the house looked like. Stupid question, I thought, it's a house. It looks like a house. It's brick and it has windows and a door. And it's easy to find because I've just given you the name of the road. I'd even given him a number, which was prominently displayed on the front of the house. What more did he want? So I decided to be sarcastic and told him, 'It looks like a church and it has a huge monkey-puzzle tree outside,' assuming he would get the joke. 'See you Saturday,' he said. Only another seventy-eight-and-a-half hours to wait.

Saturday finally arrived and so did the heart palpitations. Twenty minutes after due time of arrival, there was a ring on the doorbell. I flew down the stairs, warning off other members of my family from going anywhere near the door. After all, I wanted to spare my beloved the scrutiny of parents and siblings. He had not bestowed the same consideration upon me. I opened the door to find Elliott and a red-faced, sour woman on the doorstep. Elliott introduced his mother and I asked her how she was. Turned out she was angry. Very angry. Apparently, this woman and her son had been driving up and down Greenfield Road for the last twenty minutes looking for a house that looked like a church with a monkey-puzzle tree outside. One look at her face and I knew that a piss-take was out of the question. From that moment on, I was doomed. No amount of grovelling, apologising or explaining was going to have any effect. The mouth set in a grim slash. Steel, grey eyes frosted over. She coolly sneered a hello at me after having a go at me for being 'silly'.

A week or two later, Elliott confronted me on behalf of his mother. He wanted to know why I never asked her how she was when I telephoned to speak to him and she answered the phone. I thought I had. I was very well brought-up, you know. Too well-brought-up, I reckon. For years I was the type of person who would apologise to someone if *they* were rude to *me*. As I listened to Elliott's complaint, I sensed that this was a battle I was going to lose. I couldn't slag off his mother to him, obviously, and she had decided that she had it in for me, conveniently displacing her anger at being substituted and pinning it instead on the monkey-puzzle tree saga.

The next time I telephoned him, she answered the phone.

'Hello, Mrs Rayner. This is Emma. How are you?'

To which she pointedly and loudly replied, 'How are you?'

'Fine thanks.' I tried again. 'How are *you*, Mrs Rayner?'

I was now desperate to find out how this moose was. 'I'll get Elliott for you,' she replied.

Now, if you had been in the room with her when I called, as Elliott was, you could be forgiven for thinking that I had not enquired about the woman's health. She was winning this stupid game and, at sixteen, I was not yet adept at dealing with a reverse Oedipus complex.

A few weeks later, I was out with Elliott and I accidentally left my purse in his new car. I telephoned later in the day. Mother answered. I put on my nicest young lady voice.

'Hello. This is Emma. How are you?'

'Elliott's not here.'

'Oh well, it's just that I think I left my purse in his car and I wanted to check that he had it.'

Psycho mother turns nice and offers to look in the car to see if my purse is in the glove compartment where I think I left it. She returns to the phone and tells me, quite nicely, that she has found it and will ask Elliott to call me when he gets back. I am sickeningly profuse in my gratitude and I genuinely think I have made a breakthrough in relations, until Elliott rings me half an hour later. He is furious. 'You've really upset my mother.'

'How?' I ask weary but intrigued.

'Well, you rang up and ordered her to go and look in my car, and then when she came back to very kindly tell you that I had your purse, you didn't even bother to say thank you.'

I'm speechless. What I would like to say is 'Why doesn't your mother go fuck herself, the lying bitch,' and then I think about how much I like the prat and I start blustering, protesting my innocence. 'That is not what happened at all. God, Elliott, of course I wouldn't do that.' We make up but all is not well.

Every time I look at his face, I see his mother's mean eyes and lemon-sucking mouth. Soon I have lined up a successor, a delightful sixteen-year-old who is writing me poems ostensibly about the sun and the moon but which are apparently about his love for me. I bet he'd cringe if he read them now. I cringed at the time, but when I read them now I am almost moved to tears by their earnest purity. When Elliott rang me to arrange another date, oblivious to the existence of a poet on the scene, I told him, 'I don't want to be your girlfriend any more.'

'I hope we can be friends,' he said, all mature.

'Well, we could but I don't think my new boyfriend would like it.'

Immature, I know, but it's always been one of my favourite lines.

So that was Elliott's mother. And he is still single, by the way, unable to find a suitable mummy substitute. Could I be dealing with a similar scenario with Luca and Tina? She is certainly very involved in his life and seems to think that the sun beams from his bottom. I just know she won't like it and I work with this woman in a very small company and we get on well and do I really want to fuck it up for the sake of a smooth-talking, hairy-chested, large-cocked dreamboat? Well, I've never been the sensible type and I'd rather fuck and fuck up than not fuck at all.

The afternoon at work is relatively uneventful, although Wayne is getting rather frisky. My pheromones must be reaching him as he decides he wants to add a programme to my computer, which involves him leaning right across me yet again, this time to put a disk in my hard drive, so to speak, while I am sitting at my desk. He smells of sweat and greasy hair. I offer to move and let him take my seat. He declines and continues to stretch across me, his crotch frighteningly close to my face. I move out of my seat anyway and offer to make Tina and Wayne a cup of tea. As I stand by the doorway to the kitchen, Wayne asks me whether the temps are busy.

'Quite busy, but I had to pull Olga from a job.'

He starts giggling and I think back on what I have said. Oh yes, it must have been the 'pull' bit. Wayne is off.

'It's been a long time since I've pulled,' he says, grinning.

'Well, considering you've been married for the last ten years, perhaps that's not surprising,' I say, a little pompously.

'I wouldn't have let that stop me,' he says.

'Don't make me hate you,' I say.

'You don't know what goes on in a marriage,' he counters.

I look at Tina and she is nodding sympathetically at Wayne, before excusing herself to interview an applicant in the back office.

'You know my wife spent half the marriage in the loo,' Wayne tells me. I am not sure whether this is the start to a joke, but when I look at him, he is frowning. I don't want to be flippant but I don't quite know how to respond. Before I can stop myself, both my curiosity and social etiquette take over and I have stupidly enquired further.

'What was she doing in the loo? Was she bulimic?' I ask with vague concern.

'I don't know what she was doing. Masturbating probably,' he tells me.

I blush. The phrase 'too much information' springs to mind and I start talking about paperclips and manila envelopes. Bert appears at this moment and for once I am pleased to see him. I even offer to make him a cup of tea if he promises not to be annoying for five minutes.

He can't even manage ten seconds.

'Have you written down all the bookings this week? We don't want another Greenberg & Co. repeat. It's no good relying on memory you know,' he says.

'You are so annoying! In fact, you can make your own tea,' I say, putting his mug back.

'You two have a love-hate relationship,' Wayne comments.

'Yeah,' I say. 'He loves me and I hate him.'

Bert looks wounded and I appease my guilt by giving him a biscuit, which he greedily gobbles before asking for another.

'Why don't you ask your wife for some biscuit money?' I taunt him, before settling myself at Tina's desk and waiting for Wayne to piss off and stop fiddling with my computer.

I just want to go home and start preparing myself for an evening of love. And that's what I mean. When there's fuck all else happening in my life, work is a tonic, a distraction. At times, to be fair, it's even fun. But looking at my boss with his masturbating, soon-to-be ex-wife, and glancing over at Bert dunking his fourth biscuit in his tea, I know I would far rather be lying in bed, dreaming about Luca.

The Flatmate

I get home to find my flatmate, Simon, lying in bed with a porn magazine. Ever since he went freelance as an Italian translator, he spends weeks in bed and then seven days working round the clock. At the moment he is in one of his lulls, and this inevitably means that he actually has loads of work to do and looming deadlines. Ironically, it is when he has no work to do that he is most active. With deadlines, however, his day goes a little like this. Rise late at midday, eat cereal, go back to bed. Receive social calls in his boudoir – all calls are screened to ensure that they are social. Read magazines, masturbate and snooze. Then, at about three or four in the afternoon, it's time for some action. Trainers are located, pyjamas are magically converted into trackie bottoms (and by magic, I mean he doesn't actually change), and a cleanish sweatshirt is found. He's off to the video shop, via the cake shop for the afternoon's entertainment. He then likes to transfer some of his bedding to the lounge, where he spends the afternoon. The evening is also spent watching television, while taping something on the other side, then watching what he has taped. He often goes out much later, at eleven or twelve, and generally retires pretty late. The required translation is due in less than a week and is festering somewhere under some empty cans and Rizla packets in the corner of his bedroom. He talks about the work and how the deadline is looming and he occasionally whimpers with fear, but he makes no move to do any work at all until the deadline itself is upon him.

Once the deadline has passed, his day is quite different. He still gets up at midday, but he only went to bed two hours before because he has been working all night and all day. There are no visits to the cake shop; that would be far too healthy for his present diet of coffee and cigarettes. All calls are taken but only for a five-minute update of how incredibly hard he has been working. No time to chat, back to work. The video recorder looks forlorn and unloved. The porn mag lays strewn across his bedroom floor with a large photo of a man about to give a blow-job to a fully engorged penis and the words 'Buon Appetito' face up.

Simon's twenty-eight, four years younger than me. This means that I do occasionally feel maternal towards him and am quite good at making a fuss of him when the occasion demands it. We first met at one of those mad places in Oxford Street that teach you to teach English to foreigners, known in the trade as TEFL (Teaching English as a Foreign Language). It's the kind of thing you do when other areas in your life aren't working out (which doesn't mean that it is not a great thing to do – it's your passport outta town).

I wanted to get away from London at the time. Most people do a TEFL course so that they can run away. I had spent six years training to be a lawyer only to discover, that it really wasn't for me. After two years of commuting into the City, I dreamed of a colourful life in, say, Barcelona. I planned to teach English to support myself while I lived far, far away from life as a lawyer in the City. Simon, meanwhile, finished his degree in psychology with no clear insight into what was going on in his own mind in terms of a career ('That's the irony of a degree in psychology,' he says, 'it leaves you clueless.'). Post-graduation, he spent two years on the dole: one living with his parents in Bolton which he hated, the other living in East London with his boyfriend, who he was beginning to hate when I first met him, hence the TEFL escape route. To use a naff but accurate term, we bonded on the first day, and by the end of the month-long course we had arranged to visit each other at our respective destinations. He went to Rome –

for the men, of course. As daydreamed, I went to Barcelona. We visited each other several times during that year, wrote loads and met up in England the following Christmas. I was back in the UK for good then, while he returned to Italy in the new year where he continued to teach English for another two years before working in-house for an Italian computer company translating their manuals into English. He returned to England with some useful contacts and has been working erratically as a translator ever since. It's actually quite well-paid work, but as he's so lazy, he's mostly broke.

He's quite good-looking in a cute, boyish way: light brown hair, pale skin with a tendency towards pimples, hazel eyes, thick, long eyelashes, turned up nose and smiley, uneven mouth which twists up on one side. He's medium height and a bit on the skinny side: he's a lot closer to the concave chest end of the physique spectrum than the six-pack end. Due to the mammoth size of his organ (confirmed by his boyfriends so I know he's not bullshitting), however, he doesn't give that much of a shit about keeping in shape. I don't think he's camp, although other gay friends of mine say that he can be a little over-dramatic. The way I see it is that he doesn't hold back from fully expressing his feelings (that's part of what I love about him; I'm not into holding it all in and putting on a brave face). He's charismatic and people seem to flock to him. I think it's because he can do both entertaining talkative and non-judgemental, non-interrupting listener. He's got the cocktail for company just right.

Personally, and obviously I'd *never* say this to him, I think that his looks are waning ever so slightly. Some boys are gorgeous-looking (what you might describe as cute or cheeky), but lose it badly as they age. A classic example of this syndrome is Paul McCartney, whose boyish good looks just did not translate at all well into handsome, older man, and he now looks slightly ridiculous. He went from boy to chipmunk, missing out the attractive powerful/distinguished/debauched older man stage. My vibe is that Simon peaked about three years ago when he was twenty-five and he should hurry up and find someone before the chipmunk stage hits in.

'When's the deadline?' I ask, popping my head round the door to his bedroom, where he is semi-reclined against some pillows with his lap top and computer manual five empty mugs, a full ashtray and an empty pizza box for company.

'Yesterday,' he replies without looking up, his head darting manically from manual to laptap. 'I think.'

'How's it going?' I joke.

'Frantic. I'm almost too busy to breathe.'

I throw him a banana from the kitchen. 'Buon Appetito.' And I disappear into the bathroom for an intensive makeover.

I appear half an hour later and throw myself on his bed and demand that he takes a break.

'What did you think of Luca?'

'Yes,' he says, without looking up. 'Have you seen those herbal uppers anywhere?'

'What happened to the Pro Plus?' I enquire.

'Are you joking? Last time I took some of those, I worked furiously for five hours only to find the following morning that I had written the most meaningless crap. Someone said it looked like Icelandic. Anyway, I've gone herbal now. Will you make me a lesbian tea?' he asks.

'Camomile or peppermint?'

'Definitely peppermint. Use three bags,' he says, still not looking up, face darting maniacally from computer to manuscript.

I reappear a few minutes later with two large mugs. 'Simon, listen to me. Take a break. I need to tell you about Luca.'

'Is that Tina's son?'

'Exactly.'

'Big or small?'

'Big, I think. I will be able to tell you for certain tomorrow morning. He's coming round again tonight.'

'I thought you were celibating,' he says, in accusatory tones.

'Don't be bitter. It suits you too well.'

'Oh, all right. Emma, this is wonderful news!' And I know he means it, but I also know what is coming next. 'But when is it my turn? WHEN IS IT MY TURN?' he wails. He gets up from his computer, throws himself on the bed and starts kicking his legs, repeating his 'When is it my turn?' mantra. 'I deserve a shag. I've got a prick that wouldn't look out of place on a horse. I am loyal, kind, cute, funny, nice-looking.' Then he flings himself over onto his stomach and looks at me. 'Sorry sweetheart. Back to you. What's he like?'

'Cheeky in a saucy way as well as being a bit of a piss-taker. Yeah, cheeky rather than arrogant. Easy to talk to – a good listener and he talks, too. The kind of person where you both have so much to say that you have five topics running simultaneously. He's open-minded – you know, he listens before disagreeing. Quite funny and pays cute compliments. He told me I smelt nice which was fairly original. What else? Hairy chest. Great kisser. Good dresser. Sexually proactive.'

'Shit. Now I'm in love with him, too. Oh my God. What if I really fall for him? What does he do, job-wise?'

'He loves his job. He works as a journalist for *The Times*.'

'What section?'

'Well, that's the not quite so glamorous bit. The financial markets. I think he studied economics at university and from what I understand, Tina wanted him to do something secure and sensible like accountancy, so he compromised by writing about finance instead.'

'What time's he coming over?'

'Half an hour, and by the way, I'm not in love with him.'

'You're in denial. And please try to keep the groans down. That last dickhead you had in your bed made me feel quite sick with his squeals. Such a fucking drama queen. No-one enjoys sex *that* much. Very unconvincing and quite abhorrent.'

'Would you like me to explain to Luca that the sound of heterosexual sex disgusts my flatmate? Can't you be the type who puts a glass to the wall and masturbates to the sound of another man coming?' I ask sweetly.

'Tried that with the gorgeous David you met and I got so confused with what each hand was doing that I nearly ended up glassing my cock.'

'The only reason you liked him was because you used to hear him pestering me for the arse.'

'God, it was so frustrating hearing you turn him down. I felt like running into the room with my pants round my ankles to tell him he could have mine.'

'Darling, he would have split you in two.'

'Aaaaaaaagh!' He stamps his feet in a childish, tantrumish way. And then, 'WHEN IS IT MY TURN?' he cries.

Now it's my turn. 'Aaaaaaaaaargh!'

The Sins

...the type ... and mechanisms to determine ... and ... about later lately index ... his ...

Luca turns up on time, wearing a knee-length black leather coat – the sort of thing a stormtrooper might wear. I love it. I am a bit jittery and fluster about in the kitchen with water and lemon and gin and ice and soda. 'God,' I explain, before he thinks I am jittery on account of him, 'I am so tired from last night. I don't think I can handle another drink,' I say, pouring us both a strong one. Drink is the only way through the beginning of a new relationship. Isn't it?

I collapse onto the sofa as he stands above me with his coat on.

'What do you feel like doing tonight?' he asks.

I look up at him and think that he looks rather gorgeous. I consider his question for a while.

'Well, I feel like listening to good music. I don't want to go anywhere where there are too many people. I'd quite like a spliff. I wouldn't mind being horizontal or at least lounging on a comfortable chair. And I'd like to have an interesting but non-challenging conversation.'

He puts his hands into the pockets of his coat and for a second I think he is about to leave. Then he pulls out a large bag of grass and throws it onto the coffee table in front of me. He walks over to the stereo and scans the music collection and puts on a CD. Al Green. Funnily enough, the first track is 'I'm Tired of Being Alone'. He takes off his coat, throws it over a chair and walks across to the sofa. He lifts up my legs so that I am horizontal and then he lies down next to me, facing me.

'How does this suit you?' he asks. We lay looking at each other, both smiling, until he puts his arms around me and starts kissing my neck. After only a few minutes I hear screams coming from Simon's room. I sit bolt upright. That can only mean one thing. Simon's finished his translation. Soon, loud music is blaring from his room and he comes running into the lounge waving a computer disk.

'I've finished. I've fucking well finished. I don't believe it!' Then he catches sight of Luca's bag of grass, picks it up and suggests celebrating with a spliff. Perfect.

I introduce the boys and lie back lazily with a joint. Having a gay flatmate is a brilliant way of discovering how comfortable a man is with his own sexuality. An unfriendly, dismissive reaction from a boyfriend means that (a) the sex will be a mechanical, hands-free, dripping-chin-free affair, and, perhaps more importantly, (b) I immediately go off him and (a) becomes irrelevant. More worrying is when they are too friendly and I start to get sidelined. It's not the sidelining I mind as much as the appreciative glances Simon's crotch gets. One boyfriend used to lie in bed with me telling me how funny and cute he found Simon. 'Listen,' I said, 'I'm getting the feeling that you would prefer it if it were Simon in bed instead. Shall I get him?' 'Is he in?' was not the answer I was looking for. He still claims he was joking but I am not sure. Last time I went round to this guy's flat, he had a book on Moroccan interior design on his coffee table.

I think Luca is doing well, though. I look at Simon and Luca laughing together and realise with gratitude that Luca falls within the safety zone of liking but not too adoring. When Luca gets up to go to the loo, Simon stands up and starts energetically thrusting his groin. I take this to mean that he likes Luca, too.

'Gorgeous. If I don't find a man soon, I'm worried I'll start flirting with him and then maybe even steal him from you. Don't worry, I'll leave you two in a minute. I'm going out,' Simon says, looking in the mirror. 'Shit!' he shrieks, 'I've still got my spot cream on.'

As I look up at him through bloodshot eyes, I realise that his face is dotted with beige spots. I suppose it does look a bit weird, although I am used to Simon walking around with blobs of his beloved magic spot cream plastered over strategic areas of his face.

'Do you think he noticed?' he asks me, horrified. Simon doesn't realise that most heterosexual men wouldn't notice if you'd had your head shaved and your eyebrows waxed.

'I doubt it,' I say, lazily, kicking off my shoes and stretching.

'Oh, God,' Simon whispers to me. 'It's starting to happen and it's only the second date. I think you are turning smug.' Now I am the one to be horrified.

'God,' I hiss. 'Shit. Listen, thank you for telling me. You could be right. Fuck. How awful!' I sit up straight and slap my cheeks. 'Promise me you'll tell me if you see any other signs of smugness.'

'With pleasure,' Simon says, quickly. 'I would consider it to be my duty.'

Smugness is our enemy. It is the worse sin. We prefer theft, blackmail and sodomy – murder, even – but please, not smugness. Luca comes back from the loo, having heard Simon slagging off smugness, and asks us whether we think the seven sins are really that bad. We all agree that sloth somehow got onto the wrong list and was perhaps accidentally mixed up with modesty (definitely a vice: 'No, really, I am shit and worthless' – yawn, yawn). We all agree that sloth is a virtue and that busy, smug people are the enemy.

'I'm very anti-Gluttony,' I say. 'Definitely a sin. Greedy people over-eating. When I see it, I just want to shout out "enough already".'

'Well, if you mean the greedy bunch that are attracted to the "eat as much as you can before you vomit" offer in restaurants, then I can happily agree with you on that,' says Luca. 'I'm glad they have those signs outside the window so that I know never to contemplate eating there. It's a cheapskate idea for greedy tight-arses. There's no deal. These restaurants obviously don't care what the food tastes like . . .'

'Hence the fact the cuisine is often Mexican,' I say.

'Exactly. They just care about producing as much of the crap as possible. I don't even know why they bother with tables and chairs. They could have troughs instead. Save on the washing up and people could just kneel down and stick their heads in. Then they could charge a pound a head instead.'

'Which reminds me,' says Simon, 'of a rather disturbing thing that happened to me in McDonalds at the weekend. I don't normally eat in as the risk that I might bump into someone I know gives me violent indigestion as opposed to just mild dyspepsia. But I was south and to the east of the river so I reckoned I was safe to indulge in the luxury of actually eating a McDonalds sitting down rather than in a darkened car down an alleyway, and before the food's cold and soggy rather than lukewarm and soggy. I like to go to McDonalds very occasionally to remind myself why I only eat the stuff once every two years – that's how long it takes to forget how hideous it actually tastes. So I sit down with my tray. It's quite busy in there so I can't find an isolated table. The CD player has broken and is going crazy and no-one gives a shit. As I tuck into my burger, something strange is happening in the corner of my vision. I realise that the man at the next table is eating his chips straight from the tray! His nose was actually in the packet thing containing the chips. I'd never seen anything like it. Like a dog. I mean, surely it's not that much hard work to pick up a chip with your fingers and raise your hand to your mouth?'

'You eat low-life food and you're surrounded by low-life,' Simon says, as I am killing myself with laughter at the thought of his horror-struck face at the sight of the man eating straight from the tray. 'And no matter how many dirty looks I gave him, he just carried on. Didn't even seem embarrassed. He just looked up at me sideways from the tray and smiled.'

'OK, what about wrath?' I ask.

'Oh, anger? Natural human emotion, suppression of which is known to cause depression and the best of which can bring about social change,' Luca says.

'Lucky you said that,' says Simon. 'You need to have a positive attitude towards unfettered expressions of anger if you're going to hang around here.'

I give Simon a discreet dirty look; we had agreed a month-long no-negative-disclosure policy.

'Better out than in,' says Luca, smiling at me. 'Anyway, I'm sort of Italian,' he tells Simon. 'I'm used to lots of shouting. I was telling Emma about this passive aggressive woman at work – I seem to be the only one to see through her, which is really frustrating. Well, if she were just out and proud angry and shouted every now and then, I could probably deal with it. Instead, she talks in this highpitched baby girlie voice to fool everyone into thinking that she is really very sweet and harmless when she's actually fundamentally furious. She's a woman terrified of her own anger.'

'That's the thing about labelling something a sin. It's just demonising socially inconvenient human emotions. I mean, lust is on that list,' Simon says, indignantly. 'What's wrong with lust? You fancy your neighbour's husband so what are you supposed to do? Poke your eyes out so that you can't see him any more? Acting on it is maybe a sin, depending on whether, the wife consents, for example, but my God, just lusting after someone? Is that so bad?'

'What about pride?' I ask.

'Well, you just have to see the horrific consequences of people without pride to know that the *lack* of it should be a sin,' says Luca.

'Like what?' asks Simon.

'*Blind Date, Stars In Their Eyes* – in fact all early evening

Saturday night shows on ITV. How much pride can you have to appear on Jerry Springer? Pride just means human dignity and self-respect. How the hell can that be a sin?'

'I'm a very proud person,' I say, 'and I'm not sure if that's good, as it just means that I hate showing any weakness, so people think I'm hard rather than vulnerable.'

'Glad I know that,' says Luca. 'I've got a feeling it could come in useful. Put it on the list for further discussion.'

'Are you a proud person, Luca?' asks Simon.

'Depends what you mean by proud. Definitely too proud to go on a package holiday and wear Union Jack shorts, but not too proud to beg,' he says, looking at me. 'I don't think I'm too proud to show I'm upset or that someone has hurt me or that someone means something to me. To me, that's not pride, it's honesty.'

It takes three phone calls to find out the remaining two sins: covetousness and envy. Luca doesn't like envy, which seems illogical to me as it is just another unpleasant but natural human emotion.

'You can't help it if you want what someone else has got,' says Simon, backing me up.

'Yeah, but it's the kind of person who wants what someone else has got that makes envy a sin – normally a mean-spirited person who is never happy with what they have.'

'You mean, like a homeless person envying someone with a warm home, loving family and a fridge full of food?' I ask.

'That's not envy. The homeless person isn't wanting to take it from the other person, they just want it for themselves as well, which is really very reasonable.'

We are interrupted by the hoot of a car horn outside indicating that Simon's friends have arrived to give him a lift to their Tuesday nightclub. As he leaves, he winks at me and says 'Buon Appetito.'

Now I know that discussing a man's mother may not be the best way to seduce him, but I feel really weird about seeing my colleague's son naked and, to be honest, clothes seem to be disappearing at a pleasing rate.

'Why didn't you tell your mum you saw me last night?' I ask.

'Same reason you didn't,' he says.

'What reason would that be?' I ask.

'I don't know if I want to get my mum involved at this stage.'

I am a little hurt that he wants to keep me a secret, although, I understand that this is probably quite sensible. There's no point rocking the boat, and yet I also feel uncomfortable not telling Tina the truth. In my experience, mothers forgive their sons anything; they forgive their sons' girlfriends very little.

'Well, that's fine, but the problem is that I work with your mother and I see her every day, and when she asks me what I did last night, I will feel uncomfortable. Besides which, I am a terrible liar.'

'Glad to hear it.'

'Glad you're glad, but in the meantime, do you see my dilemma?'

'Telling your mum about a woman isn't normally done for at least a year.'

'And it's definitely not done after a second date when you haven't even decided whether you really like someone or not.'

'Oh, I've definitely decided that,' he says, pulling me towards him and kissing me.

The subject isn't mentioned again, but then we don't do much talking for the rest of the evening.

The Confession

Work is the curse of the drinking classes.
Oscar Wilde

The alarm rings at eight o'clock in the morning. I'm alone. I sent Luca home at three again so that we didn't end up having sex on the second date. When I like a guy, I hold out for as long as I physically can, and I had to get Luca out of the flat fast before we did something that only I regretted.

I also don't want to have to wake up and pretend to be a happy go-lucky person when I am actually fiendishly bad-tempered on awakening. I don't want to be scrutinised in a gleaming white bedroom in the morning with a radically altered appearance. The carefully shaded eyeshadow will have disappeared, as will the concealer covering the shadows under my eyes, the mascara will be everywhere but on my eyelashes, the bronzed sun tan along with my high cheek-bone definition will now be on the pillow case, and the lipstick will have been transferred by a series of cunning counter-moves to a completely different set of lips (still mine).

And of course, knowledge is power, and I prefer to have a little information on the person sharing my sleeping space, rather than waking up in the morning and realising I'm in bed with a virtual stranger who may or may not want to see me again.

He was really pissed off at having to go home, especially as the same thing had happened the night before and he was comfortable and he had to drive home and maybe, he said, he might even want to wake up with me. But I don't care. I don't mind kissing someone all over but I want to get to know them before I sleep with them, literally and figuratively. Rules are rules. I tried to blame it on Simon and explained to Luca that heterosexual relationships sicken and disgust Simon and we agreed before moving in together that he would not have to witness the aftermath of anything unnatural and hideous, i.e. they would be gone by the morning. Luca said this sounded like utter bullshit and I admitted that it was. I told him that he made the room look messy and he pointed at the books, CDs, knickers, trainers, Rizlas and newspapers all over the floor and told me to chill out. He was right. He wasn't too proud to beg, but I did get rid of him in the end and he was actually quite gracious and affectionate when he left, despite his bad mood.

So when the alarm goes, I am alone. My head feels fuzzy from the spliff and vodka and I am exhausted from two nights of sleep deprivation (anything less than eight hours feels deprivatory). Can I do a sickie? When did I last have one? Admittedly, it's been a while since I had a fake sickie (or mental health day, as Simon calls them), but on the other hand, I have had a few days off recently due to a bad cold. It really is tiresome when one has to use one's annual sick leave for a genuine illness. But at Search, as there is only myself and Tina running the show (Wayne doesn't count on the basis that he does fuck-all), I feel a bit mean taking days off when there is nothing really wrong with me other than that which has been self-induced. I decide to bite the bullet and go into work. If I can survive until 5.30 p.m. I will come straight home and take to my bed for the evening. I eventually get up at a quarter to nine and thank God that Simon is still in bed, where I expect to find him on my return home eight hours later, sleeping peacefully or masturbating noisily.

I stumble into work with my bottle of water, pain killers and a scone with the requested heart attack levels of butter. Tina and Wayne don't notice my sluggish manner. They are poring over the Search newsletter that Wayne has produced on his 'puter.

'What do you think, Emma?' they ask, giving me a copy.

Suddenly I really do feel quite close to vomiting and I am not sure whether it is my hangover or the newsletter. There are cheesy pictures of both Wayne and Tina smiling over computers. I had wisely refused to give him a photo as I suspected this circulated newsletter was not something with which I wanted to be publicly associated. I cringe as I read the company motto 'Believe In Yourself' plastered under Wayne's photo, while the other company motto 'The Customer Always Comes First' is printed in bold under Tina's photo. Tina's suggestive smile seems to give the motto sexual undertones of which I am sure they are both unaware, unusually for Wayne who is never one to miss the chance for a crude innuendo.

Oh my God. I notice a Mission Statement in the bottom right corner: '*Our mission is to provide Top-Quality, intelligent, competent Secretarial staff and to provide a speedy and Courteous response to your secretarial needs. We are comitted to excelence*'. Now I really do feel sick.

'Well, what do you think?' they ask again, excitedly.

'How many of these have you printed?' I want to know.

'About five hundred,' says Wayne. 'Why do you ask?'

'Well, it's full of spelling mistakes. Committed and excellence are both misspelt, which does not inspire confidence in our ability to provide "Top-Quality" staff,' I say. 'And I am not sure about the spontaneous use of capital letters. Why, for example, does courteous and not speedy get a capital letter?'

Wayne's face crumples; he looks crestfallen. For a minute I think he might burst into tears, but then his face hardens and a defiant expression begins to form. I don't care. I don't want to send this crap out. Tina reluctantly admits that perhaps it would not be a good idea to send out a newsletter stressing our excellence to clients which contains spelling mistakes. Actually the newsletter is full of immature grammatical errors as well as random apostrophes, scattered through the text in the most unlikely places. As I am detecting distinctly bullish body language in Wayne's stance, I decide it would be politic to mention these some other time.

Fortunately, we don't have time to discuss the newsletter further as Wayne has a visitor. Potential recruits to the chance-of-a-lifetime vitamin network marketing business arrive on a regular basis to the office. They are generally socially awkward men wearing shoes with man-made soles, themed socks and royal blue polyester suits. They are made to wait in the front office with Tina and myself while Wayne sits in his office drinking Coke and eating Maltesers. He is obviously of the belief that the longer his visitors are kept waiting, the more important he will appear when they are finally ushered into his office to be shown a flipchart containing key words such as 'motivation' and 'success'. The visitor emerges from Wayne's office two hours later looking dazed and disorientated as they stumble out into the sunlight, their pockets bulging with motivational literature on the wonders of the world of vitamin capsules. The truly sad ones are won over by the chance of a substitute social life at the Elstree Moathouse every week, where they will hopefully meet matching female social incompetents who might be willing to shag them.

Wayne comes out of his office beaming with self-belief, secure once again that he knows what he's doing. He has just signed up the latest desperado. As he tells us of his persuasive marketing skills, I notice he is sporting a badge on his lapel.

'What's that, Wayne?' I ask, curious as to why a grown man should be wearing badges. He looks at the badge and beams with pride.

'I was awarded this by the Executive Committee of Vita Plus. It means I have reached the next level of success. I am now a Senior Network Regional Executive Officer. I got a standing ovation at the Hilton last night.'

'Wow,' I say.

'That's great,' Tina adds. 'Congratulations.'

The newsletter is not mentioned again.

In the afternoon, Wayne calls me into his office for a chat. He is concerned that I do not offer him the respect that he feels he deserves as a boss. I am gobsmacked. I thought I could do no wrong in his eyes. After all, the figures on the temporary side of the business were up by 50 per cent with the added bonus that I thought I also made him laugh.

'Last week, for example,' he tells me, 'you told me one of my ideas was crap.' I recalled his suggestion that we have a weekly award ceremony for the temp who had worked the longest hours. Apart from the fact that I could not envisage his invitation for the temps to schlep across town to our offices on a Friday night to watch another from their ranks be awarded a £10 bonus and box of Quality Street being greeted with anything other than tired derision, I also doubted his motives. I suspected that, albeit subconsciously, he imagined taking the lucky winner out for a celebratory drink.

'Well, Wayne, I am sorry, but it was a crap idea,' I persist, perhaps unwisely.

'See what I mean!' he says. 'I think you should remember who is boss here.'

I then make a split second decision, balancing my reluctance to look for another job with an urge to tell him to grow up and fuck off.

'Look, OK. I know I can be very upfront and blunt at times. And I am sorry if I hurt your feelings. You do have some great ideas for the business,' I add, while privately wishing that he would implement at least one of them instead of dangling cherry wood desks, sofas and kitchen utilities in front of our noses and doing, or to be more precise, spending, nothing. Maybe he is traumatised by his divorce and needs to be macho at work, asserting his dominance with me. I try some reverse psychology.

'You know, we really like having you as our boss, Wayne,' I tell him.

Big mistake. He puts his hand on my knee and looks into my eyes. 'Do you?' he asks. 'You have lovely eyes, you know.' His hand is still on my knee. I start to get flustered. One minute I feel as if I am fighting for my job, the next I feel as if I should be grateful that he is being nice to me. Do I ask him to take his hand off my knee? Do I pretend it's not there? Is it a big deal? Maybe he's just reaching out? Perhaps it's just a gesture. Hang on! Am I going mad or is the hand moving up my thigh ever so slightly? I am watching his lips move, he is speaking, but I'm not focusing on a word he is saying. All I am conscious of is the hand on my leg, which is now gently patting me in a 'you're OK really' kind of way. As the conversation seems to be winding down, I start to stand up, anxious for his hand to leave my leg. He gets up too and I immediately sense a hug alert. Before I can stop him, he has planted a kiss on my cheek, ostensibly to seal the fact that we are now friends again. Maybe he is just an affectionate guy, I think, as I leave his office, my cheeks burning from embarrassment and horror and I don't know what.

When I return to my desk, Tina tells me that Luca has called and he is going to hers for dinner tonight. 'Apparently, he has something to tell me,' she says. 'I do hope he hasn't got himself into trouble with another girl,' she adds, a concerned look on her face. She notices that I look pink and odd. 'Are you alright?' she asks.

I tell her about my meeting with Wayne, suddenly delighted that I have a bona fide excuse for looking flustered while simultaneously registering the words 'trouble with another girl'. This is all too complicated. I want to go home and lie down.

Actually, I don't think I can face seeing Tina tomorrow after her dinner with Luca, when she finds out that I've been lying to her for the last two days. 'Tina,' I say tentatively, 'I want to tell you something.' The phone rings. She answers and it's for me. Robert, the practice manager at the surgery, wants me to know that Tanya has been making lengthy personal calls to her bank, daughter, the gas company and everyone else who knows her and they've asked her not to come back tomorrow. I grovel with apologies and promise to reduce our fees substantially while removing Tanya's card from my index system, tearing it in half and throwing it in the bin. I spend the next fifteen minutes looking for a replacement before settling for the domineering but professional Angela, who tells me that Bert is still sending her wages to her old bank, despite the fact that she has let him know her new bank details several times, both in a letter and over the phone. On her firm instructions (you don't argue with this lady), I take down her new bank details yet again and tell her about three times that I will pass them on to Bert, and yes, I will actually stand over him to make sure he changes the details on the computer.

When I get off the phone, I venture into the back office. I decide to launch straight in.

'Why have you repeatedly failed to change Angela's bank details?' I ask Bert, my irritation evident.

He quickly closes the FreeCell window, although not quick enough for me to miss it.

'Angela who?'

'Angela who has worked for us for over five years and the only Angela on our books.'

'Angela Connolly?'

'That's right. The one who has given you her new bank details at least twice. I've promised her that I'll watch over you while you change them.'

Bert mutters while closing down all the programmes in the most long-winded way I've ever seen before he opens up the temps' details page. Still muttering, he scans down for Angela's name and painstakingly changes her details, while I stand behind him breathing through my mouth to avoid inhaling the stench of stale sweat emanating from the space between his neck and shirt collar.

'Hasn't she got great legs?' Wayne has just entered the room and is staring at me as I lean over Bert's desk to make sure that the details are correct. He is asking the wrong person. Apart from the fact that Bert is completely unable to say anything nice ever, especially about me, he is also asexual and no doubt wrote off sex many, many years ago as an over-rated waste of time and energy. Thus, Bert continues to stare unblinkingly at the screen in front of him.

The problem is that I love receiving compliments so I'm probably not as angry as perhaps I might or should be. I quite like my legs, too, and I've been programmed to believe that it's nice to have this confirmed by the male species, albeit one from the outer reaches of classification. I'm also pleased that Wayne loves me again and that my job is safe. But at the same time, I'm aware that his comments and actions are increasingly inappropriate and I'd rather he desisted. On the other hand, I (foolishly) believe that the fact that he fancies me gives me some power over him.

Tina spends the next hour and a half interviewing applicants while I spend time in the loo planning my speech. Finally, the last applicant leaves and I make Tina a cup of tea and sit in front of her desk. I don't skirt the issue.

'I met Luca the other night and we have seen each other a couple of times.' She looks stunned, then recovers and smiles. I tell her he came to the office on Monday evening to look for her and found me instead.

'That's wonderful, Emma. You're a lovely girl. I can't believe you didn't tell me anything before now. I suppose that's why he wants to talk to me tonight.'

'God, Tina. I was so scared about how you'd react. You know I adore you but I didn't know whether you would approve, and it is a bit awkward with you being his mum and me being your colleague.'

'Sweetheart,' she says, 'I wish you luck with him, but you do know he goes through women at an alarming rate?'

'No, I didn't know,' I say, feeling depressed and then hurt in advance.

'You see, that's the thing. That's why I always keep my distance from his girlfriends. I used to get close to the girls and then they'd split up and I'd feel like I was losing a daughter.'

'What are you telling me?' I ask.

'He's just a bit flighty. I think he saw me and his father unhappily married and he's probably been put off the whole settling down thing.'

'Well, thanks for warning me. Shall we not discuss it any further?'

'It's probably best for the time being,' and I get my second kiss on the cheek for the day.

Twenty minutes later and I am in bed, the covers pulled up over my head. Tina's portrayal of her son as a random fuck machine does not match her son's description of himself as highly selective. Someone is lying. My gut feeling tells me that it's Tina. My head (or is it my pussy?) then pipes up with 'Well, you would want to believe that, wouldn't you.'

After only two evenings together I am beginning to really like Luca. Let's put it this way, I haven't discovered anything I don't like. Normally, all the bad signs are there at the beginning. You can see pretty much the whole picture on the first and second date, if you really want to; it's just that most of us would rather not. We prefer to ignore the bad signs and pretend that the man we've just met is, in fact, the man of our dreams. The one that was unfaithful? He had a girlfriend when *you* met him! The one that couldn't help himself flirting? He was eyeing up the waitress on your first date – don't tell me you didn't see! The one that never listened to a word you said? He chased you right into the bedroom as soon as you got back from the cinema! At the time you kidded yourself he was overcome with lust for you; now you realise he couldn't be bothered to have a conversation. The tight-fisted one? He screwed up his eyes to scrutinise the restaurant bill and then grimaced when he realised it was right! The inconsiderate one? He turned up half an hour late to pick you up without ringing first and without apologising! The one that got back with his ex? Come to think of it, he did talk about her an awful lot that first night!

We shouldn't blame ourselves for failing to pick up on the bad signs – who wants to start looking all over again? So much more convenient if the man in front of you is Mr Right, and if you have to twist the facts or ignore the warning signs, then so be it.

But so far, there really is nothing I have found that I don't like about Luca. I like the way he talks, dresses, kisses and holds me. I'm interested in what he has to say; I feel he is interested in what I have to say. There were no signs of stinginess in the bar or restaurant. No bad vibes with Simon being gay. No judgemental comments. No banging on about ex-girlfriends, but enough disclosure to reveal a healthy attitude towards women. Who wants someone who's never been hurt?

So say my gut feeling is right and Luca isn't lying – why would Tina want to put me off? Maybe she doesn't approve of me. Could it be that she sees me as perfectly pleasant company in the office, but that for her it ends there, hence her complete shutdown at the end of the day? As she's the kind of person who is nice to everyone, am I just one more person with whom it is politic to be friendly? But then, we do chat at a very personal level at times, and I was touched last week when she told me that no matter what happens during the day, chatting to me is always one of the nicest parts of her day. She couldn't be that fake.

I don't think it is as simple as her liking me, which I genuinely feel that she does. I have a horrible feeling that she doesn't think I am good enough for her son. He's very bright, he's very good-looking, he's very charming, and he's her first-born, and I think she has a pretty good idea of the kind of person she sees as her daughter-in-law.

She is a bit of a snob. Because she grew up and lived in NW8 until relatively recently, she sees herself as a class above most of the women who work for the agency and I think this might include me. Despite her slightly tarty style, I can see she's proud of the few relics from her old life (Chanel bag, Ferragamo shoes, Tiffany earrings, Gucci belt and fuck off diamond ring). I think she is planning on a posh bird for her son. Apart from the fact that she's into status, there is also the financial security that comes with a sensible marriage to a wealthy woman. And as we know, financial security is very important to Tina.

Please Fancy Me

I fall asleep quickly and immediately plummet into a weird and wonderful Technicolor dreamworld featuring Tina, an asymmetrical folding table and a naked man (not Luca). I awaken, confused, five hours later at eleven o'clock and unwillingly drag myself from bed to check out the answering machine to find out whether Luca has called. As I traipse into the living room, dishevelled with vertical hair, I realise with mixed feelings that Simon is still up. In a way, I am pleased as I feel quite depleted without our daily chat. On the other hand, I would ideally like to return to bed within the next five minutes before I wake up fully and become lively and then end up going to bed at two in the morning.

'Yo dude!' he shouts out.

'Has anyone called for me?' I ask him. 'Has anyone called' is our equivalent of the traditional greeting 'Hello, how are you?' It's business first, socialise later. In fact, the result of the business enquiry very often determines the nature of the socialising. When I first started living with Simon, it used to offend me that he would walk in the door after a day's absence and the first words that came out of his mouth were 'Has anyone called?' Taking offence, I would reply, 'Fine. And you?' Nine months later and I have also dispensed with accepted civilities.

'Yeah, your mum, your brother, Claudia and Sonia. They all want to know where you've been the last three days. No-one's heard from you. And somebody called about half an hour ago but I let the machine pick up. I taped *Seinfeld* and *Larry Sanders* for you.'

'Oh, darling, thank you,' I say, before scurrying into the kitchen to play the message. 'Emma, Luca, call me.' Now I feel happy and want to chat to Simon.

'It was Luca,' I tell him on my return to the living room, planning not to return Luca's call until tomorrow. Not so much of a 'treat 'em mean' policy, more of a 'not *too* keen at the beginning' policy.

'How was last night?' Simon asks. 'Did it all fall apart after I left? You know, go a bit flat?'

'No, it got much better. That's the first time in about a year that I have seen the same person two nights in a row.'

'I take it you're still a virgin.'

'Certainly am,' I tell him.

'Ooh, you make me sick. Serve you right if he never calls you again and you missed out on a great shag,' Simon says.

'Listen, if he never rings me again, I'll make your life hell for at least two weeks with my whinnying and moaning, so think carefully before you wish for that.'

'I don't wish for it. I wish for you to grab sexual satisfaction where you can. When you're an old, wrinkled granny who's gagging for it, you'll regret your abstinence last night. Perhaps if I tell you what happened to me last night, you may find the motivation you need.'

'Do I need a joint for this?'

'Yes. Now settle down and prepare to listen uninterruptedly. Last night was terrible.'

Dramatic pause.

'Terrible,' he repeats. Another pause for the impact of quite how terrible it was to sink in. I'm about to say something. He stops me with another 'Terrible.'

'Terrible?' I ask, knowing that acknowledgement is all most people want, Simon in particular.

'That's right. I found a completely new way to be humiliated. I went to B.J.s, you know, that new gay bar I told you about?'

I don't go to gay bars with Simon any more because I got fed up with being sexually invisible, an intolerable state of affairs.

'Anyway,' he continues, knowing I love his humiliation stories, 'two guys on the door gave everybody a number as they came in and then they shouted out your number on a microphone. Everyone was milling around wearing these numbers on their T-shirts. There were some really gorgeous guys there, by the way. Anyway, the idea was that you saw someone you liked and you gave your number and their number to the compère, and after an hour or so, some queen announced over the loudspeaker who liked who. Well, you can guess what happened, the same numbers kept coming up again and again and not one single person handed in my number.'

'Oh, shit, Simon. Now you know what it's like for me at these bars,' I say.

'Yes, but you're a woman. Anyway, I was beginning to feel really bad and ugly when a guy came up to me at the bar and put a piece of paper in my hand and then walked off. He was relatively cute, and without wanting to appear too uncool I immediately unfolded the piece of paper and greedily read it by the light of my cigarette lighter. I really thought my luck had changed. The note said something like "I've been watching you and I think you are absolutely fucking gorgeous. Call me and let's get together", and it had his telephone number. I scoured the room trying to find him and when I couldn't find him I thought he might have been lurking in the loos, waiting for me. I tried not to actually run as I made my way through the throngs. No sign of him in the loo, so to cheer myself up I sat down in one of the cubicles and took the note out of my pocket to reread it and remind myself that I am a sexually attractive individual. Oh God, Emma, you're not going to believe this, but under the bright lights of the toilets, I noticed, on careful scrutiny, that the piece of paper that he gave me was a fucking photocopy. I thought he had hastily scribbled the note in pencil in his mad, hungry lust for me. Turns out this guy must have photocopied this love letter, probably fifty times or something, and has been handing it out indiscriminately all evening.'

I start laughing and, soon enough, he joins me. Lately, his stories start pretty much the same way, with hope and unarguably good signs, and end up pretty much the same way, with varying degrees of humiliation, but even I could not have guessed the ending to that one.

'Aaaaaaaargh! God, that's awful. Listen, why don't you give up for a while. You've actually reached the "please look at me stage",' I tell him. He groans.

'You're right. No-one is even looking at me. But I can't give up. I want a man really bad,' he whimpers, snatching the joint from me.

'Even more reason why you should give up. You'll end up with a wanker. That's the best you can hope for when you're this desperate,' I add.

The 'please look at me' phase is the worst stage to reach, and there is no way out from this one for the foreseeable future, as Simon knows.

The optimum stage is to automatically assume that everybody wants to go to bed with you. That's the 'everyone wants to go to bed with me' stage. The irony of this stage is that it usually occurs when you are madly in love with someone (your eyes are shining, your gait takes on an unconscious but discernible wiggle, your pheromones are raging, etc., etc.), and the last thing on your mind is shagging someone else. You are so happy that you don't even need the affirmation of everyone fancying you, which isn't to say you don't enjoy it (who wouldn't?), it's just that you take it in your stride. At its most extreme, you can attract men, women and children. During one brief but memorable stint at this stage a few years ago, confirmed heterosexual women were flirting with me and I was seriously harassed at a bus stop by a group of very cute ten-year-old boys.

The next stage down is to be pleasantly, although not altogether surprised when somebody wants to go to bed with you. I suppose this is a constant stage for people with healthy self-esteem. It's not until you've been binned, lost your job or suffered some other serious setback to your self-esteem that you slide down to the less desirable stages, described below.

The next stage is known as 'please fancy me'. You will actually give off mild desperation vibes and have to work pretty hard to get somebody to want to go to bed with you. You arrive at a party and know that however technically attractive you thought you looked in the mirror before leaving home, it's going to be an uphill struggle. Rejection is certain; it's just a matter of how much rejection you are prepared to suffer before either going home or pulling. The quality of the pull is irrelevant and to enquire further in this regard shows you are missing the point. It's not about whether you fancy them (although admittedly this does help when it comes to follow-through), it's about whether they fancy *you*. The *raison d'être* of the pull is to establish whether anyone could possibly fancy you again. The motivation behind the pull is to prove that someone, somewhere does. If you don't actually manage to persuade anyone to fancy you for more than three consecutive months, you end up at the bottom of the ladder – the 'please look at me' stage.

This is where Simon currently finds himself, and the desperation vibes are so strong that they can be smelled at more than fifty paces. The usual response is a universal aversion of eye contact, just in case anyone else should be infected through any form of contact with you. The only reason a guy will ever willingly approach you is to find out whether your friend is single. If you try and chat someone up, they will make their excuses and leave immediately. You turn up at parties and, literally, no-one looks at you. You don't even merit a glance. You are invisible. You don't exist, and at the end of the evening you go home and pinch yourself just to prove that you do. It is normally during this stage that you find out that your emergency husband (a rather unattractive but kindly ex-boyfriend who you assume will love you forever and who you may consider if things get desperate and you are single in your late-thirties) has met and fallen madly in love with someone. He'll still talk to you at a party during the 'please look at me' stage, but only to lord it over you that he's met someone and no longer needs to be patronised by you.

The good news is that you can make a vertical ascent up the ladder once you've reached the bottom, and people have been known to skip a few of the lower stages and end up near the top of the sexual attractiveness ladder. The bad news is that I can never remember how to get up from the 'please look at me' stage. The other bit of bad news is that no-one can actually determine how long one will languish there. When I was seventeen, I spent a whole year there, although I then managed to miraculously leapfrog the in-between stages and spent the next two years at the top of the ladder at the 'everyone wants to go to bed with me' stage. They are now referred to with reverence as the glory years.

I urge Simon to surrender to his lowly place at the bottom of the sexual attractiveness ladder.

'It could be worse, I suppose,' he says, sighing.

I am stunned. Worse than the 'please look at me' stage?

'To what stage could you possibly be referring?' I ask, horrified in advance.

'I could reach the "please *don't* look at me" stage. You know, where I am filled with self-loathing and disgust.'

Once I have cheered him up by reminiscing about his top of the ladder months, I tell him about Wayne's chat and kiss and cuddle. Simon tells me, once again, that Wayne is a creep and waves aside my assurances that, apart from the kisses and cuddles and lewd comments, he is really a great boss, shouting 'Creep!' every time I try to say something in Wayne's defence.

The Creep

The next morning I wake up on time and feel wonderfully refreshed after my thirteen-hour sleep marathon. I arrive in the office early to find Tina already there. I notice during the day that she is not quite herself with me. She is still lovely and kind and helpful, but she does not confide in me at all. We normally chat about our evenings, what we ate, who we saw, what we watched, but today neither of us offers any information about what we did the night before. Wayne arrives late, as usual, and hides himself in his office, unwilling to engage in any way with the business he has bought, despite the fact that due to Tina's and my own hard work, canvassing and schmoozing new clients, the business is desperately busy and our only problem now is finding people to send out to our new and old clients who match up to our boasts of excellence.

The temps desk is desperately busy all morning and Tina helps me out. I really appreciate this. She could just let me tear my hair out; she doesn't make any money from putting her own work on hold by spending the morning trying to find a legal secretary, a French translator and someone who knows shorthand for my urgent temporary bookings. We're a great team, I think, as we manage to find someone semi-suitable for each client.

In return for her help, I offer to spend the afternoon brainstorming the permanent positions with her. She hasn't made a decent placement for nearly ten weeks and I can tell she's panicking. We are normally very productive during these brainstorming sessions, as I often think of candidates she's overlooked. The truth is that I think I am a better judge of character than her and can therefore suss out who is right for which job. Normally she'd jump at the offer.

'Very sweet of you darling, but I'm alright at the moment,' she says.

I have registered her refusal of help but feel too confused to do much with it, except immediately repress it.

'Well in that case, I'm going out to get something for lunch. Do you want anything?' I ask, rummaging through my bag so that she can't see the hurt expression on my face.

'If you're going to the deli I'll have a salad niçoise, and if you go to the café a baked potato with cottage cheese,' she says, standing up. 'Here, let me give you some money.'

'But you never take any money off me. Let me get it – my treat,' I implore her.

'Don't be silly, darling. Please. Take the money.'

So I do. She always insists on paying and I can't decide whether it's generosity or largesse. Normally, I don't mind, although the 'take the money' arguments can become a little tiresome. Today, however, it feels mildly insulting, as if she won't let me give her anything.

While I'm out of the office, I ring Luca on his mobile. I'm a bit nervous. To be honest, I am very nervous. I really like him and hope that the last twenty-four hours haven't done anything to affect the magic of the first two dates. He picks up after the second ring.

'Emma! I was just about to ring you. How are you?'

'Great thanks. You?'

'Horny as hell.'

'When do you want to come over?'

'Can't we change the "when" to a "where"?'

'I'm in a queue in a café!' I whisper. 'Did you see your mum last night?'

'Yeah, I told her we'd met and that we were friends.'

'So that's what we are?'

'That's what I told *her*. You don't understand; it's better that she doesn't think it's serious as then she'll start getting involved and interfering and I just don't want that. Past experiences. Honest.'

'One minute we're friends, next it's serious.'

'We're seriously friendly. That's right, isn't it?'

'I thought I was your girlfriend after the other night. Anyway, it doesn't really affect things, except the sex, obviously, as I don't sleep with friends.'

The man in front of me in the queue turns round to check me out.

'I don't want you to sleep with me. I want you to stay awake all night. I want to know what I have to do to get to spend the night with you.'

'We've only met each other twice! What's the hurry?'

'I've already had about ten wanks since we last saw each other.'

'I'm still in the café.'

'What are you doing tonight?' he asks.

'What? So you can harass me? I get enough of that during the day.'

The man in front turns round to have another look at me.

'This is turning vicious. You're comparing me to Wayne. I feel sick. Listen, I've got tickets for a great gig at the Watford Hilton tonight. There'll be loads of drugs there.'

'You don't mean vitamins, do you?'

'Yeah, sorry, vitamins. Do you fancy it?'

'I can't, I'm washing my friend's hair.'

'Seriously, I've got preview cinema tickets – freebies from work. Shall I pick you up?'

'I'd love to, but I am actually washing my friend's hair. I promised I'd do her roots for her. It's my bezzy mate and it's been in the diary for a while. You know the kind of person who dumps their mates when they meet someone?'

'And you're not like that. OK. It's good for you to see your friend; you can tell her all about me. Are you going to mention my hairy back or are you going to make out that I'm perfect?'

'I'm not a liar, and anyway, it's not what I would call a hairy back. It is a back and it does have some hair on it but I normally think of hairy backs as being literally coated with hair. One of my friends went out with someone whose back was so hairy that when she woke up in the middle of the night, she couldn't tell whether he was facing her or had his back to her.'

'Who is he? The Wolfman?' Luca asks.

'No, an Iranian with a penchant for handcuffs and anal sex.'

'My kind of guy. Let's all go out for the evening.'

'He's long gone.'

'Why? He sounds lovely.'

'Salad niçoise and a chicken salad mayo on granary, please.'

'They really split up over that? Who wanted what?'

'Can I call you later?'

'No. I want to talk to you now.'

'I know you're used to getting your own way but what's more important, you or food?'

'Me, obviously.'

'You're right,' I say. 'Sorry, I'm hanging up,' I tell the deli man, who is getting almost as angry as the people standing behind me in the queue.

'I'll call you later.'

'Bye.'

I'm in love and practically dance, skip and jump back to the office. Obviously, I tone it down for Tina and try not to look too happy as I sense my excitement may offend her. In my great mood, I am able to see things from her point of view. For someone who likes to keep their boundaries so firmly intact and who works so hard to maintain them, arriving at work and finding out that they are well and truly fucked must be rather disheartening. I should imagine that she is pretty angry with Luca but cannot, I imagine, admit this to herself. It is easier to be offish with me than to bear any negative feelings towards her perfect son. She may be worried that he will be mean to me, and where will that leave her, when she still has to work with me?

The day passes quickly and I am left alone in the office with Wayne at six o'clock. I have been on my best behaviour with him during the day: no sarcastic comments, no 'bollocks' at his comments and no 'crap' at his suggestions. I've been quiet, dignified and professional. As I stand by the fax machine, feeding through our terms and conditions to a new client won over by Tina's cold-calling charisma and with whom we have just placed the only really good temp on our books, Wayne sits on Tina's desk opposite me, his eyes roaming unself-consciously up and down my body. I don't like it. We are rarely alone in the office together as Tina normally works much later than I do, and due to his vitamin commitments at various suicide-inducing hell-holes out of town, Wayne is rarely in the office beyond 5.30 p.m. I feel instinctively nervous and uncomfortable and determine to keep the conversation on a strictly professional basis. He obviously picks up on the vibe and decides the professional route is the best way to start the ball rolling.

'How are the temp bookings this week?' he asks, smiling at me.

I resist the temptation to reply that I'm surprised he is asking since I thought he wanted nothing to do with the business. He uses the equipment, has a desk here, holds meetings in his office, presumably withdraws a salary, and yet contributes absolutely nothing to the business whatsoever (apart from crummy newsletters).

'Really well, actually. It's a record month for us. Did I tell you my brother's advertising agency is using three of our women and paying great rates?' I reply instead.

'Using them for what?'

'What do you think for, bearing in mind this is a secretarial agency?' I say, adding 'Boss,' with a forced grin.

'I wouldn't mind three women on a month-long booking,' he says, actually winking at me.

'Got something in your eye?' I ask, losing the battle to refrain from sarcastic disrespect.

To give him some credit, he does laugh.

'You're doing brilliantly, Emma,' he says, looking at the temp sheet after a minute's silence. 'I've been going through the figures with Bert and I'm delighted. To be honest, it's the temp side that's keeping the business going. Tina hasn't made a permanent placement for nearly two and a half months and I'm getting worried. Problem is that I like Tina very much and I like having her around. We're a great team, but I don't know how much longer I can give it without rethinking the situation.'

I almost feel like congratulating him for managing to break a completely new boundary. What is he doing confiding in me? How am I supposed to react to Tina tomorrow knowing that her job might be in danger? Is he mad? Or just immature and stupid?

It is true that Tina hasn't made a placement for ages, and admittedly, since Wayne took over the business, her record has been appalling: she has only made three placements. One was a friend of mine that I effectively set up, while the others were for substantially reduced commission payments. She's also had her share of bad luck: another three placements fell through at the last minute. Tina keeps referring to a curse, but it has occurred to me that she has a mental block due to her constant fear that Wayne is going to replace her with a younger model, and it is almost as if she is unconsciously fulfilling her own prophecy.

I take the loyal colleague route.

'Firstly, Tina is fantastic at canvassing clients. Much better than me. You should have heard her on the phone to the new client that I'm faxing now. It was a charm onslaught – even I was melting and desperately racking my brains to find a reason to employ my own secretary. She was fantastic. She picks up most of the new clients, you know. The weird thing is that while Mr Fox was here, she was doing much better than me in terms of making money. I'm sure it's just a temporary situation.'

'Well, let's hope so.'

'But the thing is, Wayne, you shouldn't really be talking to me about this. You should talk it through with Tina, not me. I'd hate it if you talked like this to her about me,' I say, earnestly.

'You're right. Sorry to put you in an uncomfortable situation. You really are completely right. I suppose it's just that I feel a closeness to you. We've got a special understanding.'

I decide it is best to ignore the last comment. As I sit down at my desk to shut down my computer, he continues to chat to me.

'What are you doing tonight? Any plans?' he asks, all casual like. 'We should go out for dinner sometime.'

'I've got someone coming round for dinner so I'd better run.' I ignore the invitation.

'Man or woman?' he asks.

Instead of telling him to mind his own business, I reply, 'Woman.'

'Why haven't you got a boyfriend, Emma?' he asks. Once again, instead of telling him to mind his own business, I answer with my standard retort to this standard question.

'I suppose I haven't met the right man yet.'

Then I think of Luca and feel weak at the knees with accompanying flutters in my stomach and a shooting sensation in my knickers.

And he's off.

'God, I wish I had waited until I'd found the right person. I married Lisa when I was thirty-two and I was panicking that all my friends were getting married and I was feeling left behind. I think I knew on the wedding night that I'd made a mistake, but then she changed the day we married.'

He obviously wants to talk, but I decide it would be unwise

to enquire further. I want to leave the office as soon as possible without appearing rude. I am a little torn between wishing to consolidate my position in his good books after yesterday's little chat and knowing instinctively that intimate conversations with Wayne are likely to end excruciatingly. I grab my handbag and stuff my mobile, keys and diary into it.

'You're a very attractive girl, you know,' he says, leaning forward and staring into my eyes. 'I should've married someone like you instead. Much more fun than my boring wife whose only interests are ready-prepared meals and lunch with her mother.'

I smile, blush and put on my coat. Why do I smile? I should have scowled. Must be embarrassment.

'And you've got a great pair of tits. I'd love to see you in that T-shirt without your bra on.'

The smile leaves my face. I am completely gobsmacked. For a minute or two, I am simply too shocked to reply.

'Wayne, you have absolutely no right to make comments like that. In fact, I want an apology.' I am seriously angry but he is laughing, pleased that he has riled me.

He gives me a half-hearted apology. 'Look, I am sorry if I upset you.'

'There is no "if" about it. That was completely inappropriate.'

'I was trying to be nice. It was a compliment, for God's sake. What's going on when you can't pay a lady a compliment? This whole PC thing is out of control; it takes all the fun out of being a man and a woman. God, have I got to watch everything I say?'

'You're the one who's out of control, Wayne.'

And with that I storm out of the office, fuming and fearful of the destruction that will be unleashed by my fury if I say another word. I often escape from angry situations. Instead of staying and expressing my anger, I just walk out. Why is it so hard to tell someone how I feel? In the present situation,

I really do think that I am too scared at what will flow should I freely express myself. So instead I leave and carry the anger home with me for the evening, like an unwanted visitor.

The Office Shag

I am still fuming when I get home and ring Claudia to check whether she is still coming round for dinner and dye.

'You sound pissed off,' she says. 'What's up?'

'I'll tell you about it when you come round. Eight o'clock OK?'

'Yeah. See you then.'

I think about ringing Luca to tell him what has happened. In one way, it is so easy to get used to the idea of having a man in my life who I can tell everything to and who, one hopes, will be on my side. But I don't want to fall into the trap of leaning on someone and expecting a boyfriend to make everything OK. There is also the fact that in the past, whenever I have rung a boyfriend for reassurance or support, I have rarely been reassured or supported. Perhaps men are genetically unable to offer support, but I suspect that it's a daddy thing (the kinder the daddy, the more supportive and reassuring the boyfriend). I then decide that it's too soon to have any such expectations or make such demands and I therefore resist the temptation to collapse into his arms.

Claudia arrives and I fill her in on the Wayne nonsense. I dye Claudia's roots for her every month or so and we tend to make an evening of it. I've made a beautiful mushroom risotto, filled the flat with flowers, put on a Dean Martin CD, filled the oil burners with lavender and utilised every candle in the living room. I love making a fuss of my friends.

The good thing about dyeing Claudia's hair is that I have a captive audience. Firstly, she is grateful that I save her the cash by doing it, especially as the peroxide stinks, so she tends to make it worth my while by focusing the conversation on me while I'm parting and coating. Secondly, she can't move and I am in possession of a sharp comb if the conversation takes an unscheduled turn.

She is thoroughly indignant on my behalf. It really helps to have someone acknowledge that his comments are inappropriate, although it is a shame that I need someone else to validate my belief that this is not a correct or fair way for him to treat me. Until Wayne's bra comment today, I have always regarded his lecherous comments and surreptitious gropes as irritating but minor transgressions rather than deeply offensive assaults.

'You know what? You should have stamped this shit out much earlier,' she says, sipping her gin and tonic and inhaling decisively on a cigarette.

'God, you are so right. Shit. I just let it go on and on,' I reply.

'But why? It really isn't like you to be the quietly suffering martyr. What's been going on?'

'I think I just pitied him. I thought he was an immature man with a small penis who was suffering a mid-life crisis. I suppose I thought it wouldn't escalate beyond harmless innuendo.'

'Oh, come on, it was on the cards. You told me he brushed past your tits the other day. He's not done that before has he?'

'No. Not actual hand-to-tit contact. Eye-to-tit contact, yes. Frequently.'

'This is what I'm telling you. He's hotting up. He's preparing for a major lunge.'

'Tina did point out last week that his daily game of pocket billiards is increasing in frequency and intensity.'

'Yuck. I hate standing in front of men who blatantly fiddle with their balls. Where are you supposed to look?'

We're quiet for a while. Then Claudia pipes up, 'Do you like the attention? Be honest.'

'What? From that grotesque gnome?' I say, indignantly. Then, 'A bit, I suppose, but I'd rather he just didn't say or do anything sexual at all.'

'I only asked cause you've been single for a while and sometimes it's nice to have someone fancy you and make a fuss of you.'

'I suppose, it has been vaguely flattering, although I don't know why as he is completely indiscriminating.'

'So you just let it go.'

'You sound like you're blaming me,' I say, poking her scalp with the comb.

'I'm not. I'm just surprised that you've not been more ballsy, so to speak.'

'It's really difficult when it's your boss. You're right, normally I would definitely say something if I thought someone was being too over-familiar. Or say it was a colleague rather than a boss, I'd give as good as I got or just tell them to piss off, depending on whether I fancied them. I've treated this situation differently because he's my boss.'

'Why do you see yourself as the underdog with no power and no rights when it comes to bosses, Emma? You do realise that this has happened before?'

'I don't know why. Technically, I know we're equals, but it just doesn't feel that way somehow. And they do have the power – they pay us.'

'Wrong. In this case, you hold the power.'

'What do you mean?'

'You run that business for him. Tina's not made any money for months, he doesn't know the first thing about recruitment and temps, all the clients know you and love you, you get on with the women, you are brilliant at charming people that come in. He'd be lost without you and don't forget it.'

'I'll try to remember that,' I say meekly.

'You must. He should be seriously rethinking his behaviour tonight. I should think he's pretty worried that you'll walk.

Actually, why don't you just look for another job and get away from the creep?'

'Would you believe me if I told you I like my job? I know that doesn't sound like me, but finally I've found a job that I enjoy. Well, when I say enjoy, I mean I don't mind going in and I never clock watch. I don't want it to come to this.'

'Then nip it in the bud as soon as possible. You've let it go on too long.'

'I'm going to write a memo telling him not to make any more personal comments. Get it back on a professional basis. I won't laugh at his jokes any more and I won't smile at his compliments. I'll be polite, slightly cold and great at my job.'

'Why don't you just talk to him?'

'God, I couldn't possibly. I really can't face him at the moment. I'll keep it formal. Anyway, if I speak to him, I don't know whether he'll take me seriously. He'll turn it into a joke or wave me aside. If I show him I'm serious, you know, by putting it in writing, he'll take the situation a lot more seriously and hopefully stop mucking about. Up until today, I've found it more of a nuisance than anything else, but today I was actually offended and I do feel angry.'

'I had sex in the office on Monday night,' Claudia says. 'Sorry to change the subject. Did you want to continue ranting about Wayne?'

'No! I want to hear about your office shag. I've never had sex in the office. What? Where? When? Who? Why?'

'God, it was really horny. It happened more out of urgent necessity. You know Monday was the day I met Ben after our three-week break? So things were both a bit uncertain and exciting when we met in a bar near my office after work. We talked and groped and snogged. At about nine, we decided we couldn't get home quick enough and stood outside in the freezing bloody cold to wait for a cab. But after half an hour of waiting, all the passion was ebbing away. We went to my office to call a taxi and wait in the warm, and as soon as we got to my desk I realised that I needed to have sex that instant. I had a sniff round our open-plan office to look for a spot but there were no hidden corners. The security team are pretty diligent: as well as the CCTV, they also walk round the floors of the building ten times a day. We were lucky, though, as a security guard walked past and nodded to me. I knew we must have some time until the next tour. You know Fergus? You met him at my Christmas party. Well, he's having his own office built, and although it isn't quite complete – no doors, no windows, no ceiling, no privacy – it nearly had four walls. I beckoned Ben into the office – he had no idea what was on my mind. He couldn't understand why I was so keen for him to see Fergus's new office, but once I suggested an office shag, we were on the floor within seconds. The absolute minimum was removed to ensure that the shag could take place: one boot, one leg of tights, knickers half on, top lifted, one trouser leg, skirt up. It was amazing. It was fast, thrusting, wild and over in about five minutes. It was obviously very loud, though, as while we were readjusting our clothing, another security guard suddenly appeared out of nowhere. He nodded, and although he was grinning I thought he could only have been suspicious rather than certain of our indiscretion. But when I rolled into work yesterday, I realised that this wasn't the case. Every single member of the security team said good morning to me and used my first name. Some of them even seemed to make special trips to my floor as there were far more visits than normal. Every time I looked up I saw one of these grinning security guards smiling at me. The one that caught us no doubt told all the others. Probably made their week.'

'Either that or they've all been watching the CCTV video,' I suggest, perhaps a little meanly.

'That has occurred to me, too, but the thought of a bunch of old, past-it ex-coppers sitting round watching me screwing is too awful to contemplate and I have refused to think about it since.'

'Good idea'.

Luca calls me on his way home from the cinema and is completely adorable. I had this idea that he wouldn't be interested in hearing my problems at this early stage in our relationship, but he listens to me intently as I tell him the Wayne story, not interrupting once. He is taking Wayne's behaviour seriously and suggests I do the same, although he doesn't think the memo is a good idea. He reckons that I should go and speak to Wayne and tell him that his behaviour has pissed me off, rather than resorting to writing notes.

'You know what it's like when you live with someone and get home to find they have left you a note telling you not to do something, I don't know, piss on the carpet, for example. Then you leave them a note and everybody's seething, whereas if they just had a quick word with you, the whole thing would be dealt with and then blow over. Do you see what I mean?' he asks.

'Have you been pissing on the carpet again?' I don't finish the sentence with a comment about his mum not being around to clear it up as he is being supportive and I don't want to annoy him. 'I don't want to speak to him. I can't face him. If I leave him a memo, he'll know he has to stop and then I can carry on as normal.'

'I suppose you've got to do what you feel comfortable doing. I thought you were spunkier.'

'I am spunky, I promise. I'm just not as hard and impenetrable as I seem.'

'You're not hard but you are impenetrable.'

'What do you mean, I'm not hard?'

'Hard? You're a complete pussy cat! I'm not even remotely

fooled by the tough exterior. It's completely transparent. Surely I'm not the first person to tell you that.'

'The first person to tell me that has only known me for three days.'

'You mean it's our three-day anniversary already? In that case, I'm taking you out for dinner tomorrow night.'

'How long are you this wonderful for?'

'About another four days or so.'

'As long as that?'

'No, I'm actually really, really nice and thoughtful and loving and romantic all the time.'

'Thank God for that. I thought you were one of those men who are totally amazing for the first month and then transform overnight into a monosyllabic agrophobe.'

'Are you suggesting that my behaviour so far has been totally amazing?'

'Well, you are being quite nice,' I say, becoming a little embarrassed.

'I can be much nicer than this.'

'Then why aren't you being much nicer?'

'When you're nicer, I'll be nicer.'

'You think I'm not nice because we haven't had sex yet?'

'It's not really the sex,' he says. 'It's more not being allowed to stay the night.'

'Maybe on our six-month anniversary.'

'See what I mean!'

'Not at all. I'm happy to go out for dinner with you tomorrow night. That's very nice of me.'

'Why? Are you paying?'

That stumps me.

'Are you still there?'

'Yes,' I say, quietly. I hate being lost for words.

'So where are you taking me?' he persists.

'I know a nice Mexican where you can eat until you puke for a pound.'

'I'll pick you up at eight.'

'I can't wait.'

'Really?' he says, sounding unsure but chuffed.

'Really. I'm really looking forward to seeing you.'

'Me too.'

Thank Fuck it's Friday

Contrary to Luca's advice, I leave a memo on Wayne's desk the following morning explaining that I would appreciate it if he refrained from making any more personal comments about my appearance. He ignores me for the rest of the day. I have told Tina what happened with Wayne yesterday, and although she tells me that she is disgusted, she still rushes into his office within five minutes of him arriving in the office that morning with a cup of tea and some biscuits.

Then I think something that I haven't thought for a while – thank God it's Friday. I can't wait to get away from Tina's arse-licking, Wayne's immaturity, Bert's misogyny, the clients' complaints and the temps' demands. I can't wait to have a lie-in, read the papers in bed, slob in front of the television, hang out with Simon and do what the hell I want when I want. And most of all, I can't wait to see my arse-licking colleague's son.

By the time 5.30 arrives, I practically fly through the door, hurling a few 'have a good weekend's over my shoulder.

Luca picks me up in a cab at eight and takes me to a gorgeous Thai restaurant in Islington and then on to the Medicine Bar down the road for a couple of drinks. By the time we get back to the flat at one, Simon is already home from a night at The Cage, having finally taken my advice about not bothering to attempt to pull.

'See anyone you like the look of?' Luca asks Simon, trying to be au fait with the situation.

'I saw plenty of people I liked the look of. The problem was that no-one liked the look of me, apart from one old bloke with big hair, a sun-bed tan and a really lined face.'

'An exquisitely coiffeured bollock, in other words,' says Luca

'You know the type. The awful thing is that when I first got there, I thought someone was actually giving me the eye. Has Emma told you my current relationship status?'

'She told me you're at the "please look at me" stage'

'Emma!' says Simon, looking mortified. 'How could you?'

'Luca!' I say. 'How could you?'

'Oh, come on. We've all been there,' says Luca.

'I haven't,' I say, lying but desperate to appear incontrovertibly gorgeous in front of my new man.

'Except Emma, who languishes permanently at the "everybody" stage,' Luca says, while Simon stifles a snigger.

'Yeah, right. Anyway, every time I look up, this bloke is looking at me. I've seen him in there a few times over the past couple of weeks and he always stares at me in this kind of adoring trance. He's no oil painting, but he's not a three bagger, either.'

'I know what a two bagger is, but I've never heard of a three bagger,' says Luca.

'One bag for their head, one for yours and one to throw up in afterwards.'

'Of course. Makes perfect sense.'

'Have you ever slept with a three bagger?' I ask Luca.

'The truth, please, Mr Moretti' insists Simon.

'Not for a long, long time. I promised myself a few years ago that I would only have sex with people I fancy.' says Luca

'I wish I had that luxury. So there we both are, sitting adjacent to each other at the bar, me and the one-and-a-half bagger, and he's gazing at me and I decide, what the hell, I've got to climb back up that ladder and if it means starting at the bottom, then so be it.'

'Well, a friend of mine has this theory that if you're going through a really barren patch with women and nothing's working, you should go out with someone who you consider way below you on the desirability stakes to get your confidence going. He says the gratitude and adoration you receive is a huge boost to your ego and this then allows you to dump them while giving you the confidence to go for someone generally more attractive. He says it works. You just keep moving on up, trading up each time.' Says Luca, trying to be helpful.

'Sounds charming,' I say.

'Don't be a hypocrite!' cries Simon. 'What the hell do you think I was doing tonight? No difference at all.'

'I don't agree with your attitude, either. Maybe it's a male thing. I don't like the idea of grading people according to their looks, with the ugliest people being used, abused and discarded,' I say.

'Can I *please* finish the story?' shouts Simon.

'Wish you would,' I say.

'Right. So I go up to him and say something along the lines of – "You're always staring at me."'

'What was the actual line you used?' I ask, intrigued.

'Far too cringey to tell you. So he looks back at me blankly as if I'm a complete nutter. I say I've seen him in the club a few times before. And get this, he says he's never seen me before in his life and claims that he hadn't even noticed me until I went up to him. We actually stood there arguing for a bit about whether he fancied me, with me insisting that he did. Eventually, it turns out he's short-sighted and doesn't wear glasses to clubs, hence the glassy stare. Can you believe it? Then he excused himself to greet his new boyfriend, leaving me on my own.'

'Ouch. Are you going to start wearing *your* glasses to clubs from now on?' I want to know.

'No, next time I'll remain in blissful ignorance and walk around in a trance myself, believing that everyone fancies me.'

'Works for me,' says Luca.

'God, you're like that guy in *The Fast Show* who agrees with whatever anyone around you is saying.'

'You're right,' he says.

'He's just trying to get in with you by getting in with me,' says Simon. 'Don't be mean to him.'

'Yeah, don't be mean to me,' Luca says, pulling me towards him until I am sitting on his knee. I vaguely catch sight of him mouthing something to Simon, who then kisses me goodnight and leaves the room.

'Blimey,' I say, 'you've really charmed the pants off him.'

'Now I've just got to do the same to you,' he says, kissing my ear.

His charm is clearly bisexual as when I wake up in the morning, he's fast asleep next to me. We have one of those weekends where you only get out of bed to either go to the loo or to get something to eat. I love the fact that (a) he is able to surrender himself so easily to sloth, and (b) I don't have that nagging fear that he is planning a getaway after the next shag. In fact, when it gets to Sunday lunchtime and he has still made no move to leave the flat, I start to feel a little stir-crazy myself, but when I mention fresh air he recoils in horror and drags me back into bed. Simon becomes our unofficial butler, making us a huge fry-up on Sunday morning, buying the papers and fielding calls while maintaining a discreet distance. It's the best weekend I've had in years. Everything we do together, whether it is talking, having sex, kissing or cuddling, is heaven. I couldn't be any happier, and as the time passes, one hour flying by after the other, I realise that I am dreading Monday morning and my return to work. Obviously, I'd prefer to lounge around in bed for the rest of the week daydreaming about each of the phenomenal fucks with Luca. Instead, I have to work for a wanker whom I am beginning to despise.

Luca leaves me at ten on Sunday evening. I consider begging

him not to go but decide that it would be unwise as well as lacking in pride. It always seems to be men who decide when to break up the party, and experience has taught me that a temper tantrum makes things worse (although I think they probably like the ego boost). And anyway, he also has work and I suppose he needs to go back to his flat to iron shirts, drink beer and discuss football.

As we stand at the door, we are unable to stop kissing each other.

'I've had a brilliant time,' he says.

'Me too. The best in ages,'

'You're addictive. I don't want to leave you.'

'But you must?'

'Yeah, I need to touch base and iron shirts and things.'

'Course. Well, see you around,' I say, trying to be nonchalant.

'Maybe, yeah,' he says, smiling and kissing me again. 'I'll ring you tomorrow. Good luck with Wayne.'

The Sack

Monday morning arrives and I trudge to work, dreading seeing the lot of them. Bert gives me my salary slip mid-morning and it is not until I look at it more carefully over lunch that I notice I am about £200 short on the commission that I had calculated I was due. I'd had a monster month and I was looking forward to seeing my hard work reflected in increased commission in my salary. The shortfall could either be a coincidence, Bert's incompetence, my miscalculation or Wayne's revenge. Once I've double-checked my figures, I go into Wayne's office to tell him that Bert has made a mistake with my salary. I decide against approaching Bert with such a query as I suspect the best case scenario will be frustration, while the worst case will be a possible breakdown and/or facial twitch. Wayne used to smile and joke when I went into his office and we'd normally have a short but jovial chat about our weekends. This morning, however, he avoids eye contact with me while telling me abruptly that he will deal with it. Knowing Wayne's track record regarding 'dealing with it', I am not hopeful that anything will actually ever happen. I thought that he would take an error in salary seriously (after all, Tina and I are 'the business'), although the more I think about it, I suspect that doing absolutely fuck all will be his revenge for my memo to him. I am reluctant to leave his office without a more convincing assurance that he really will remedy the shortfall, but his vibes are mildly menacing and it's easier to simply leave the room and hope for the best.

I'm not a terribly conciliatory person, particularly when I feel I am in the right, as I do in this situation. I suppose those who hate an atmosphere would want to smooth things over with Wayne and try to patch up the lift. But I'm experienced at enduring long periods of hostile silence (my childhood was full of them) and I am therefore fully prepared to sit this out until Wayne cracks, apologises and confesses that he's been a fool, that he needs me, that I'm doing a great job, and then promises that his pitiful behaviour will cease forthwith. I'm also principled rather than pragmatic, which doesn't help the situation. I am aware that sensible, smart, mature people, who understand the world of work and are prepared to play the necessary games to ensure their survival, would probably be charming to Wayne while managing to hide their disdain. They ultimately get ahead by putting up and shutting up. I am just not like this. If I repress my anger for more than a couple of days, I end up depressed, sometimes with backache and a couple of nasty spots, followed by a small explosion. So instead of helping myself by being extra nice to Wayne while firmly but politely making my point, I am self-righteously indignant (and justifiably so, in my opinion) and completely unwilling to pander to him in any way or under any circumstances.

Sensing that Wayne will do nothing about my salary and feeling resentful that I have not been paid what is rightfully owed to me, I decide to approach him once again. Halfway through the afternoon, I tentatively knock on his office door and politely ask him whether he has had a chance to speak to Bert about the shortfall in my salary.

Now he stares at me with cold, beady eyes. 'Emma, I said I was dealing with it,' he says, sternly.

'I know. But when can I expect an answer?' I persist.

'When I have looked into the matter and not before. Now I am busy.'

He turns away from me and goes back to doing something to do with his vitamin business on his computer. I might have known that he wasn't busy working at making Search a success. I feel I have no choice but to drop the matter for the time being and hope that he comes back to me soon before things turn really nasty.

Naturally, Wayne doesn't deal with the matter of my commission and I leave the office once again at 5.30 p.m. on the dot with a bad feeling that I am going to be punished for daring to leave that memo on his desk.

When I speak to Luca in the evening, I have to reluctantly agree that perhaps the memo wasn't the best way of dealing with the situation.

'Has your mum said anything to you about it?' I ask him, before I can stop myself.

'Mum never talks about work, you know that.'

'Or me, I suppose.'

'It's better that way.'

'Why?'

'Trust me, it is. You don't know my mum as well as I do.'

'My initial instinct when someone tells me to trust them is to distrust them completely.'

'OK, don't trust me. I trust you, though.'

'Do you?'

'Yeah. I feel really good about you. You're honest, I know where I stand with you. You're too upfront to be crafty. Although I take your point about the "trust me" line. It is a bit bullshitty.'

'It's like when people say "I'm not angry, honestly, but . . ." and you can tell they're just seething underneath.'

'What about when they say "I really don't mind you going" after a gorgeous weekend together?'

'They are definitely bullshitting.'

'Thought so.'

A few of his friends are going ice-skating tomorrow evening and he asks whether I would like to come. I haven't been ice-skating for years. I remember not ever being able to get the right size skates and either wobbling wildly from side to side or ending up with no sensation at all in my toes. The rest of the Brownie pack (or whoever I was with) would be shrieking with delight as they learned to skate, while I'd be queuing in the cloakroom for my fifth pair of boots. There's probably something in that but I'd rather not dwell on it. Once Luca's promised to pick up my fingers should someone skate over them and put them in his pocket until they can be sewn back on, I agree to come.

As I put the phone down, I try to figure out why it is that the arrival of a new boyfriend should coincide so unhappily with a change of fortune at work. Rationally, they can't be connected, but it somehow feels as though they are. Could it be that at an unconscious level I am unwilling to allow myself to have it all? Why has it always been so difficult for me to maintain the hot job, hot lover, hot apartment triad simultaneously? I torment myself along these lines for the evening, with intermittent feelings of joy and excitement about Luca.

At work the next day I decide to leave the matter of my salary and wait to see whether Wayne will address the matter. I am sure you will not be surprised to learn that my salary deficit is not mentioned and, once again, Wayne hides himself away in his office for most of the day. In desperation I moot the idea of discussing the shortfall with Bert, but as Tina points out, previous experience has shown that not only will he be as obstructive as possible, he will derive great pleasure from doing so. Tina is sympathetic, while waving aside my fears that Wayne is going to sack me. She tells me that he can't afford to get rid of me, that I am doing a great job, that the clients and the temps love me and that this will all blow over. And then she goes into the kitchen area and prepares a nice lunch for Wayne, just in case he is thinking of getting rid of her, too.

I am getting progressively more pissed off, and when Wayne

leaves early for a vitamin seminar, I sit hunched over my desk feeling apprehensive and angry. Instead of behaving as if he is keen to keep me on, Wayne is clearly unperturbed that his star employee is upset and is acting instead as if he were the injured party.

The one good thing is that Tina has warmed up towards me (although we now never discuss either son). She can afford to be nice to me; for once, she feels secure in her job. As Wayne's not really communicating with me, he's being extra sweet to her and she absolutely loves it. She's not openly sickening about it. There's no gloating or obvious brown-nosing going on. I can just tell by the way she sweeps into his office with a cup of tea, stays for a while and then quietly exits, looking faintly smug, benign and in control.

At six o'clock, after Bert has left and the phones have finally stopped ringing, feeling reluctant but nonetheless compelled, I ask her whether Wayne has discussed me with her (inwardly noting with irony that it was less than a week ago that the tables were turned and I was defending Tina to him).

'I mentioned the matter to him, actually,' she says.

'You're joking.'

'I'm not. Not the T-shirt and bra thing but the money. I think it's very wrong that he's not sorting it out.'

'What did he say?'

'He said he was incredibly busy at the moment but that when he had a spare moment he would look in to it.'

'A spare moment!' I say, becoming agitated. 'That's just not good enough. He should be apologising and putting it right immediately. I'm owed that money. I've worked bloody hard and I don't expect to have to haggle over getting paid the right amount.'

'I totally agree with you. Emma, listen my darling. He's a little boy and he's sulking. He'll be fine in a couple of days, I promise you. It will all blow over. His ego is hurt. Men of that generation think they can say whatever they like to a woman without any repercussions.'

'I disagree. I think men are either lecherous and fundamentally disrespectful to women or they are not. I know that my father, for instance, would never dream of making such lewd comments to a woman. Anyway, don't make excuses for him.'

'OK, OK. I'd probably have broken a chair over his head if he'd said that to me.'

'There you go,' I say, knowing full well that Tina is one of those sensible, pragmatic, smart, mature people to whom I referred earlier, and I somehow sense that she'd never even find herself in this position. Must be something to do with those cast-iron boundaries of hers.

The following morning, I decide I need to sort out the salary issue before I do any more work for this arsehole. I have to wait until Wayne finally arrives at the office just before lunchtime. I knock on his door, armed with paperwork to demonstrate my assertion that I have been under-paid. Wayne is still not making direct eye contact with me and stares at his computer screen while I tell him that I want to discuss my salary shortfall. The longer we leave it, I tell him, the less chance we have of remedying it. I show Wayne the figures and watch his bald, scaly head as he pores over them. I feel thoroughly repulsed by him. Having studied the figures for ages while I wait, willing myself to remain calm and neither cry nor shout, he leans back in his chair, his stomach stretching his shirt buttons to capacity. He is definitely enjoying the master/servant divide, evidenced by the fact that he is sitting at his desk acting as judge and jury, while I stand before him, a petitioner dependent upon his goodwill. Finally, he looks up at me with a sneer.

'These figures are wrong.' He gestures dismissively at the paperwork that I have provided him with.

'Which figures are wrong?' I ask, feeling hot and sticky under my arms.

'You don't get fifteen per cent commission on anything. Your commission is ten per cent and you know that.'

'What?' I ask, incredulously. 'We agreed that my commission would go up to fifteen per cent when I invoiced more than five grand a week.'

'Have you got the paperwork to show that?' he asks, smugly.

'What?' I ask again. I can't believe my ears. *You disgusting piece of shit.* 'Wayne, we agreed that three months ago when we reworked my commission structure. This is the first time that I've billed well over five grand and it was for precisely when I worked this hard that you said you wanted to reward me.'

And then I remembered that, as per fucking usual, I was still waiting for a fresh contract from him with the new agreed figures.

'I don't remember agreeing anything. And I would certainly never agree that you should get fifteen per cent commission,' he says, looking very pleased with himself.

'I can't believe you are doing this. We agreed the new rate and you know it and now you are lying,' I say, getting increasingly heated and red in the face.

'I don't like the way you are speaking to me,' he says.

'And I don't like the way you are lying to me,' I say.

'Just remember that *you* work for *me*,' he adds, pointing his short, little finger at me.

Although I am boiling with rage, I manage to keep calm as I say to him, 'No, Wayne, we work together. This is not a matter of who works for who.'

'Well, I am beginning to think that it is not working at all,' he says.

I realise there is no point arguing. This is not about the commission structure. He is lying about the commission and he knows that I know and he doesn't care. This is about the memo I sent him. The working relationship is over. I walk out of his office without saying another word. I pick up my bag and tell Tina that I am going out for lunch. I sit in the café opposite, chain-smoking and staring into space, unwilling to face up to the reality of my work situation. I am not thinking about resigning or being sacked. I am just quietly fuming about the fact that this motherfucker has just lied to me and cheated me out of my money.

When I go back to the office half an hour later, I tell Tina what has happened. She is incredulous. She remembers me telling her that Wayne and I had agreed a new commission rate for me to reflect all the work I was bringing to Search. She can't believe he is blatantly lying about it and she suddenly starts fishing through her drawers to look for her contract. She then remembers that Wayne never did get round to giving her a final version. I tell her not to worry about it; as long as she doesn't object to him making impertinent remarks to her (which I know he wouldn't dare do, and anyway, he only targets younger women), her job is safe. As we sit whispering about what I am going to do, Wayne calls me into his office.

I feel wobbly, but I enter with dignity.

'I'm going to have to let you go. With immediate effect. I have prepared a written memo stating the reasons and here is your P45,' he says, without looking at me.

I feel numb. I take the memo and my P45 and all I say is, 'I'll be taking advice on this.'

'None of us can put up with your difficult, insolent behaviour any longer. I need to work with people I can trust.'

I wish I could tell you that I then told him to fuck off, but I am simply too stunned and humiliated to respond.

As I walk out of his office towards my desk, Tina asks me, 'Did you get everything sorted out?'

'Sort of,' I say. 'He sacked me.'

Her jaw drops. She doesn't get up to comfort me. She just sits there with her mouth open. I quickly go through my drawers, taking out my personal stuff. I pick up my coat and as I walk out, all the telephone lines start ringing at once.

Part Two

And yet as a path to happiness work is not valued very highly by men. They do not run after it as they do after other opportunities for gratification. The great majority work only when forced by necessity, and this natural human aversion to work gives rise to the most difficult social problems.

Sigmund Freud, *Civilisation and Its Discontent*, 1930

What do You Want to do When You Grow Up?

1978. Woodgrange Primary School, North London, fourth year juniors. I am ten years old. Mrs Wells asks us what we want to do when we grow up.

'Put up your hand if you want to be a doctor?' A couple of boys' hands shoot up. 'Put up your hand if you want to be a nurse?' A couple of girls' hands shoot up. She runs through various standard occupations and is clearly perturbed that a few of us have wilfully refused to commit ourselves to pursuing a career as an accountant, air hostess or fireman. I have not put up my hand and neither has my adorably vacant best friend, Tara Kass.

'Well, what do you want to be when you grow up, Tara?' she asks, impatiently. There is silence and I watch Tara racking her brains for something acceptable. Her face brightens.

'A bank,' she says.

Mrs Wells is indignant. 'What? You want to be a building!'

Tara looks confused, then crushed, and mumbles something about wanting to work in a bank, but Mrs Wells has moved on to me.

'What about you Emma?'

'I'd like to write stories.' Mrs Wells is pleased with this answer, says 'Good' and that's all I remember.

When you're that age, you don't really know what you want to do, do you? I mean, how can a child of ten know what they want to do for the rest of their lives? Over twenty years later and I still don't know.

When I was fifteen, I landed my first job. I was very excited.

Mr Nash, the newsagent round the corner, agreed to employ me on Saturdays as his assistant. I was attracted to the job by both the idea of having my own money each week and the opportunities afforded by being surrounded by chocolate and sweets all day.

Earlier that year, someone in authority at school had made the mistake of appointing me head of the junior school tuck shop for a term. I am afraid I was guilty of pilfering large amounts of stock. I was no longer bringing in a nutritious packed lunch, but choosing three or four bars of chocolate from my locker stash instead. I was also eating a bar at each of the three breaktimes during the school day and taking home a bar for the bus journey and maybe a bar for the evening, too.

Nobody ever accused me of stealing but the keys for the tuck shop were taken away from me at the end of term and it was never suggested that I work in the shop again, despite my numerous pleas to do so.

The next dental visit after this term at school was rather disturbing. My dentist spent a worryingly long time peering into my mouth. 'What's your diet like?' he asked, sounding puzzled. 'Good,' I lied, then, 'I do like a bit of chocolate.' He hummed, then told me that I needed *eight* fillings.

However, like all addicts, I didn't care about the consequences of my habit. I was only interested in finding new opportunities to freely indulge. I was fifteen. I had not discovered drugs or alcohol. Chocolate was my life.

I thought my Saturday job was perfect – until I started work. Mr Nash was a miserable, misogynistic, tight bastard. He worked me very hard without even offering me a bar of chocolate. I told him I'd like a cream egg. He quoted me full market price and then told me that I could not eat it in the shop. It was torture. I was surrounded by chocolate and I wasn't allowed to even suck a slab. Other kids came in, carefully making their selection, tearing off the wrappers and happily tucking in before leaving the shop, while I looked on forlornly. I soon became an opportunistic chocolate thief during heart-palpitating stock-opening sessions in the back of the shop when Mr Nash would leave me alone for a few seconds. Unfortunately, the only place to consume the stolen chocolate was in the shop's filthy outside toilet which was almost knee-high in sticky top-shelf girlie magazines.

I began to hate Mr Nash, and having to work in such close proximity to him made my flesh crawl (I was more upset about the chocolate stinginess than the pornography). I think I lasted another couple of weeks then made up some bullshit about too much school work.

And that was my first job. It was a disappointing entry into the world of work, yet it set a pattern: initial excitement before the job starts followed by disillusion with either the work or the boss, but usually both.

Mr Nash has appeared in various guises in my many jobs.

The Ideal Job

Exams were passed, universities considered, a path chosen. I don't think I gave more than five minutes thought to the career that would occupy me mentally, physically, emotionally and spiritually for the next fifty years or so. I was going to be a lawyer and that was that. Everyone else thought I would be a good lawyer and I couldn't really be bothered to think about whether this was true, or whether I actually wanted to be one.

Part of the problem arose from the fact that I was only interested in escaping suburban home life and finding myself in exciting new social situations. I spent hours poring over the sections on the social side of each university in an unofficial guide to universities, written by the students, while giving the course description only a cursory glance. Was I in serious denial? Perhaps I thought law would be stimulating. I certainly thought it was reasonably glamorous (really!). I think I thought I'd be doing lots of articulate, powerful arguing on behalf of wronged clients. People would respect me for being an important person in the community. I mentioned law to my parents and teachers and they enthusiastically encouraged the idea. No-one tries to persuade you *not* to be a lawyer. They may persuade you not to be an artist, an actress or a writer, but a lawyer gets the thumbs-up.

It didn't occur to me that I needed to enjoy my chosen occupation. It was a job. No-one enjoys working, it's something you have to do to live. The important thing was to find something well-paid, and what else was there apart from medicine (not clever enough plus squeamish) or accountancy (found maths a struggle and a bore)?

So that was settled. I would go to university, do a law degree, spend a year at law school and then do my articles (now called 'a training contract') with a law firm for two years until qualification. I would then work as a lawyer, probably meet another lawyer, get married, have kids, retire and then die. That was the basic plan.

In order to fund my lifestyle while studying at university, I worked during the holidays. I did quite a lot of waitressing. I even did one fashion lunch for Princess Diana, although I wasn't allowed to serve her table as my fingernails were too short. I also waitressed at a massive party for Michael Jackson in the dinosaur room at the National History Museum. It was around the time that Michael was dating a monkey. I remember serving the monkey.

I learned silver service waitressing, where you serve with a spoon and fork at the same time. I found that the best way to get people to move out of your way when you are carrying a very heavy tray laden with food is to touch their shoulder with the scorching hot tray. This is especially effective with ladies wearing backless dresses. I always made sure when serving profiteroles, etc., that I left back at least two for myself. At one very exclusive £200-a-head lunch party, where Michelin star chefs did the cooking, I even ate the guests' leftovers.

I worked at a computer place at the start of the computer boom when the industry attracted people who had failed at everything else. The boss hadn't gone to university, felt bitter about this and was very angry with me for being a student. If I didn't know something, he would take great pleasure in snarling something like 'Don't they teach you that at your fancy university?' or 'Cor, I am glad I didn't go to university if they take the likes of you.' I was too young/bemused/offended to reply.

I worked as a filing clerk for a surveyor who sniffed all day.

I was too unassuming (at the time) to offer him a tissue so I just sat there wanting to stab him instead. After four weeks in the job, I became less conscientious and filed half the paperwork in my handbag. It was the kind of job where you constantly look at your watch, convinced that at least an hour must have passed since you last looked. Instead, four minutes have passed and you have another 286 to go.

I worked for a fashion house where my duties included making lunch for the in-house models (mostly crisps and chocolate rather than salads and fruit) and helping out with finishing some of the garments. I once had to iron forty velvet dresses, which would have been OK – it's just that I suffer from an aversion to velvet. Some people squirm and shiver at the thought of fingernails scraping a blackboard. I'm fine with that. However, I do have a major problem with velvet, velour, coarse-knit wool, tweed and corduroy. I would have had a nervous breakdown on a textiles course. I was forced to overcome my velvet aversion, but more than compensated for this horror by helping myself to large amounts of smoked salmon, meant for the fashion buyers' lunches.

I did some market research for Pepe jeans. I stood in Camden Town feeling completely unloved as everyone I approached for their views on how to pronounce 'Pepe' scurried past me. I ended up turning a bit schizo on the train back up to university as I tried to take on the imaginary characteristics of fifty people to answer the outstanding questionnaires myself.

What else? I worked as a receptionist/secretary for a cosmetic surgeon who specialised in breast augmentations, breast reductions and bat ears. I spent most of my day staring at the before and after photos. Every time the surgeon or one of the patients approached the reception desk, I would be caught unawares, pawing the Polaroids, staring intently at the tits. I couldn't help it. It was fascinating. People brought in pictures from magazines of what they wanted their breasts to look like, but all the enlarged breasts looked exactly the same and were never any sexier. I felt sorry for the women and I didn't like the cold surgeon who was now mega-minted as a result of their imagined inadequacies. What a sad way to make money, don't you think?

I didn't last long as a sales assistant at Simpson's of Piccadilly. I hated being on my feet all day and when I told my supervisor that I understood that by law I was allowed to sit down for ten minutes every hour, she ignored me until later that day when she informed me that Friday would be my last day. I think being a shop assistant is the pits. Nobody likes being asked if they 'need any help' when they want to browse. The alternative is to simply shift weight from one foot to another. *For seven hours.*

I have left my favourite holiday job to last. In fact, I think it takes the prize as my all-time favourite job. During the Easter break of my second year at university, my dad's solicitor offered me some court clerk work in Norfolk. One afternoon, I took a tube to Chancery Lane where I met his colleague who instructed me on my duties. I was to go to Thetford, a pretty little village near Norwich, the following Monday and attend the trial of ten Arsenal football hooligans who had been very naughty at a pub in Norwich after a football game (which, I assume, Arsenal lost). My job was to take notes of the case and basically to represent the solicitors on behalf of two of the hooligans. The barrister was there to argue the case for them. I was given details of the hotel where I was to stay for the two-week hearing.

I was an extremely immature twenty-year-old. I had gone from a fairly cosseted middle-class suburban home life and an academic single sex girls' school to university halls of residence and then a shared flat with other girls and boys. I was pretty naïve in the ways of the world and two weeks on my own in a hotel in Norfolk as a court clerk seemed like a very grown-up thing to do. It was actually the most responsibility I had ever been given.

I arrived at the hotel on the Sunday evening before the trial. I got the train and then a taxi *on my own*. I dumped my bags and, as I was starving, I decided to brave the dining room. I sat on my own and studied the menu. The restaurant was not very busy and there were hushed conversations at the few occupied tables. It seemed quite posh and I didn't understand most of the menu, so I ordered a fruit juice to start and fillet of beef for my main course.

The fruit juice arrived and I drank it. Then something arrived that I had not ordered: A wide-rimmed glass filled with champagne (I think) and sorbet on a saucer with a teaspoon. I was confused not only by its unannounced and unexpected arrival, but also by what the fuck I was supposed to do with it. Was I supposed to drink it? Eat it? Drink it and then eat it or eat it and then drink it? I looked around for clues but I was met with what I felt were deliberately obtuse faces. I felt foolish in advance as I suspected I was going to do the wrong thing with the drink/dessert. The cruel waiter left me there with the damn thing for about fifteen minutes while I sat eyeing it resentfully. I decided the best thing would be to leave it. The glass was eventually removed with a raised eyebrow from the waiter. Maybe he wasn't cruel as he gave me my get-out clause. 'Don't you like it?' he asked. 'No, I don't,' I said, and during my stay at the hotel I was never given the palate cleanser again.

And that was the worst thing that happened to me over the next two weeks. I had a delicious time. My work day went something like this. Wake up at eight-thirty, get dressed and stroll down to breakfast in the dining room, picking up the newspaper I had ordered from the reception desk en route. Eat a leisurely cooked breakfast and retire to my bedroom for a rerun of *Dallas* and a lie down after my brekkie. Meander down to the court for a ten o'clock start. The court house was a ten-minute stroll from the hotel and involved a pretty river with swans and a bridge.

I would take the odd note of the proceedings in the morning. There were five different barristers, each representing two of the defendants, and I only had to take notes when my barrister was speaking, which wasn't that often. I would enjoy sitting there having pornographic fantasies about my sexy clients. The two guys on whose behalf I was there were what some might call a bit of rough, but whom I preferred to think of as cheeky chappies. They were charged with assault, something called affray, and one of them with possession of cannabis. With an indulgent smile, I told one of the other clerks that I thought they were just being playful, but she wryly commented that she felt that throwing a heavy glass ashtray at someone's head and breaking a snooker cue over someone else's nose was slightly more aggressive than mere high spirits. I looked over at one of my boys in the dock and he winked at me. Aggressive? Surely not. I thought he was adorable.

The court broke for a two-hour lunch at midday. As my entire hotel bill was covered by expenses, it was more economical for me to eat at the hotel. Sometimes I would have a ploughman's in the bar with the barristers and other clerks. As I was not a proper adult, I wasn't really up to making valuable contributions to the learned and witty conversations, so sometimes it was easier to sit in my room, watch TV and order room service. This was also quite nice. I might even have a little siesta.

I took a newspaper back to the court with me as I liked to do the crossword in the afternoon session. It seemed to take such a long time for anything to happen in the court and I didn't understand much of the interminable speeches made by the barristers, despite having studied law for two years. Once again, I refused to acknowledge the fact that I had demonstrated zero interest in the judicial process.

I was no better at university. We only had eleven hours of lectures a week and I barely made it to half of them. When I did make it to a lecture, I was more interested in sussing out who on the course was fucking who. My lack of interest in the law is so obvious in retrospect, but at the time I refused to admit to myself that I was bored rigid by every aspect of my legal studies. I think I thought that *learning* law was going to be boring while *practising* it would be wildly exciting. In any case, my boyfriend at university studied politics and philosophy and he didn't seem particularly interested in his course either, so I just assumed that we'd all had enough of studying. I was having such a good time generally at university that it seemed only right that I pay some penance in terms of attending boring lectures a few times a week. I thought it was a fair deal.

Anyway, the court session finished at around four o'clock in the afternoon. Can you believe it? My official day's work consisted of four hours. I wasn't skiving off early or turning up late. I think it was the only job for which I have never been late, although admittedly it was only for two weeks, and who knows what would have happened after that, especially if my fantasised lunchtime siestas with my naughty boys had become a reality.

After court I would go for a wander around the pretty little town where I was staying. Back in my room I'd kick back until dinner. I think the restaurant staff loved me. I became much more adventurous and ended up choosing delicious, expensive à la carte meals, guided by the waiter. After a couple of nights, the chef came out to meet the woman who was allowing him to indulge in a more Parisian style of cuisine as opposed to being simply confined to the customary orders of chicken or steak and chips. Soon, a conference was held at the beginning of each meal to discuss what I would be having, the chef making suggestions with the waiter in attendance, ready to suggest a complementary wine. Each course would be delivered with a flourish and removed with a polite but interested enquiry into whether madam had enjoyed the food. It was heaven. Other customers looked on in astonishment, wondering whether I was a precocious food critic.

After dinner I'd retire to my bedroom, either with a liqueur or a cup of coffee. I spent the evening reading, watching television or boasting to friends on the phone about my job. My boyfriend at the time, Joe, was also working during the university break, however his experience was somewhat different to mine. Joe was helping to erect marquees for a big event, can't remember what, in the Midlands. He was putting in twelve-hour days; none of this sitting down doing crosswords lark, but heavy, demanding manual work from seven in the morning until seven at night. He was sleeping in a tent with twenty other dirty, sweaty, farting, snoring men, one of whom accidentally urinated over his sleeping bag one night when he came back pissed from the pub. While I was eating flambéed Steak Diane, he was emptying a tin of baked beans into a tin pot over a little calor gas flame. And while I was sipping cognac in my bed, watching television, he was walking the three miles to a free phone box to call me to hear me describe my luxurious hotel, cordon bleu food, cute criminals, leisurely lunches, the swans in the river, the pretty little bridge on the short walk to the court, lie-ins, cooked breakfasts and what had happened in *Dallas* that morning. (Don't feel too sorry for him. He got the last laugh by dumping me six months later, and not even a month's stay at the hotel in Thetford would have helped make me feel better.)

So that was my ideal job. Unsurprisingly, nothing has ever come close.

The Real World

The year at law school came and went. Once again, I showed zero interest in my studies, preferring to spend lectures replying to flirtatious notes from the guy sitting next to me. I passed, he failed (and so did his girlfriend, who found out about the flirtatious notes shortly before the finals).

Next stop was the law firm which had agreed to employ me for the next two years and provide training in three key areas of law. Before I start talking about law firms, I hope you won't feel patronised if I explain some things about the legal world to avoid confusion. If you think you know everything (either because you are a lawyer or a know-all) you can skip this bit.

There are two different types of lawyer: a solicitor and a barristers. Barristers are the ones who wear the wigs and gowns and appear in court with pompous, booming voices. Probably no-one listened to them as children so they chose jobs where people would be forced, literally, by law, to listen to them now. Everyone thinks that the job of a barrister is very glamorous and I suppose you could argue that about the court side of things. However, what you probably don't realise is that most of their time is actually spent closeted away in a draughty room researching obscure points of law on behalf of solicitors. Thus their time is divided between providing opinions on obtuse points of law, based on these long, lonely hours of research, and the odd appearance in court.

The other ones, solicitors, were the gang I was aiming to join. It's much easier to become a solicitor as the training is more straightforward. There is one year at law school which involves horrendous amounts of learning but which is not, if you are reasonably clever, conceptually difficult. Then a two-year training contract, which used to be called articles. A trainee lawyer used to be called an articled clerk. When I trained, I was called an articled clerk and I think it changed straight after I qualified.

What else? A law firm is not a company but a partnership, and when I talk about partners I mean the big bosses of the law firm rather than the PC equivalent of the person you are screwing. Litigation is the area of law where you sue someone, and conveyancing is the property side of law. Company/commercial is the area where lawyers meddle in company affairs, complicating matters. That's about it.

I somehow ended up working for a very English, public school, well-respected, well-established law firm. It was a large firm with eighty partners and a total of 250 employees. Everyone was white with the exception of five black secretaries and a black trainee, who was not retained after his training contract expired. He may have been completely crap for all I know, but so were lots of other people and they were kept on.

I'd had quite a few interviews on what is known as the milk round, where law firms come to universities to find the cream of the crop to recruit. Needless to say, I didn't manage to find anywhere prepared to take me on, being too immature and ill-prepared for the grown-up interview process. I began to panic that I had not found anywhere halfway through the third year, especially as I heard that law firms were prepared to pay the hefty law school fees. I needed to find somewhere so I did what I normally do when faced with a new and strange situation. I went to the library. I took out two or three books on job interview techniques, realised where I'd been going wrong and swotted up on appearing as if I was doing them the favour by turning up for the interview.

I decided to go traditional and invested a wad of cash in a

smart, navy blue interview suit from Harvey Nichols, which, for some reason, my boyfriend found a major turn-on, and soon we couldn't have sex without me wearing it. From being apathetic about jobs in general (he didn't know what he wanted to do), he was suddenly more than happy to stage mock interviews with me, as long as I wore my interview suit and the interview ended with me sucking him off or us fucking. By the time it came to the real thing, I half expected the interviews at these stuffy law firms to end the same way and I felt strangely incomplete and dissatisfied as I simply shook their hands as I left.

I had two interviews and received two offers. One was from a small but flash firm that took itself very seriously, and although I managed to feign wide-eyed enthusiasm for their global plans in an hour-long interview, I knew that I didn't have the hungry ambition required for a stab at world domination.

The other firm, Coopers, had a more laid back, low key arrogance, which I felt would be less demanding and more in-keeping with my style. It was also bigger and this meant I could fade more easily into the system without anyone noticing that I wasn't doing much work. I was also swayed by the good-looking partner who interviewed me, and the thought of late-night meetings with him would, I knew, do wonders for my willingness to work long hours and thus my chances of advancement. I'd asked the good-looking partner some rather cute questions, one of which was whether the firm had a motto. He'd laughed, said 'good question', leaned back in his chair, gave me a piercing sexy look and then said, 'Firm but Fair'. I told him that I liked the motto and that I would be very happy to work for his firm, and he smiled and said I would hear from them shortly.

A year and a half, a degree and law final examinations later, I started at Coopers, City law firm. Fifteen of us started at the same time. I looked at the other new kids and wondered with whom I would end up being friends. They looked like a motley bunch of losers to me, but experience told me that I would probably end up being best mates with the person I hated most on first sight. We spent the first week on training courses; what is known as 'induction week'. It still felt as though the world of work was miles away and I couldn't imagine that anything would be expected of me for quite some time.

Once again, when partners came to explain what went on in their departments, whether it be conveyancing, wills, shipping, banking or litigation, I found myself paying absolutely no attention. I sat at the back of the room trying to figure out my place in the pecking order of shagworthy articled clerks. I perked up when I heard Stephen Kennedy, the partner in charge of articled clerks, telling us how we were all carefully selected and how we represented the future of the firm, and if there were any problems we shouldn't hesitate to contact either himself or the personnel officer, Sue Grange.

There was quite a lot of socialising at Coopers and I liked that side of things. My first friend was Thomas, who made a sly comment to me at one of the cocktail parties that revealed he was also taking a sceptical but humorous view of our new employers. This was in contract to the bright-eyed, bushy-tailed, star-struck gratitude of our fellow trainees. I think he described one of the camp American partners as 'fruity'. This was the first unorthodox comment I had heard in nearly a week and, for some reason, it had me in stitches. I'd only had a glass of wine and I was laughing hysterically. I could see other solicitors looking at me disapprovingly. Hushed conversation with quiet, corporate laughter was allowed; unscheduled, raucous laughter was not.

The following Monday, real work finally began. I was designated to sit with a litigation partner, Angus McFadden, who everyone told me was lovely. I arrived on time on Monday morning and waited in his room for him to arrive. I had been shown to my desk by a second year, sensible but nice, articled clerk who worked in the same department as me. Angus walked in, all smiles and hand shakes, and within three minutes his phone started ringing.

As he took the call, I had a chance to suss out the man whose office I would be sharing for the next six months. He had light brown curly hair with a red tinge that suited his freckled face and brown eyes. He didn't have that sun stroke Scottish look. He didn't have the accent either; like every other partner I'd met since arriving, apart from the camp American, he spoke with a posh, public school accent. And, when he'd leaned over his desk to answer the phone, I couldn't help noticing that he had the most gorgeous bum I'd seen in ages. It was firm, chunky and rounded and asking to be pinched. Obviously, I knew that pinching his arse would result in me leaving the firm, but I'm just telling you, it was that damn gorgeous and capable, I am sure, of plenty of heavy-weight pumping action.

He was without doubt the nicest man I worked for at Coopers, while being the worst lawyer.

Angus was in the middle of a huge court case, and he spent an afternoon going through it with me. He was acting on behalf of a huge and well-known British corporation who were suing an even huger American corporation. He was clearly very excited about this and explained that I would be mostly involved with compiling evidence for the case over the next six months. As he explained the details of the case and the various points of law, it struck me that the case contained a fatal flaw. This doubt surfaced again and again over the next six months, but since this troubled neither Angus, a partner for five years at a top City law firm, nor two assistant solicitors also working on the case, nor two very well-paid and confident barristers, I thought I must have got it wrong. What did I know, a fresh young graduate with zero experience in the tough, intellectual world of commercial contract law? One day I raised my query with Angus, who explained dismissively why

I was completely wrong. So I left it and got on with the tedious task of filing evidence into hundreds of lever arch files. Six months later, when the case came to trial, our client was so resoundingly beaten that Angus started smoking again after ten years of abstinence.

Once we were let loose into our various departments, the word on the street was very different from the 'you are very important – you are the future' speech that we received during our induction week. It was soon made clear to us trainees that, in the hierarchical order of the firm, we were way below the secretaries and a small step above the lizards in the basement who sorted and delivered the firm's mail. We were supposed to be seen and not heard. Not only were we given the most mundane and shitty jobs to do (e.g. filing evidence into hundreds of lever arch files), we were also the personal slaves of the partners for whom we worked. On one occasion, Angus sent me to get him a load of bullets for his weekend shoot. I was allowed to get a taxi back to the office with this heavy box that came up to my waist. I managed to haul the box out of the taxi and drag it into the office via a side door on the ground floor. I returned to the office and sat down once again to file our client's invoices for the last ten years. Angus comes in the office and beams when I tell him that I bought the bullets, no problem. 'Where are they?' he asked me. 'On the ground floor by the side door.' 'What?' he shouted, with incredulity. 'You left two kilos of live ammo by a door?' And with that he rushed downstairs to retrieve the box. I am a suburban North London Jewess. What do I know about 'ammo'? I realised I had entered a different world.

The Crew

I had started to make friends with other trainees and within the month a gang had formed. My co-leader Tariq was, like me, an outsider, I felt. A Muslim from Walthamstow. The first and only Asian lawyer in the firm. You could see times were changing. Even a year ago, I am sure they would never have allowed anyone in the firm who wore dark green wide boy suits and flash kipper ties. Tariq had also trained as a boxer and had the physique of a street fighter. He was fucking bright, very funny, left wing and quietly studying for a masters in immigration law.

Then there was Alasdair who was more in the correct mould. Ex-public school with the right voice but the wrong suits. He looked ten years older than he actually was, he was balding with glasses and had a slightly furry nose. Despite this, he possessed some weird kind of sex appeal that made women flock to him when they were pissed. I think it was because he was manly (he even had hair on his nose, for God's sake) and because he played the piano very sexily. He was also irreverent and a great audience, with a warm, loud, encouraging laugh. Prior to starting at Coopers, he had been in a rock band touring scuzzy pubs in London. Starting work at Coopers was his final admission that he hadn't made it in the rock world.

Then there was young Timmy. Now here, the mould was perfect: right size, right colour, right everything. Coopers had recruited from among their own. Timmy went to Westminster School, Bristol University, and passed his law school examinations with honours. Good-looking in a slightly effete way: floppy hair, kitten hips, delicate ankles, big blue eyes that whimpered *please hurt me* and dimples. Timmy adored me for being everything he wasn't. Where he was cautious, I was impulsive. Where he was completely deferential to the partners of Coopers, I was familiar. Where he was conservative, I was outrageous. And I adored him for adoring me and for being pretty adorable himself. He was an amazing impersonator, kind, generous, well read and self-effacing. He came from a wealthy, English, liberal, left wing background. The type that love blacks but hate Jews (too nouveau) and Pakistanis (unfashionable). Timmy, however, was too intelligent to hold such prejudices and was devoted, in private at least, to myself and Tariq.

There was also mad Sally Smith, who I brought on board precisely because she was mad. She was going out with a very annoying guy who had gone to the same university as me and who she met at law school. I was sure, knowing this guy, that he would be shagging at least five other women besides her, but as she was acting like they were on the verge of getting engaged, I didn't think it was appropriate to mention his track record. Socially, she was also an arriviste. Her parents were Cor Blimey but had done incredibly well and sent her to a private school. She therefore had a foot in both worlds. She was one of those women who you just knew needed loads and loads of sex to keep them sane. She also liked having her bottom bitten very hard.

Finally, Tessa. The last member of the gang was not actually a trainee solicitor but what is known as the outdoor clerk. An outdoor clerk's function is to serve all the documents at court. With the huge litigation department, writs, defences, counter-claims and all types of notices needed to be served at court. This involved queuing up for ages at various counters at the High Court for the documents to be stamped and put on file. Tessa is one of the most unforgettable characters I have ever met. I'll start with her appearance. For those of you that remember Bessie Bunter, that will probably suffice.

For those of you that don't, Tessa was about five foot four and about fifteen stone. She had long dark hair and thick, large round glasses that magnified her eyes. I also think she had an extreme oral fixation. If she wasn't smoking a cigarette, she was sucking a lozenge or a mint or a sweet or chewing gum or biting her fingernails. At lunchtime, her diet meals were an hilarious mix of health consciousness and gluttony. For example, she would think that she was being really good by having a baked potato, as opposed to, say, a takeaway pizza or an Indian (everyone else ate sandwiches). However, with the baked potato she would mash in half a pound of butter until the potato was in liquid form. She would bring in five biscuits from home, neatly wrapped in cling film. But once they were eaten she would bring out the rest of the packet from her handbag and say that she'd brought them with her, just in case. It sounds mean to mock at what was obviously some kind of cry for help, but each lunchtime I would watch in disbelief at what was only tucked away.

Personality wise, and this may sound like a cliché, she also had a large, warm, bubbly personality that knew no limits. She'd greet men in the pub with a flash of her tits. She had the longest cleavage I've ever seen. Everyone at court knew her and we loved her. She was the best laugh in the firm. She had a great voice and she'd always end up on the table at the end of the evening, belting out naff songs. And finally, she was unhappily married to a good-looking policeman who adored her but with whom she was clearly bored.

Lunchtimes were the highlight of our day, often taking place at our local, The Heaving Bum. The rest of the day was so numbingly boring that we were ready to go wild at lunch. Although we were only supposed to take one hour, we would meet every day at a quarter to one in reception and not make our way back to our desks until gone two. Every minute of freedom was precious. It's impossible to explain how hilarious these lunchtimes were to anyone now. I have never experienced anything like it since.

We became infamous within the firm as a subversive group, and Timmy took to leaving our lunches five minutes early so that he would not be seen returning to the office with us and therefore be associated us. We'd always shout out after him so that he drew even more attention to himself. As he was the goody-goody perfect one that all the gay partners were in love with, we'd also torment him in other ways. Tariq and Simon would wait for Timmy's partner to leave the room and then slip in to see Timmy, fart for a while and then run out, so that by the time Timmy's partner returned to the room, it would stink and Timmy would be too embarrassed to deny it was him.

None of us was ready to grow up.

The Revelation

> A great deal of harm is being done in the modern world by
> belief in the virtuousness of WORK ... the road to happi-
> ness and prosperity lies in the organised diminution of work.
>
> Bertrand Russell, *In Praise of Idleness*

Two months into life at Coopers and us trainees were awaiting
our law society final examination results. Can you believe it?
You start work somewhere on what you hope and imagine
to be a two-year contract, at the end of which you are
a fully qualified solicitor. Then, two months in, after you
have started to make friends, ingratiated yourself with the
secretaries, schmoozed the partners, flirted with the security
guard, you find out you have failed your professional exams
and you have to leave. The law firm may or may not take
you back after you've passed the exams next year. A fairly
humiliating scenario, I am sure you'll agree.

The results appear first in all the broadsheet newspapers.
Crowds of anxious trainee solicitors gather at all the major
British Rail stations where the next day's papers are delivered
at around ten o'clock in the evening. I had a contact (the editor)
at one of the newspapers and had discovered the day before
that I had passed my exams. I did not want to go around
telling people until I had seen it myself, confirmed in black and
white. Instead, I made smug, self-satisfied, annoying comments
to other trainees all day at work, things like 'I don't know what
you're all worrying about. I'm sure we've all passed, in fact,
I am certain *I* have' or 'I've just got a really strong feeling
that I've passed the exams, yeah, I'm feeling confident.' Ashen
faces, contorted in worry, looked forlornly back at me.

Sure enough, my name appeared in black and white in *The
Times* that evening. An inexplicable depression descended

the following day. I couldn't understand it. Shouldn't I be celebrating like everyone else? Shouldn't I be proud of myself? Shouldn't I be relieved that I was staying at Coopers for my two-year training contract? Wasn't I delighted that I was going to be a solicitor?

Angus, sweetly, became concerned at my lack of spirits and took fifteen minutes out of his hectic work day to talk with me about my gloom. He shut the office door and diverted his phone – the first time I had ever seen him do this. As his hourly charge out rate was about £200 per hour, I appreciated the gesture. I was unable to explain to him quite why I felt so depressed at passing my law exams. He told me that perhaps it was all just an anti-climax after months of anxious waiting.

At no time during this month-long period of depression following my exam results did I connect the feelings of gloom with my now unfettered path to becoming a solicitor. I used every available defence mechanism to deny the glaring truth that I did not want to be a solicitor. I used 'rationalisation', whereby I persuaded myself that being a solicitor was a wonderful, worthwhile, stimulating and financially rewarding profession. I certainly used denial – I failed to ask myself exactly why I was unhappy, preferring to gnash and wail unquestioningly. It may have helped if one other legal person had been able to express doubts about their career path, but we all remained silent in our repression. I swung wildly between admiration for the partners at the firm, with their self-assured, polished confidence, and contempt for their pompous, smug arrogance. I didn't know what to think.

I was also beginning to realise that the career path was never ending. To use a metaphor, it felt like climbing a steep hill where you are kept going by the sight of the summit, where you expect to feel a sense of arrival, before settling to enjoy the view. You struggle your way to the top, tired and looking forward to the rest, only to discover that the summit is not, in fact, the summit, but a small and uncomfortable ridge where you can rest for a short time before pressing on to further heights in your mission to reach the top, kick back and relax.

I had kept going over each hurdle: passing A-levels, getting into university, obtaining a degree, being accepted by a law firm, getting into law school and finally passing the law finals. Having spent two months at this law firm, I realised that not only was I a long way from the peak, I was also hanging on rather precariously to a crumbling ridge.

Once you enter a City law firm, a whole new set of hurdles stretches before you. As the first year trainees were congratulating themselves on passing their exams, the second year trainees were beginning to panic about whether they would be kept on at the firm at the end of their two-year training contract. Not everyone is kept on after articles and you are told about three months before the end of the two years that the powers that be do not see a future for you at the firm. This gives you three months to wander around the firm in leper garments, waving a bell, silently shouting 'Unfit to practice law'. The rejects enter lifts and everyone stops talking. Clusters regroup around them at firm lunches. Their inability to succeed could be infectious.

Understandably, people that have been 'let go' are reluctant to admit their fate to other members of staff. If outed, they often pretend it was *their* choice and talk optimistically about their plans to join other City firms. No-one is convinced. Soon after joining the firm, you unwittingly undergo a brainwashing, whereby you soon believe that life outside a City law firm is unthinkable. Coopers becomes the centre of the universe, and to be banished from the City is to enter purdah, a shameful no-man's land of cowboy West End law firms and reduced salaries.

So, once you've reached the next plateau of being allowed to remain in the kingdom of the blessed, you work your balls off for between three and five years before hearing whether you've passed the next hurdle. Will you be made a partner of the firm or will you continue as a bog standard associate solicitor? You thought you were already a member of the club but you ain't nowhere near it until you join the ranks of the partners. The advantages of becoming a partner are: more money, more prestige, more status, your own secretary (as opposed to sharing one), your own trainee solicitor to do the shitty stuff you can't be bothered with any more, and, most importantly, your name on the firm's headed paper. Having your name on the headed paper is an invaluable way of letting your university and law school contemporaries know that you have made it.

So, you've become a partner. You can relax now, right? Sorry – not until you've become an 'equity' partner, as opposed to a 'salaried' partner. An equity partner is entitled to a share of the profits and a say in things, whereas a salaried partner is a partner in name only. To become an equity partner, it is not enough to simply be a very good lawyer – you also have to bring big business to the firm. In fact, even if you are a completely shit lawyer, if you net a nice big, fat fish of a client, you're very close to that pinnacle and can seriously start thinking about unfurling that picnic mat and removing the cling film from your packed sandwiches.

OK, say you've brought in the business and you've put in the hours, you might be allowed to graze on the equity partner plateau for a while. There is, however, one last hike. The zenith is the managing committee, where all the really important decisions about the running of the firm are made. It is the inner circle and the power-house engine of the firm. Unless you're in the managing committee, you are really just a lackey, albeit a very well paid and tired one.

So this, at least, is one thing that I am realising as the ladder stretches up endlessly in front of me. I can't even see the top of it, although I imagine some God bloke is there looking down, like our own senior partner, Mr Cooper. A white-haired, sophisticated, elder gentleman who is 'Firm but Fair' unless he is crossed, in which case his cold, calm fury is renowned for reducing otherwise reasonably confident people into quivering, sweating freaks. Just like the guy in the Old Testament. The one thing this steep climb really entails is working incredibly long hours. Joke hours. Hours that suggest that it isn't so much that you enjoy work but that you don't like going home. There was a real machismo, I noticed, about working ridiculous hours in the high-pressured company/commercial department. To be able to say that you were working through the night was the equivalent of holding two perfect cheezer conkers when you were seven. We're talking serious respect.

I sat with Elizabeth, an austere female partner who had the most gorgeous-looking, devoted boyfriend but who nevertheless worked until at least eight o'clock every evening. As I was her trainee, I was often given work to do at 5.30 p.m. when most of my chums in other departments were going home. Other workaholic partners would saunter in and out of her office during the evening to exchange self-congratulatory martyred sentiments. I would sit quietly at my desk in the corner, resentment at my enforced presence seething inside me. One smarmy lawyer, Eric, really irritated me as he seemed to spend most of his evenings talking to other swotty lawyers rather than doing any urgent work. On one particular evening, he strolled into Elizabeth's office and lowered himself into a chair with a stifled yawn. 'Why is it, Elizabeth,' he pronounced with self-satisfaction, 'that it is always you and I who are working late?' I piped up from my corner, breaking my not seen nor heard vow. 'Perhaps it takes you longer to do things than it takes other people,' I said, in an innocent tone. Silence. Eric looked over at me with a sneer. 'Then why are you still here?' he asked. 'To keep Elizabeth company,' I shot straight back, looking at Elizabeth. I was never asked to stay late unnecessarily again.

No-one seems to think that workaholism is a problem. We

work harder in Britain than anywhere else in Europe and no-one seems to mind. No-one seems to mind that there are seven days in the week and we devote five of them to work. I mean, come on. Be fair. What about the boss having four days, say, and the rest of us three? I mean, isn't that fairer while still weighted in the boss's favour? Come on guys. Please. Be reasonable.

As well as working emotion-repressing hours, we also had timesheets, whereby we had to account for every six minutes of our time so that clients could be charged according to work done. I do not disagree that this is a fair system. In fact, throughout my undistinguished legal career, I never once saw a client over-charged, despite the perception that all lawyers are rip-off crooks. The depression induced by the idea of having to justify every six minutes of my existence at work for the rest of my life, coupled with a personality type completely lacking any discipline, could only spell timesheet disaster.

You know when you have a job you really hate doing, you delay and delay doing it, even though you know for a fact that the longer you leave this job, the worse it will be when you actually get round to it. A classic example is washing up. You are either the kind of person who eats and then thinks that it would be a good idea to wash up now before everything dries on the plates, saucepans and utensils, making the task much harder and more time-consuming, so you give everything a quick rinse and sit, self-satisfied but relaxed, in front of the television for the rest of the evening. Or you are the kind of person who eats, feels full and lazy, gets up from the table and wanders to the sofa, swearing to do the washing up 'in a bit' before forgetting completely until you hit the kitchen later to discover an unholy mess that is too depressing to think about, let alone tackle. This state of affairs continues until there are no clean plates, mugs, saucers, saucepans, cutlery, etc., left and the flat is starting to smell. Well, I am one of the latter, so fulfilling my timesheet obligations every six minutes was never really going to happen. The consequence of this failure was sick panic every month when I would rack my brains trying to remember whether I had been perusing, filing, telephoning, noting, attending or researching, for how long and on whose behalf.

One final whinge. After taking all those exams: entrance exams, end of school year exams, O-levels, A-levels, degree exams and law finals, I thought I could finally stop studying. Not so. Some swotty creep decided that lawyers need to keep up to date with legal developments and thought up a continuing education programme with which to torment us. This is based on a points programme: the more mind-numbingly, leg-chewingly boring the lecture, the more points. Shortly after qualifying, we were required to attend a legal accounts course and then take *another* exam. Feeling defiant, I turned up, registered my name for attendance record purposes, left after the first lecture, went shopping and copied a friend's answers a week later. As is the way with copying a friend's homework, he got 76 per cent and I got 67 per cent. I really had no right to feel indignant, but I did.

For the rest of my professional life, I would now be required to earn continuing education points by attending lectures, seminars and conferences on a regular basis. Some of these lectures were held in-house. I had yet to attend any of these lectures, once again employing the defence mechanism of denial, whereby my intense aversion to absorbing more legal mumbo jumbo buried the painful necessity of gaining these sodding points.

In fact, one of the only lectures I ever attended was given by the police on women's safety. Halfway through the lecture, the policewoman asked one of us to tell the rest of the room, in detail, about our last sexual encounter. I suddenly remembered being on all fours during a sex with the ex session as he attempted to wedge his short but fat cock into my arse. I then heard the policewoman say that she was going to 'volunteer' someone. For some reason, perhaps because I have very short, blonde hair and look distinctive, I am often picked out on such occasions. I immediately panicked. I looked to one side and saw Elizabeth and two other female partners. I looked to the other side and saw Sue Grange, Head of Personnel, and a mousy trainee called Anita who didn't look like she'd have much to talk about. Where the hell was Mad Sally Smith when you needed her? Months later, on describing the details of my reaction to the policewoman's request to a psychologist (deafness, sweating, heart palpitations, nausea), I was informed that I had suffered a panic attack. Due to the deafness, I did not hear the policeman follow her threat to pick someone out with the explanation that this was a humorous technique used to convey the horror of relating a sexual encounter to strangers, something unfortunately required from rape victims.

As the senior partner, Mr Cooper, was speaking at one in-house lecture, I decided to check him out and attend. The room soon filled with all those eager to (be seen to) support the big boss. There must have been over a hundred lawyers present. Halfway through the rather tedious lecture, I looked around at my colleagues. It suddenly dawned on me that everyone, and I mean *everyone*, was wearing black or navy blue. Except me. I was in an orange trouser suit. If you had come into that room and been asked to pick out one person who did not fit in, you'd have pointed straight at me without any hesitation.

My moment of revelation had finally arrived. I did not belong in this place. It felt both alienating and liberating. I hadn't consciously decided not to wear the uniform; it was just that I loved wearing colours and still do. With all the beautiful, vibrant colours in the world, it always amazes me that so many people wear black. I knew from that moment on that I wouldn't be staying beyond my two-year contract.

The decision was mutual. Three months before the end of my articles, I attended a meeting with two people from the pinnacle. With a sympathetic nod and sigh, I was informed that there would not be a position for me in Coopers once my training contract expired. Despite my decision a while ago to leave Coopers in any case, my pride was still dealt a blow. 'Actually,' I said, breezily, 'I've got a job in New York working for my friend's father's fashion business.' It wasn't actually true, although I did have plans to live abroad for a while. 'Well, I hope you have a great time, but Emma, you need to realise that when you come back to England to practise law, you will need to adopt a more professional attitude.' I was annoyed at the time and gave him a speech about how it wasn't a professional attitude I needed but subservience and the sacrifice of my personal life.

In retrospect, I think we were both right.

The Descent

I left Coopers with mixed feelings. I was off the conveyor belt. The problem was that, in a sense, I had never left school. All my decisions had been made for me. School, university, law school and articles. The headmistress had been replaced by the senior partner, the teachers by the partners, the prefects by the senior solicitors and my classmates by my colleagues. There was still homework, detention and a uniform.

I decided to take some time out, booked a one-way flight to Barcelona and lived there for a year, teaching English. As I settled into my new life abroad, Coopers seemed like a million miles away. I lived the life I'd dreamed of during my drudging commute into the City and my restless hours checking legal documents for typos. I partied like mad, dated furiously and, very occasionally, wondered how my ex-colleagues at Coopers were doing (although not for very long).

After a year of adventures, I felt ready to return to London to pursue a career. Unwilling to concede that I had wasted six years qualifying as a solicitor, I convinced myself that it wasn't law I disliked, but working in a large, stuffy City law firm. I decided to join the cowboys and applied to a few West End firms. Having a firm like Coopers on my CV helped and I soon found a job at a firm called Taylor Goodman.

The interview was an informal affair with plenty of laughs. Things went swimmingly for the first couple of months. Mr Taylor and Mr Goodman regularly told me how delighted they were with their decision to employ me, and I congratulated myself at being a grown-up solicitor. However, once the novelty of having my own workload wore off, I was faced with the mundane reality of actually doing the job.

Faced as I was with Mr Taylor and Mr Goodman's faith in the hot shot whiz-kid they had recruited from the City, I was reluctant to admit that I didn't know an awful lot apart from filing invoices and checking documents for typos. What little I had retained after the binge and vomit method of learning at law school had faded during the photocopying years at Coopers and then vapourised entirely from alcohol, spliff and sex sessions in Barcelona.

I tried to muddle through but soon found myself spending most of my day lying. I lied to my clients ('yes, the contract's in the post to you'), I lied to my bosses ('yes, I've drafted the contract and it's in the post to the client'), and I lied to the solicitors on the other side ('yes, the contract is with the client'). I also lied to my secretary, a miserable cow who hated working for a junior solicitor as well as for Mr Goodman ('yes, I do know what I am doing'). I have never lied so much in my life.

As my lack of expertise became apparent to Mr Taylor and Mr Goodman, they transformed from kindly, benevolent elder statesmen of law to grotesque ogres. Taylor was basically a spoilt brat and regularly destroyed office furniture by hurling it across the room. I think he'd gone through three desk lamps that year. He was also a tit starer and took to addressing my breasts rather than my face, which was disconcerting. I was too young and lacking in basic self-worth to confront him with this, and stood before him, embarrassed yet angry.

The other one, Goodman, I had mistaken for a charming but flirtatious bachelor. On closer inspection, he turned out to be a woman hater. His repressed abhorrence for women was congealing his stomach juices, and his breath should have been bottled by the Ministry of Defence and used as a final measure against enemy troops. Instant surrender guaranteed.

'It really sickens me that everyone goes on about women

having babies, as if it requires some special quality. Anyone can have a child,' he said, scornfully, one day.

'You can't,' I said.

He won, though, by sighing over me. I reeled back and quickly left the room.

I lasted six months. Taylor and Goodman weren't interested in investing any time at all in training me and, to be honest, I found my mind wandering to my new biker boyfriend's trouser package when I should have been investigating the sewer and cess pit situation of a client's proposed house purchase. My final booboo involved over-paying a client £10,000 from the firm's office account on a house sale. I left Mr Goodman with the embarrassing task of having to ask the client for the money back. An unusual state of affairs followed whereby the client failed to return his solicitor's calls. The client was clearly enjoying the reversal of roles.

As I was handed my P45 and my last salary cheque, Mr Goodman kindly informed me that I was not suitable to practise as a solicitor as I lacked any sense of professional responsibility.

'Save the lecture,' I said, 'and give me the money.'

I was deeply despondent at this state of affairs. I was also simultaneously binned by the biker boyfriend, which did nothing to alleviate my fears that I was a loser. I signed on and dropped out for a while. When I say 'a while', I mean a year. I decided I had had enough of the world of work. I also decided that I needed a rich boyfriend.

As I wasn't working, I devoted myself completely to looking good and socialising. While other people were forging ahead with their careers, I was swimming, walking, resting and drinking pints of carrot juice. Physically, I was in tip top shape. While other people cried off full-scale mid-week partying, I was always able to stay up and carouse.

It was during this frantic socialising that I met the rich boyfriend for whom I had prayed. Russell was loaded, and my favourite kind of loaded: self-made. Like most self-made entrepreneurial millionaires, he hadn't gone to university, deeming it, quite rightly, a waste of time. I met him on the balcony at a friend of a friend's cousin's best friend's party. I had gone out to get some air after a spot of exhibitionistic dancing and there he was, sitting on his own, drink and cigarette in hand. I sat straight down on his lap, helping myself to his cigarette and beer.

'Who are you?' I asked.

'Russell. And you?'

'Emma.'

'Comfortable?'

'Not really, plus I can't see you,' I said, standing up to face him. It was dark, but I could make out that he was well dressed, with fair cropped hair, blue eyes and a beautiful but cruel mouth. He stood up, too.

'Who do you know here?' he asked.

'You,' I said.

'I don't know you yet,' he said. 'What do you do?'

'I don't do,' I said, 'I am.'

He laughed and said, 'What would you like to do?'

'With you?' I asked.

'Yeah, with me.'

'A kiss would be nice.'

And that was how I met my rich boyfriend. It was one of those intense from the word go kind of relationships. I saw him nearly every night for the following few weeks until we decided that I might as well move in with him. I was delighted to put career decisions on hold indefinitely while I serviced his every need. In fact, as I was living with him and he was paying for everything (restaurants, theatre, cinema and clothes), I felt duty bound to service his every need. His voracious sexual appetite was, at first, a dream come true. However, after six months of five times a day, I began to tire of all that fucking. Problem was that if I said no, he became moody and difficult.

So I often ended up shagging with a 'pull my nightie down when you've finished' attitude.

The other problem was that he was very possessive and, as it was his flat, whenever my friends came round I felt very awkward. Male friends coming over always caused a fight, and life with Russell became increasingly stressful. If I spoke to other men at parties I would be subjected to hours of interrogation when we left – that was if he hadn't already stormed out of the party.

I realised that being a kept woman also meant being a possessed woman, with no independence and very few rights. I occasionally contemplated a future without him, but knew that being independent meant getting a job, something which terrified me. My two legal experiences had paralysed me professionally and my brittle self-confidence was a very fragile front. I told myself I loved Russell, which was an easy way out, especially as he told me that he loved me all the time.

Ten months down the line, we attended his cousin's wedding. As we stood outside the synagogue, he asked me to marry him. Without pausing for thought, I heard myself say no. We both looked at each other, shocked. It was becoming clear that I needed to find a job and a way out. A month later I took the plunge and moved out and into Simon's flat in West Hampstead. It took a while to shake Russell off. He was a man used to getting his own way and I don't think he could quite believe that someone had walked out on him. His increasingly menacing phone calls convinced me I had done the right thing.

Suddenly, all those people that didn't know what they wanted to do when they left university now had great jobs in journalism, advertising, film and TV. A friend got me a short-term contract at the BBC, working as a researcher for a consumer affairs programme. Everyone was very nice, very smug and very ambitious. They made the power hungry tigers at Coopers look like meek, mealy mouthed saps. Not only did I not care enough about the dangers of cordless phones during electrical storms, I didn't care enough about the job to pretend to care enough. The three-month contract expired and was not renewed. All I could do was breathe a sigh of relief that I no longer had to schlep to White City every day and feel awed that I was working at the greatest broadcasting corporation in the world.

Another friend got me a job working at a small publishing company, selling rights and negotiating contracts. This was more fun, although so badly paid that the joy of being surrounded by books all day soon wore off. I didn't like the job much, but I liked my colleagues a lot, although the company suffered dreadfully from a lack of suitable flirting material. The no-money no-men combo ultimately proved fatal to my career there. I had been with the company for a year, and I knew it was time to move on as the promotion prospects were limited. An advertisement in the media section of *The Guardian* caught my eye: *Solicitor required for prestigious media agency*. The salary was good so I applied.

The first interview was with the big boss and I absolutely gave it my best shot. I was offered the job and I accepted.

Now, this was a classic case of listening to my head rather than my heart. My heart said that I would find another legal job leg-chewingly, mind-numbingly boring. My head said that it would be sensible to put all that legal training to use. Negotiating the small print in contracts, whether for houses, shares, widgets or script-writing services, was something which made my heart sigh and sink. My head said wouldn't it be nice to have the kudos of being a lawyer at an agency in Notting Hill, responsible for 50 per cent of the drama output on television. My heart said that there was something vaguely unpleasant and inhumane about the head of the agency. My head said that this man was impressed with me so he obviously had impeccable taste.

And after all, I didn't need to marry the guy, just work for him.

The Fuck Pig

I started the job with one of the biggest handicaps imaginable – a competent and popular predecessor. Lucy was perfect. I could see as much during handover. Naturally straight, naturally blonde hair, large, clear blue eyes, slim, petite and casually but elegantly dressed. She was leaving work so that she could devote herself body and soul to looking after her adorable, soft-skinned, fluffy haired, six-month-old baby in her divine four-bedroomed house in Fulham. Her good-looking, rugby playing, intelligent, popular, rich husband was a City lawyer. The fact that he was a City lawyer gave me some, albeit small, satisfaction, as I knew that he would be absent from home most evenings and weekends (confirmed by her after some gentle prodding from me).

She told me that despite the agency offering her every conceivable deal, from part-time to working at home to a year's leave, she was determined to quit work and become a full-time mum. Yikes. She must be really, really good. They were clearly desperate to keep her. As she was extremely nice and helpful to me, it was hard to get a handle on any justifiable hatred of her.

During the one (measly) handover day, she was bombarded by colleagues expressing their dismay at her leaving. I presented a smiling, convivial face at these scenes, while inwardly cursing the fact that I was replacing Little Mrs Perfect. The agents all confirmed that not only was she a pleasure to be around, she was also a shit-hot lawyer. I had not practised law for some time, and even then, 'practise', in its literal sense, was an accurate description of what I was doing since

I had no real idea of what grown-up lawyers actually did. As well as being rusty at not being a proper lawyer, I had no experience of drafting and negotiating script-writing contracts and film option agreements. I hadn't even lied about this in the interview. Lucy Perfect convinced both the agents and myself that the law part of things was very straightforward and eminently pickupable.

She was right. I sat quietly for a while going through her amendments to various contracts, some of which I discovered and then confirmed with lawyer friends were completely unnecessary. I even made a few amendments of my own. I sat in silence in my room for three days with no visitors at all. I was the serious, professional owl of the agency, and unfortunately left alone to work in peace.

While making myself a cup of tea on the third day, I picked up one of those Far Side mugs in the kitchen. The illustration was of two large men shaking hands, with miniature people hovering around their feet. The caption said something like 'Well, that's a deal – let the little people sort out the details'. After my dreams and aspirations, my studying, my search for a fulfilling career, here I was. This is what I had become. A little person.

Twice a week, I was required to attend a lunchtime meeting. Not much had changed from my days as a trainee solicitor. While everyone else sat there having informed, intelligent, grown-up conversations, I was eyeing up the biscuits. The agents represented the cream of British screen-and playwriting talent. Rightly, I believe, I had little to contribute, and apart from nodding and smiling in the right places, I kept shtum. Unfortunately, the more silent I was, the harder I found it to contribute anything at all. Occasionally, I would be asked for my advice on a legal point. With my mouth full of tarte provencale and my mind empty of clever legal jargon, I fear I did not acquit myself with any degree of gravitas.

The managing director was the most sinister character there

and, in my opinion, quite vile. Lloyd's father was a moderately successful theatre impresario, and he had sensibly decided to exploit all his father's contacts and set up an agency. He certainly hadn't managed to achieve anything through his own charisma. Lloyd was unfriendly to the point of hostility (after all, there was no point being friendly to 'the little people'). He also had nasty, acrid smell about him. I couldn't put my finger on it (nor would I have wished to), but it was a mixture of TCP, mothballs, grime and garlic. I suppose I should have been relieved that he kept his distance.

Lloyd thought he was witty as hell and had a number of natty catchphrases, which he thought hilarious but which I found tiresome. One such phrase was: 'the words "chance" and "no" come to mind'. This was said in response to any request he found unreasonable. The 'come to mind' gag was used daily, as in 'the words "money" "much" and "more" come to mind' when discussing contract rates, and 'the words "hit" and "huge" come to mind' when discussing a new play's prospects.

That was his humorous side. His cold abhorrence of humanity revealed itself in his choice of swearwords. His ultimate expression of contempt was to call someone a 'fuck pig'. When I first heard him call someone a 'fuck pig', I was actually amused. It seemed such a shockingly horrible thing to call someone. Maybe because I am semi-kosher and have been brainwashed to consider pigs dirty and disgusting beasts, I was struck by the level of loathing that the word carried. It seems like a pretty venomous, vicious thing to call someone. A fuck pig.

I splashed out on a media law book in an attempt to appear more knowledgeable. However, the book was so utterly boring, I never seemed to get beyond the first chapter.

I also made the mistake of fraternising with the wrong elements in the company. The agents were all far too busy to have a conversation with little people and, being a sociable person, I looked to make friends elsewhere. The person whose sense of humour matched mine most promisingly was the receptionist, Laura. We soon became friends, and when I wasn't eating freebie tarts I was lunching in the park with Laura. Why do I always get on better with the secretaries and receptionists? I suppose us little people stick together.

Actually, two of the female agents were simpatica, if a little fraught and distant. The male agent, Toby, was a chronic tit starer, despite his credentials as a liberal, politically correct member of the media world. What really gets me about these tit starers is that they don't even have the decency or respect to hide what they are doing. I am not averse to checking someone out, but I've got the social sense to do it without getting caught.

Another of the female agents, Thea, was the most horribly ambitious person I have ever come across. I realised that people like her don't get to the top of their profession by being even remotely nice (except, of course, to her clients – a medley of the most respected playwrights and script-writers in the country, who were under the mistaken belief that she was a genuinely nice person simply because she schmoozed them unconditionally).

What I am trying to say is that I thought she was a bitch. And I don't mean a catty, mischievous, you-love-her-for-it kind of bitch. I mean someone who's self-advancement is their complete *raison d'être*, and it's your sad, tough luck if you are the sap who gets in her way.

A native New Yorker (maybe it's not time efficient to be nice there), her hoik up the career ladder was in stark contrast to my series of fuck-up moves down a series of complete and utter snakes. Her curriculum vitae was accessible on the company computer network. I read it with a mixture of admiration and envy. She had started as a publishing assistant on *The New Yorker*, moved into films as an assistant producer on a number of major blockbuster films, where I am sure she had no problem kicking ass when appropriate. She then effortlessly set up her own agency representing script-writers at a precociously young age. As I read down the bullet-pointed list of achievements under each post, I knew with a sinking feeling that she hadn't made up a thing. Again, I mused, this was in stark contrast to the CV packed with exaggerations and omissions that I had doctored to get myself the job.

I am guessing that she moved to England because she met a guy, her husband, with whom she had adopted two children. Now, what angered me here was that, as far as I could see, she lived in the office. Her office was next to mine and she was always in way before me, and I had not managed, in six months, to leave later than her. What I wanted to know was when did she actually get to see her kids, two rather sorrowful-looking boys of six and eight? Why bother going to the trouble of actually adopting kids if you are unwilling to give them any time? Unless, as I cynically deduced, they were lifestyle trappings.

One evening, for some bizarre reason, I was working late. Thea popped her head round the corner of my office, announced that she was leaving early and would I like a lift? She lived in Hampstead, and in our one short non-work conversation soon after I had joined, I had mentioned that I lived in West Hampstead. I foolishly accepted. By the time she dropped me off, I wished I'd asked her to run me over on her way home to finish the job.

She began the tortuous journey by telling me her of plan to become the best agent in the western hemisphere and to sign the few remaining high-profile playwrights and script-writers that had so far eluded her. Instead of asking her, as I was to ask myself a few hours later, why she had to be 'the best' and why she couldn't be happy being 'among the best', I sank into my chair feeling depressed at my own lack of master plan for world domination. This woman is shit-hot and I am just shit, I thought.

'It will mean working longer hours, of course,' she said, 'if I want to represent one hundred per cent of the cream of British talent rather than the seventy-five per cent I currently act for.'

'Gosh, you already work long hours,' I commented.

'You have to, if you want to be the best. I take home manuscripts to read every night as it is. I'll just have to get up even earlier,' she said, robustly.

'What about your children?' I blurted out.

'Well, we have help. Admittedly, Jon's out a lot, too, but I try to spend quality time with them at the weekend and they're happy kids.'

I think of the mournful faces in the frames on her desk. Those kids looked lost, confused and vaguely unkempt. They really didn't look like happy kids.

I decided to change the subject.

'How do you think I am doing at the agency?'

'You want the truth?'

And before I could answer, she was off.

'Well, frankly, I am a little disappointed. Apparently you interviewed well, but you really haven't lived up to the hype. I mean, Lucy was just wonderful. You knew if you asked her to do something, she would just do the most competent job possible. I had absolute faith in her and believe me, I tried everything to get her to stay. But you know, she wanted to do her earth mother thing and, hey, it's not for me, but I am sure she's as fabulous a mother as she was a lawyer. I don't have that confidence with you. Sure, you negotiate contracts for us in a satisfactory way, I guess. It's just that you don't seem that confident and self-assured about what you are doing. You don't seem to be dynamic. You don't take the lead, the initiative. I guess we just don't have the same confidence in you that we had in Lucy. It's such a shame she left, really.'

As she finished her speech, we drew up to a set of traffic lights. There was silence in the car. I had shrivelled up inside and my eyes had glazed over with tears. All the agents were obviously of the same opinion, hence the 'we' dropped in at the end.

During the silence, I wondered whether she was aware of the traumatic impact of her answer to my question.

A few more minutes silence, then she reached for her mobile.

'Hi Jon, honey. Yeah, yeah, mmmm, sure, I agree. Absolutely, they should be in bed by now. Listen, I'll be home in ten. Just dropping someone off.'

I was not a colleague. I was not Emma who works in the room next to her for eight hours a day. I was just a 'someone' in this high-powered, high-achieving, high-earning bitch's life. I was surprised she was willing to breathe the same air as me in such a confined space. Having adopted this woman's version of reality, I thought that I was not someone, I was no-one.

And then I did something I now bitterly regret. With her high up on her pedestal and me cowering under the pedestal on the floor below her, a shrunken, unworthy nobody, I decided to hand her a heavy paving stone with which to flatten me completely.

'Have you got any tips to help me improve my performance?' I asked, meekly.

She sighed a 'Where the fuck do I start?' sigh. 'Well, I don't know. You should be reading trade magazines to give you a wider picture. You need to be up on all the latest developments in the law so that we are always one step ahead of the competition. I mean, the digital revolution is happening already, but it seems to be passing you by. You need to be able to cover every angle of digitalisation in our contracts. You see, the thing with Lucy was that we knew she was going to give us the best possible advice. You need to manoeuvre yourself into that position. If you can.' She didn't sound convinced.

'I'm just on the right here,' I said, pointing to an off-licence, into which I intended to stumble if my legs still worked.

'Thanks for the lift,' I said, as I got out of the car.

'Oh, it's nothing,' she said, turning on the radio to stimulate her busy brain for the remaining three-minute journey home.

I considered running in front of her car as she pulled off, but I was too sluggish to shift it.

Now in my thirties, I look back on that journey with astonishment. My self-esteem was carpet level and I just absorbed her low opinion of me as gospel. I forgot all about the partner at Coopers with a double first at Cambridge who told me I was the brightest trainee solicitor he had ever come across. This woman thought I was shit, therefore I was.

If I had my time again, what would I have done differently? Would I have told her to fuck off and got out of the car? Would I have gently but cruelly examined her clearly neurotic need to be numero uno? Would I have defended myself by pointing out that I had only been at the agency for six months? Would I have pointed out that the agents knew I did not have media experience when I joined? Actually, I don't think I would have got out of the car, but waited until she had taken me to the door and then told her to fuck herself.

Following on from Thea's helpful advice, I decided that I was going to turn things around for myself. I turned up an hour earlier for work the next day. Thea was already in. I noisily pulled up my blinds and banged a few books so that she knew I was there. I looked at my in-tray with dread. There was nothing in it that even remotely interested me. I wandered out to reception and picked up that week's trade magazines. I made myself a cup of tea and trudged back to my office. As I sat there, drinking tea and flicking listlessly through the magazines looking for something vaguely interesting to read, Lloyd popped his head round the door.

'The words "work" and "no" come to mind,' he said.

'Just reading the trade mags,' I said, showing him the cover of *The Stage*. 'I thought—'

He interrupted me. 'An advertisement wrongly quoting one of my client's works has been drawn to my attention. What's our legal remedy?'

He seemed to think I was a walking textbook. All of a sudden I am supposed to be an expert on advertising law and copyright. The words 'clue', 'fucking' and 'no' came to mind, but I didn't voice them.

'I'll find out and get back to you this morning,' I said.

I thought this a perfectly reasonable response. His sour look of disdain indicated that he felt otherwise. I then heard him go into Thea's room. He shut the door behind him. All of sudden, the mouse turned. I felt angry at the situation and determined to go and speak to him at the earliest opportunity.

Once I had found out the answer to his earlier query, I made my way to his office. I felt a little shaky. He was on the phone when I appeared at his door and I was waved away dismissively. I stood outside talking to his PA, Belinda, a perfectly pleasant if completely self-absorbed Notting Hill babe. The day before, at the agents' lunch, I had learned that she was about to be axed and I felt a stab of pity as I talked to her. She whispered to me that she felt she could do nothing right in Lloyd's eyes and that he had started to ignore her most of the time and did I know anything? I deflected the question by asking her if she was happy working for him. Before she had time to answer, I was summoned into his office by the shout of my name.

I walked in, calmly shutting the door behind me.

'I've written you a short memo on your client's legal position and remedies,' I said, handing him the piece of paper.

He didn't look at it as it landed on a pile of other unread memos.

I launched straight in. 'Lloyd, I am not entirely happy about how things are working out here.'

His face was completely impassive and unreadable.

'I know that you all thought that Lucy was wonderful and I

am sure she was, but I feel that I have been unfairly compared to her from the word go. She worked for you for nearly three years and was clearly very experienced and knowledgeable. You knew that I had limited media experience before coming here and my lower starting salary reflected that. I would like to point out that, as Lucy was going on holiday, I only had one day's handover, which is not very much considering she was the only person in the company that did what she did. It's not like I can ask anyone else. There is only one company lawyer and I've pretty much had to learn from scratch. We both knew it would be a steep learning curve, but I am bright you know and I pick things up quickly. I have already made several key amendments to our standard contract – I just don't go around shouting about it. Perhaps I should. Not you, or any other agent here, has spent any time at all with me explaining how things work. Perhaps I should have insisted on it, but I knew you were busy and so I figured things out for myself.'

He was still impassive, although I noticed his face had got a little flushed. I continued.

'I have found the lack of support very demoralising, and if things are going to improve I need fewer unfavourable comparisons to Lucy and a little more help.'

I stopped, drew breath and looked at him. His face was now purple. With rage.

'How dare you walk into my office and impose your demands on me. How dare you criticise Lucy, who was more of a lawyer than you will ever hope to be. She was a wonderful girl and I will not have a word said against her. Now listen to me, young lady. If you don't think you are up to the job, perhaps you had better say so now rather than wasting my time. I have neither the time nor the inclination to justify the way I work to you. You either fit in or you leave.'

A split second decision.

'I'll leave,' I said.

As I walked to the door, I turned round and looked at him.

'The words "pig" and "fuck" come to mind,' I said.

A week later, I signed on at Search. As a temp. I was on their books for eight months until Mr Fox recruited me to work as the temp controller.

And that was how I had ended up at Search.

Part Three

Why Work for the Cunt When You Can Sue Him?

I've been sacked by Wayne. I can't believe it. I've got no job. He's told me that none of them want to work with me. I am difficult and insolent. I am unable to keep a job. I can't function in the world of work. I don't know how to do it.

I run down West End Lane. I am in pain. I must get home where I can fall apart in the privacy of my own bedroom. I keep repeating the 'I am a fuck-up failure who can't keep a job' mantra. As I get in through the door, the phone is ringing. It is Luca.

'Mum just told me the news. How are you?'

'Shit,' I say. 'Numb, angry, pessimistic, humiliated, devastated, negative, depressed, shocked. Listen, I'm running out of adjectives. Can I call you back? I need to get my head round this.'

'No, you can't call me back. I'm coming round. I'll tell work I've got to interview someone. I want to be with you.'

Although I would love to see him, I know that I need to fall apart and cry and be fucked up, and I don't want my new boyfriend to see me this way, at least not this early in the relationship.

'Luca, I really, really appreciate your offer. It means a lot to me, it really does. But I just need to be alone for a bit to cry and freak.'

'What happens when you freak?' he asks, sounding intrigued.

'If you're still around in another month or so, I'll tell you.'

'OK, I'll leave you to freak out in private, if that's what you want. I've seen plenty of people freak before. I've done it myself plenty of times. I can handle it. I want to be there for you.'

'You are fucking gorgeous,' I say, trying not to cry.

'So are you.'

'I'm not,' I say, feeling worthless. 'Listen, I've got to call you back.'

'I'll call you in a bit,' he says, and then, 'I love you.'

As I put down the phone, I burst into tears.

Simon wanders out of his bedroom, still in his pyjamas.

'What's going on? Why are you home so early?' he asks, rushing over to me on the sofa. He sits down next to me with his arms around me.

'I've been sacked,' I say, between sobs.

'That fucking *creep*. Emma, I am really sorry.'

'It's all my fault,' I wail. 'I can't keep a job. My work life is a fucking disaster. I'll never get another job after this. I won't get a reference. He still owes me commission. This is all because of the memo. Simon, I am a fucking failure loser fuck-up disaster.'

Simon sits and listens to me maliciously berating myself. He gives me fifteen minutes to self-destruct before firmly intervening and taking a practical approach.

'Did you say he gave you a memo?' he asks.

'Yeah, it's in my bag. I haven't dared look at it yet,' I say, fishing around in my rucksack for Wayne's memo. I read it with disbelief. I can't believe what he has written. It is utter bullshit. I read it out to Simon.

Dear Emma,

I regret I am unable to continue employing you at Search. Your personal phone calls have escalated over the last few months and this is unacceptable. I am also unwilling to accept your behaviour towards me which demonstrates a lack of co-operation and respect. Finally, with regard to your most unwelcome memo to me, please expect comments from any employer when you come to work inappropriately dressed.

I wish you well in the future.

Yours sincerely,

Wayne Burns

Now, for those of you who didn't realise and thought I sounded like a confident, together kind of person and who are now shocked at how quickly this façade has crashed and burned, I would only say that the more confident a person appears, the less confident they truly feel. However, on reading the pathetic memo from Wayne, my self-pity turns to angry indignation.

'The arsehole. As if I had time to make personal calls at that place. I was too busy schmoozing clients and placating the temps,' I shout.

'I know. I never bothered to call you at work for a chat. The other phones were always ringing and it was so annoying being put on hold for five minutes while you gave someone intellectually subnormal a detailed description of how to find the correct office unit in a sprawling warehouse park in Colindale. And you never used to ring here for a chat, either. So, for a start, that's not true. What was the next thing?'

'My unco-operative behaviour and lack of respect. Does failing to co-operate mean failing to sleep with him? How could I respect a sleazeball like him?'

'Well, quite,' says Simon. 'I couldn't agree more.'

'And as for the last comment about my "most unwelcome" memo. It was a one-line memo asking him not to make any more personal comments about my appearance. What a joke. How was I inappropriately dressed? Does the fact that I wear mini-skirts in the office mean that I have to expect comments on my legs? If I wear fitted white T-shirts in the summer do I have to put up with remarks about the size and shape of my tits?'

'Absolutely not,' says Simon. 'Did you get any notice pay?'

'I hadn't thought of that. He didn't give me any money. My salary was paid up till last Friday. I haven't been paid for today, for any notice period or for any untaken holiday. He still hasn't paid me my full commission for March.'

'You know what I am thinking?' Simon says, smiling. 'Why work for the cunt when you can sue him?'

'That hadn't occurred to me,' I say.

'Well, what did you think you were going to do?' he asks.

'Sign on, mope and mourn and lie in bed a lot,' I suggest. 'I suppose I thought I would write him a letter pointing out how unfairly I have been treated, and then I could ask for some notice money and the rest of my holiday pay and commission.'

'Emma, sue him,' Simon urges me.

'Oh, I couldn't,' I say, getting timid. 'He'll just point out my previous job record – he knows that I've had about two hundred jobs. He'll deny he ever made any comments about my tits and legs. He'll say I am a difficult, argumentative bitch and that I was eminently sackable. I can't face the aggravation of a court case.'

'You feel like that now, darling. But when you wake up tomorrow morning, you are going to be angry. You have a very good case and it will be fun, I promise you. Just think about how stressed he'll be having to fight a sex discrimination case.'

'Especially with his divorce going on at the same time,' I add gleefully, warming to the idea of tormenting Wayne.

'Listen,' Simon continues excitedly, 'it could be your hobby. You know, while you are not working. Something to motivate you and keep you occupied. You were a lawyer, you could do the case yourself.'

'Oh, I don't know about that. I can't remember a thing about employment law. Maybe I could find a no-win, no-fee firm of lawyers to take the case on for me,' I wonder aloud.

'That's my girl!' Simon says, cuddling me. 'Now, get into

the bath then get dressed. I am taking you out for a drink to celebrate you being a lady of leisure. You've got half an hour and then we're off out. No arguments.'

So, feeling a little shaky, I hop into the bath and scrub every particle of the Search Employment Agency from my body. I can hear the phone ringing and Simon telling Tina that I will call her back. 'I want to speak to her,' I shout out, so Simon brings the phone into the bathroom and lets me know that I have only five minutes to speak as the taxi is picking us up in fifteen. Tina keeps repeating 'I can't believe it', and I end up reassuring her that I am OK, that no, I don't know what I will be doing yet, and that I don't think that Wayne's going to sack her, too. Then, surprisingly, she starts crying and says that she will miss me dreadfully.

'What sort of person am I working for Emma?' she asks me. Simon's voice immediately enters my head and all I say, quite unemotionally, is 'a creep'. I tell her I have to go and she says she will ring the following evening for a more in-depth chat.

Then I ring Luca to tell him that Simon is taking me out to get me pissed and that I won't be back until late. I don't know why I should feel guilty for not letting him come round. After all, we've only been together for a week and a half. It's just one of those rare relationships that seems fairly serious right from the beginning. Perhaps that has happened here because, in one sense, the timing is right. We have both been on our own for a while and were both looking for a relationship. You know how you can meet someone and just know it ain't going to work out – they've just come out of a long-term relationship and they want to revel in their freedom and randomly screw around without ties. Or they've just started a new job and need to put in the hours there rather than committing time and energy to a new relationship. Or they're coming off drugs or getting into them. Whatever. Timing issues.

I suppose it's a sort of rejection when someone wants to be there for you and you don't allow them to be. I've never had a truly supportive boyfriend before and I feel too fragile right now to allow myself to be vulnerable in front of Luca. I don't want him to see me as needy and full of self-doubt. It's too soon and I think it would irrevocably alter the dynamics of the relationship. I'd feel that he'd have one over on me. Basically, I daren't trust myself to trust him.

As I get ready to go out with Simon, my mind is still swirling with the idea of taking Wayne to court and writing vengeful letters, interspersed with thoughts of failure, rejection and humiliation. Simon must sense that I am quietly withdrawing as he puts on some loud, funky music and writhes around in my room, gyrating his hips and imitating a naff Seventies crooner. I am just applying my new lips, fuller and juicier, with the help of a lip liner and dark purple lipstick, when the taxi arrives. Simon bangs on the answering machine and we are off.

We decide to go to Montgomery's, a new gay bar in Chalk Farm, where we will begin with a quick, quiet drink before moving on to somewhere more proactive. As soon as we enter the bar, I am filled with excitement. The air is alive with infectious, predatory, sexually charged pheromones. I feel as if I am entering a different arena, one where anything is possible. And I am straight, so I can only imagine something of the promise that Simon feels each time he goes to a gay bar.

Simon daren't look around the bar in case no-one is looking at him. We sit down and order doubles. Simon proposes a toast to my new life as a layabout and we clink glasses to 'Why work for the cunt when you can sue him!'

It's probably quite good that I am there as I am able to take Simon's mind off looking at younger, better-looking men suggestively eyeballing each other. One hour, four drinks and two packets of peanuts later, I announce to Simon that I will be leaving him on his own for a moment while I go to the loo (which is not as easy as you would think – I need to get a key for the ladies' loo from behind the bar. I feel very grown-up to be entrusted with it). As I emerge from the ladies', I see a skinhead consulting an A–Z map and looking a little lost and forlorn. Considering myself something of a Route Mistress when it comes to finding my way around London (one of the few advantages of having had so many jobs in different parts of the capital), I offer to help.

His name is Lorenzo, he's from Milan, he speaks adorable English not too badly and he needs to get back to his sister's in South Kensington for dinner at eight o'clock. We both look at our watches and note that it is now ten past eight. 'Look,' I say, 'why don't you borrow my mobile and tell her that you are going to be late. Meanwhile, my friend speaks fluent Italian and he can explain to you how to get home from here.' Now I wouldn't describe Lorenzo as bellissimo, but he has gorgeous brown eyes and looks perfectly cute in a skinhead kind of way. He is also so friendly and warm that I find myself insisting that he come and meet Simon. As I approach Simon at the bar, I can see from his face that he is pissed off that I have been gone for so long. Then he catches a glimpse of Lorenzo behind me and his expression changes from annoyance to hope. 'Have you bought me a present?' he whispers. I introduce Lorenzo to Simon and they start babbling in Italian until I put my foot down and insist on being included in the conversation. I guess that Simon likes Lorenzo as he is being argumentative and overly sensitive. His sarcastic comment quota has increased dramatically and the conversation has taken a combative direction, hinting at a passionate kiss and make up session later on (I've seen it many times before). Lorenzo is provocative and easy going at the same time. I can see he is teasing Simon, who is getting worked up about something rather trivial, while Lorenzo sits back and smiles. Actually, we both really hit it off with Lorenzo and another three drinks, four bags of crisps and a mobile phone call to his sister later, we have decided that he will be staying at our flat tonight.

When we arrive home, we give Lorenzo a tour, starting with Simon's bedroom with its huge king-size bed. In fact, the bed looks so inviting that both Simon and I jump onto it and sprawl out. 'Keep your boots on,' I say to Lorenzo, beckoning him onto the bed. I am not enforcing my rule of Shoes Staying On here, but responding to Simon's confessed fantasy that he fancied tussling on the bed with Lorenzo and his, vicious, twenty-four hole Doctor Martens.

Suddenly, I notice Lorenzo looking very uncomfortable and making no attempt at all to join the party on the bed. 'Is this a triangle?' he asks nervously. I switch on to his fears and reassure him that I am not in on the deal, sexually speaking. So he joins us on the bed and we chat and smoke and continue drinking for another hour or so. I decide it's time to leave when they start kissing and Lorenzo uses my neck for leverage, so that he can grind more effectively against Simon's groin.

I fall into bed, pissed out of my head, thankful that I am not working the next day and then feeling suddenly terribly afraid and cast out. I start wondering what the hell is going to become of me, and then I feel excited at the thought of my unknown future. I can't get my mood quite right. Before I have time to establish a positive mind-set, I have fallen asleep. I wake up in the middle of the night, immediately think to myself 'I've been sacked', and then fall back to a long and troubled sleep.

The Spit Roast

When I wake in the morning, once again, the first thing I think is 'I've been sacked', and I feel a bit sick. Then I realise that part of the reason I feel sick is that I drank excessive amounts of alcohol the night before. And then I feel incredibly grateful that I don't have to go to work. I stumble into the kitchen where I see the answering machine winking at me. I force myself to eat some cereal. I can't deal with the answering machine at the moment, my head is too full, so I make myself a large mug of herbal tea and get back into bed. I have a wonderful sleep until almost lunchtime, when I am awoken by angry Italian voices. I decide to get up officially now and find out who has upset who. It would appear that Lorenzo has found Simon's Kylie Minogue CD collection and is tormenting Simon, who has become so defensive that he looks like he might wear himself out with indignation. I stop the argument with an 'I've been sacked', and both of them enquire kindly as to whether I am OK. I say I am not sure. I am certainly pleased not to have to go to work feeling like I currently do.

'What will you do?' Lorenzo asks, grimacing at the instant coffee he is being forced to drink. I like the fact that he seems genuinely interested in my welfare the morning after the night before. Sometimes when you meet people out and about and you've all been drinking and forged a great bonhomie, it can be a shock the next time you see them to realise that they were only being warm for the evening, a warmth that was clearly only sustainable by large quantities of alcohol. Lorenzo really is acting as if last night was the first step towards a solid friendship.

'Sign on and think about it,' I say.

'Very good idea. Now let's all go out for lunch,' Simon suggests.

'I'd better wear dark glasses,' I say. 'I don't want to bump into Wayne, Bert or Tina.' And off we go.

Actually, it turned into rather a lovely day. We went for lunch at a nice little café round the corner from Search and I even had the nerve to sit outside. Afterwards, the boys went back to bed and I decided to indulge in one of my all-time favourite pastimes – going to the cinema in the afternoon. Alone.

Some people think I am odd for wanting to go to the cinema on my own. I try to explain that going to the cinema alone allows me to avoid absorbing other people's discontent, thus ruining the film for me. Many times I have been quite happily enjoying a film, when I am suddenly aware that my cinema partner is huffing and puffing, quietly at first and then less self-consciously. I turn to them and raise my eyebrows, as if to say, 'Is everything OK?' The cinema partner grimaces to show that they are not enjoying the film. I make a sympathetic noise and then return my attention to the film, which now does not seem quite as engrossing as it did a few moments before. After ten minutes or so, I am recaptivated, however, and this continues until my cinema partner then changes his or her seating position every five seconds. I now raise my eyebrows in a 'shut the fuck up' kind of way. It is very distracting. The odd critical comment is quietly whispered in my ear, poisoning the film for me. I suppose what I am saying is that I am too weak-willed not to be influenced by the reactions of other people, and I have therefore come to the sensible conclusion that I am better off on my own, free to form my own opinions without distraction.

Actually, what is worse than my companion disliking a film that I like is my companion liking the film that I dislike. I've occasionally gone to see a big Hollywood blockbuster (against my better judgement) whose plot I have found insultingly banal and manipulative, only to discover that my companion is glassy eyed with emotion and wonder in the foyer at the end of the film. All respect has gone. Sadly, we are not on the same wavelength after all.

And I could easily fall out with someone who laughed in the wrong places. I went to see Mike Leigh's *Secrets and Lies* with someone who guffawed loudly at all the poignant moments, revealing a shameful lack of emotional sophistication. I was aware of other people in the cinema giving poisonous eyeball action to my companion, communicating 'Shut the fuck up, you moron, this bit isn't supposed to be funny.' My companion, however, was oblivious to such subtleties.

'Don't you want to discuss the film with anyone afterwards?' sceptics ask. 'Not particularly,' I say, knowing that I do not have the kind of friends with whom I have in-depth discussions about anything other than the state of our love and work lives.

'Aren't you embarrassed about going in your own?' they ask. 'A bit,' I reply, and that's why I have two tactical moves which help to alleviate my self-consciousness at daring to do something alone. I only go in the afternoon when the cinema is relatively empty. I think I would find it mildly distressing to see a film on my own and emerge from the cinema at night at the same time as jolly couples hugging each other before going home to have warm and loving sexual intercourse.

My other top tip for going to the cinema alone is to find out beforehand what time the actual film starts, as opposed to the programme. That way, you can slip into the auditorium under cover of darkness and quietly tiptoe out as the credits roll. The absolute deliciousness of sitting in an empty cinema when everyone else is beavering away at work is extremely satisfying. It is also important to find a civilised cinema so that you don't get caught sitting in front of someone chomping popcorn in your ear for the first hour and a half (I find that

that is how long it takes someone to munch their way through even the smallest bucket of salted cardboard).

Luckily, I have found somewhere that caters to my taste. I go to a cinema in North London which serves tea and home-made cake. The auditorium is ornately carved and tasteful rather than an unimaginative rectangular box, and the seats are widely spaced and comfortable. It also happens to be cheap. The ushers are polite and informed film buffs rather than the teenage automatons you find elsewhere. The only downside is that there is no parking, but I reckon this is a small price to pay to avoid the depressing and tacky multiplex cinema villages, with their hot dogs and giant puke size only bags of sweets.

Oh yes, one more vital top tip. Don't even think about going to the cinema in the afternoon during the school holidays. I made this mistake one year on a day off, when I foolishly ended up going to a multiplex cinema. I needed medication by the time I left. I noted with alarm as I entered the cinema that row upon row of seats were filled with excitable miniature people. For the first hour of the film I could barely make out a word of the dialogue due to the deafening sound of crackling sweet bags being opened. After attention spans began to reach the end of their natural life (about twenty minutes), I could make out popcorn being thrown around. There was a steady but constant background chitter chatter, and within half an hour these children were swapping seats and darting all over the cinema. I looked around for someone to control the situation but the ushers were nowhere to be seen. Every fifteen minutes throughout the film (and often at crucial moments in the plot) there was an exodus to the loo. Young girls that came up to my waist in height, wearing crop tops, mini-skirts and make-up, scurried past me every now and then, no doubt heading for the loo in order to reapply their lipstick. The girls would invariably be followed a few minutes later by two small boys who were probably the same age but half the size of the girls. These boys were clearly game as they sprinted past me every ten minutes in search of the girls. I used to like boys like that when I was ten years old, but now I am just glad that we are not allowed to carry guns in this country as I am sure I would have opened fire on the lot of them halfway through the film.

I have since issued, free of charge, government health warnings to other childfree adults, urging them to avoid afternoon cinema during school holidays at all costs. Claudia recently admitted that she listened to my advice but decided to ignore it on the basis that she was a much more tolerant, loving and carefree human being than me. She made her way to the cinema one afternoon during a school holiday, parked in the car park (ignoring but subconsciously noting the high proportion of those ugly people-carrier cars) and briskly walked to the cinema entrance. She opened the door to the cinema and surveyed the scene with horror. The foyer was packed with children, loads and loads of them, buying sweets, screaming to each other and their parents, running to the loo and generally having a wonderful time. She stood mesmerised by the scene in the foyer, momentarily paralysed by the horror of it all, realised that no film was worth the aggravation, then turned and fled, sprinting back to the car park, my words ringing in her ears.

You've been warned.

So this afternoon, unemployed and with suppressed feelings of being unemployable due to my defective character, I made my way to my favourite cinema. I arrived just as the film started and noted with satisfaction that most people there were on their own. I spent two hours immersed in a different world and, as I came blinking into the street, I felt liberated rather than sacked.

Luca takes me out for dinner in the evening to a beautiful restaurant in Primrose Hill with lots of mirrors and cubby holes. As we study the menu, he asks me if I've ever had a spit-roast.

'Quite a few times. Why do you ask? Is it a speciality here?'

He bursts out laughing and tells me the story of an outwardly prissy secretary at work who ended up on a pub binge last Friday. Apparently, a group of them had gone straight to the pub after work and this girl had been persuaded to join this posse of hard-core drinkers.

'Are you in this gang?' I want to know.

'I go with them about once a month because basically that is all I can handle. I'm nearly always sick and then I have the piss taken out of me for a week afterwards. I'm just not interested in drinking to oblivion any more.'

'Who is?'

'These guys. They go out nearly every night after work and down pint after pint.'

'Alcoholics?'

'Probably, actually, yes. But a really good laugh. Fantastically funny; fast, cruel humour, very sexist. You'd hate it.'

'Maybe. I bet if you sat down and had a meaningful conversation with any sexist guy, though, you'd find a man with a broken heart.'

'Well, if you meet them you can ask them, but I'm telling you, they are pretty rowdy, and if you were to ask them a question like that in front of their mates they'd tear you apart. So this girl, Naomi, is really sweet and quiet and lives in Kent with her mother. She ends up being dragged along to the pub, drinking loads and then gets chatting to members of a stag party who are in the same pub. Then she disappears, along with the groom and the best man. One of the girls from the office finds her an hour later in one of the loos sliding around on a mixture of vomit and spunk. Naomi told this girl that she'd given the groom a blow job while the best man had taken her from behind.'

'So that's what you meant by a spit-roast? The girl who told everyone, the one that found her, she sounds like a real bitch.'

'Possibly, but remember she was pissed too and a good story is a good story.'

'She's not a sister.'

'Not to her sisters, I agree, but she was a definitely a sister to her brothers.'

'So is anything worth it for a good story?' I ask, suddenly concerned at Luca's possible lack of morals.

'There's a bench on Hampstead Heath that commemorates the journalist who said "If I don't do it, someone else will" and I hate that mentality. I just think that is a low-down, cowardly, immoral excuse for being an arsehole. But Naomi doesn't know that people know. Obviously, the guys were sworn to secrecy and they've actually got a weird code of honour.'

'It's bound to spread. You weren't there and you know about it.'

'True.'

'She'll have to leave.'

'By the way, was Naomi a sister to the groom's bride?'

'When you're that pissed . . .'

'The same could be said for Linda, the girl who told the boys what she'd witnessed in the loo.'

'Look I'm not the most discreet person in the world, but I think it is a bit mean to tell that to a group of rowdy, sexist men. Would you ever have another work relationship?'

'No. I don't shit where I eat any more.'

'You'd never believe we're in a restaurant having a romantic meal.'

'Well, being serious for a minute, maybe that is the one obvious good thing about you not working at Search any more. You know, my mother and my girlfriend are not in the same work place.'

'You're right. Hang on a minute, did you set the whole thing up to make a messy situation tidy? I'm not complaining, though. When we split up, I won't have to see your mum any more.'

'Can we change the when to an if?'

'Good idea.'

It's probably lucky that we're in a hidden corner of the restaurant as we're kissing madly by the second course and by dessert, and after a quick visit to the loo, my knickers are in my handbag.

As I know that Lorenzo will be staying with Simon, I decide to take the plunge and stay at Luca's flat this time. I am nervous about meeting his flatmates, but as they are from the grunt school of communication, I need not have worried about making a good impression. After a short but satisfying conclusion to the restaurant passion, Luca and I stay up talking for ages about my case for unfair dismissal and sexual discrimination. He's done some research on the matter and excitedly shows me some newspaper clippings on new employment legislation that has reduced the qualifying length of employment from two years to one year, thus allowing me to qualify.

As we snuggle up in bed together, Luca asks me whether I will be leaving in the middle of the night. He says that he is thinking of setting the alarm so that I don't risk waking up with him again in the morning.

'How would you feel about being asked to get up and leave now?' he asks me, as we lie warm and entwined.

'I wouldn't like it at all.'

'I wasn't too keen on it, either. Are you my girlfriend?'

'Why do you ask?'

'I just want to know whether it's OK for me to screw other people.'

'Sure,' I tell him. 'I hope so anyway, because I had sex with someone last night.'

He sits bolt upright and switches on the light.

'Emma, are you serious?'

'Yes,' I say. 'So now you are free to screw around.'

'But I don't want to,' he whines.

'So why did you ask?'

'Because I am really falling for you.'

'Oh, well,' I say, 'in that case, I didn't really screw anyone last night.'

'I'm a one woman man. I just want to make that clear right from the start. If you're not happy with me, tell me, but please don't cheat on me.'

'I'm the same, actually. I finished with someone once just for kissing someone else.'

'You were fifteen at the time, right?'

'Eighteen actually, but the principle remains.'

'Good. So we're clear on that.'

I am full of love for him, but I don't tell him. I need a face-to-face declaration of love before I also put myself on the line. Instead, I tell him that I think he is wonderful and that I really, really, really like him. He doesn't say anything, just pulls me incredibly close to him.

The Dole

After a week of not working, I am settling quite nicely into my life of leisure. I survive signing on, a depressing experience to say the least. I fill in form after form, booklet after booklet. I gather together bank statements, tenancy agreements, P45s and P60s, payslips, employment contracts and passport. I have a phoney conversation with a Job Adviser, telling him of my many and varied plans to seek new employment. I end up promising to update my CV, write letters to ten prospective employers, register with five employment agencies and scour the job pages of *The Guardian* on a Monday, *The Independent* on a Thursday and *The Evening Standard* every night. I leave the Job Adviser open-mouthed at my determination to immediately seek alternative employment. And then I go home to bed to rest after my ordeal, knowing that I will do precisely nothing for many months to come.

In fact, the only positive step I take towards remuneration is to ring the number of a firm of no-win, no-fee lawyers in Kilburn who specialise in employment cases. I relate the significant events of my employment with Wayne. 'What do you think?' I ask when I have finished, prepared to hear that my allegations amount to nothing more than friendly office banter from which I have taken unnecessary offence. 'You've got a good case,' Peter says. 'We'll take it on. This Wayne character is in trouble. He's been a naughty boy.' We agree that I will write them a full report of all incidents of sexual innuendo and unwanted physical contact.

Every now and then I experience an unpleasant twinge, and then I find myself feeling incredibly lucky. I am enjoying myself. I go for walks on the Heath in the morning. I buy a newspaper on the way home and sit in a café and drink tea. I go home and friends ring mid-morning and we chat, me reclining on the sofa, them tired and stressed at work. I have met a friend of a friend, David, who is also not working and we hang out together in the afternoon sometimes. I get a bus up to various art galleries and wander around, feeling relaxed yet absorbed. I go to the library and catch up on my reading. I am discovering wonderful new books and am totally up to date on current cultural events. I listen to the radio again and I reacquaint myself with fresh, new music. I visit my parents regularly and spend quality time with them. I have long, relaxing baths. My skin has never felt softer after lengthy exfoliating and moisturising sessions. I have the time, energy and inclination to remove my make-up, wear face masks and use moisturiser twice a day. The flat is tidy, I have cleaned out my wardrobe and I now know where pretty much everything is. I have had time to bargain hunt for cool things to spice the flat up. I have customised some beautiful terracotta pots and filled the flat with plants. I make delicious nutritious meals in the evening and experiment with new dishes. I have sorted out my admin and am totally up to date with all my correspondence. And I see Luca quite a lot in the evenings. And Lorenzo, our new unofficial flatmate. Things are ticking along quite merrily.

However, I do find that if I sit still for a moment, undistracted by the television, a book or the radio, I start to feel either very angry or very dejected by the whole messy end to my employment at Search. I start to realise that I never leave myself in silence for even a minute in order to avoid unpleasant emotions. I wake up in the morning and go straight to the Heath, where I sometimes meet David for an hour's walk. I read the newspaper while eating breakfast. The minute I go home I have a compulsion to use the phone to speak to someone and, don't forget, Simon is in a lot too, so there is always someone around. I go to bed either with Luca or the radio. While in the bath, I read. When I cook, I listen to the radio. I can't even crap without a distraction. I am becoming aware that I can't bear to be on my own.

One afternoon, I attempt a radical experiment and try to sit in silence for fifteen minutes. It is unbearable. I can't even manage *five* minutes. As I sit on the sofa, I start to mull over events at Search over the last few months and I fume.

I have not heard from Tina since the day I was sacked. When I spoke to her that evening, she said she'd call me the next day. I heard nothing for another three days. Then I got a message on my answering machine saying she was thinking of me and would call me later. Again, nothing for a couple of days, so I decided to ring her back. I left a couple of messages on her machine. I sense that she's one of those people who screen every call. It's probably years since she has picked up the phone when it has rung. Anyway, she doesn't return the calls and I decide to leave it. She obviously feels very uncomfortable as she's still working for Wayne, but I can't help feeling bitterly disappointed. I can't believe that she has not been in touch, especially after her tears and distress on the phone the last time we spoke.

I don't normally like to talk about Tina with Luca, as I know how awkward he feels when I bring up the subject of his mother. Whether this is because he is embarrassed about her abandonment of me or because he is fiercely protective of her, I have yet to ascertain. To be honest, I have made the odd snide remark about her being a let-down which Luca pretends not to hear. This actually makes the matter worse as the more I repress my hostility, the more dangerously it bubbles away inside me. We have so far managed to avoid an honest discussion of my feelings, but one Sunday afternoon he comes to see me straight after he's had lunch at her house. My period is due in a couple of days and perhaps I want to have an argument. Perhaps, however, I want to clear the air. The ghost of Tina has been hovering over us ever since I lost my job and I don't like it.

'How is your mother?' I ask, as Luca plonks himself down next to me on the sofa.

'Fine. She asked about you. I said you're enjoying your freedom.'

'Did she say why she hasn't bothered to call me?'

Silence.

'Oi, cloth ears,' I say, jokingly, giving him a kiss.

'We've been through this before.'

'Not properly. We haven't had a proper talk about it. Am I never allowed to bring it up?'

'Of course you can.'

'That's not what you just said.'

'OK, I admit it. I hate talking about it.'

'Why?'

'Why do you think?'

'Do you want me to have this conversation for you?'

'Because I'm in the middle and I hate it and it reminds me of my mum and dad and I felt in the middle with those two as well. Dad would come into mine and Mario's bedroom very early in the morning and show me how much money he'd won at poker that night and I'd have to promise not to tell Mum, and she'd be bitching about him and I fucking hated it.'

Now I am quiet. It's the first time he's talked about his home life.

'Luca, I'm really sorry to put you in the middle. It's wrong of me. It really is and it's just not fair on you.'

'I don't know what to say to you. I'm sorry she hasn't called you. I'll tell you something, though. Mum is terrified of losing her job. I know that doesn't help you but it's a fact. She's over fifty and she wrongly believes that she won't be able to get a job elsewhere should Wayne decide to get rid of her, too. You know how grateful she was that Wayne decided to keep her on when Mr Fox sold the business. You have to understand that she lost practically everything when we had to sell the house when Dad incurred his huge gambling debts. You could say that she's ruthless now. She doesn't really put herself out for anyone apart from me and Mario. I'm not saying she's mean to anyone, but with something like this, she just won't get involved.'

'I'm not asking her to get involved, just ring me and see how I am. I miss her, Luca. We worked together for a year and a half. I spent more time with her than with anyone. We confided in each other. We laughed a lot together. I know that we didn't socialise outside work but I thought that we were friends. I really liked her. And she hasn't called once since that first day. And that's what really gets me. All I want is one call or a letter to tell me that she doesn't feel comfortable about keeping in touch at the moment. It's just the complete cut off that I find a little brutal. I just can't imagine not ringing a colleague, especially one to whom I've been so close, just to offer a few words of support.'

'I know. I also know that she really likes you, too. As you know, she doesn't talk about work, but she did used to mention you every now and again and it was always in glowing terms. Why do you think I turned up at the agency that day? I'd been dying to meet you.'

'Really?'

'Really. I thought you sounded cute.'

'Cute how?'

'Direct, down to earth, polite, friendly but distant. No words wasted. Efficient. Competent. Not posh and not cockney. And, of course, there was the little picture of you on the website, sitting next to Wayne but leaning away from him.'

'Well, I didn't feel I could flirt in front of your mum. I was dying to meet you too, though.'

'I thought you seemed a bit flustered when I came up to the office.'

'Not at all. You're imagining things again,' I say, smiling and pulling him towards me for a cuddle.

'I don't mean to switch off over Mum, but I don't know what else to say apart from the fact that she is terrified that Wayne will find out you've been in touch.'

'Listen, I'm really sorry for putting you in this position. I know I didn't actually put you in it, but you are in the middle, yet again, and it must be really difficult for you. I'm not against your mum. I told you, I miss her. After all, we spent eight hours a day, five days a week together. I miss hearing updates on her love life. I miss her sense of humour and warmth. We had great bitching sessions. She was always very caring and supported me through my ups and downs. We never argued, which doesn't mean to say that we always agreed with each other, but we always made an effort to understand and respect each other's point of view. Anyway, she must be alright if she produced someone as gorgeous as you.'

And I mean it, he really is gorgeous and I am reluctant to spoil things between us by banging on about his mother, as everything else is just as I would wish it. He is supportive without being clingy and possessive. He is entertaining while also letting me shine. He is intelligent but not above *EastEnders*. And he's great in bed. His worst fault is that he expects me to do things for him, just like he was used to at home. I always make the tea, cook dinner and clean up after him. This leads to the occasional shouting match about him being a lazy, macho slob, with Luca, being naturally argumentative, confrontational but easy going and rational, arguing back and then finally succumbing to reason and making me a cup of tea and promising to make dinner one day.

So I let it go and confide my disappointment to my friends instead. It's just that he is a constant reminder of her failure to keep in touch. There is one other thing that I don't feel I can mention to him. And that is that I am not just a colleague, or rather an ex-colleague, I am now her son's girlfriend, and her unwillingness to embrace me as such also hurts me. Is she hoping that I'll go away? She must be praying that Luca and I don't work out. I don't want to raise this with him as it is still early days and I don't want to draw his attention to the fact that his mother may not approve of me. I had always understood that if the mother didn't like you, it was really only a matter of time before you were history. I told you the monkey-puzzle tree story. That's what it's like. Piss off the mother and you might as well put yourself back on the market.

Claudia reckons I shouldn't take it personally. She thinks that Tina's fear is based on the fact that I know details of her sex life and she's terrified that I'll tell Luca (as if!). He'd never talk to me again. I once tactlessly told a male friend of mine that I'd heard his mother had slept with someone I knew and he went ballistic (and he didn't even like his mother!). Understandably, Tina hides that part of her life from her sons and her 'men friends' (as she coyly terms them) never stay the night. She always told me that they were fed and then despunked well away from the boys.

Claudia may be right. However, I also think Tina is too closely involved with her sons and that any woman might be perceived as a threat to her. I have never heard her talk about their girlfriends, except in vaguely disparaging terms. I cringe when I remember her saying, 'Let's get married, darling' to Luca when he was upset about the woman last year. I laughed along at the time. Now I think it's sick. On Sunday, Simon read out a piece from a magazine that stated that something like nine out of ten marriages in Italy fail due to mother-in-law problems. That didn't help the queasy feelings, either.

The Headmaster

We don't have any glasses in the flat at the moment. Last night, Lorenzo came round, one month to the day since we first picked him up in Montgomery's, and told Simon that he didn't actually want to be in a relationship. It was nothing personal, he didn't want a relationship full stop, despite the fact that he liked Simon very much. Luca and I were sitting in the lounge, minding our own business and quietly indulging in a mid-week coke fest, when Lorenzo suddenly rushed past us and out of the door. I heard him hurling himself so fast down the communal stairway that I was worried for a moment that he was going to end up breaking his neck. Two minutes later, Simon appeared in the lounge, wordlessly en route to the kitchen, where all is silent for a few seconds. Luca looked at me and I looked at him. And then the smashing started. Simon threw something against the wall. A few seconds later, something else hit the wall. I decided it was safer to stay where I was and so, apparently, did Luca. Minutes later, Simon appeared in the lounge with a glass in his hand. He looked defiant. 'There are only two glasses left after this one,' he told me. 'Go for it,' I said, amused by the melodrama. 'Actually,' I said, suddenly leaping up from the sofa, 'can I have a go? I've always wanted to throw a glass.' Luca jumped up after me, shouting, 'I want a go' and we both picked up a glass and hurled them across the room.

It is so cathartic giving in to one's destructive instincts, as long as someone else does the cleaning up.

As we surveyed the glass all over the kitchen floor I looked at Simon.

'You're cleaning this up, right?'

'Sure,' he said, calmly, and we retired to the lounge for more drugs and booze.

Last night was the second time that Lorenzo has told Simon that he is not able to commit to a monogamous relationship with him. Last time, after much reconsidering by and begging from Lorenzo, Simon took him back and let him back into his heart, life and bottom. Just when Simon has relaxed and thinks that things have got back to normal, Lorenzo announces that although he has tried, he really can't do it. My theory is that if Lorenzo were to have a real relationship with another man, it would mean that he was a real, one hundred per cent, no turning back homosexual, whereas having sex with male strangers in dark rooms in clubs means that his homosexuality can be confined to repressible ten-minute slots.

I feel really sad for Simon as I know he really fell for Lorenzo, but I am also sad for myself. I have grown to adore Lorenzo. He has such an innate curiosity about other people, such a rare quality but one that is pleasurable to be around. He asks you so many interesting and searching questions, the sort of questions no-one has ever thought to ask you, and seems to be genuinely engaged by your answers. How often do you meet someone who is fascinated by you? That's exactly how you feel with Lorenzo. He listens intently, remembers everything that you've told him and has the wonderful gift of easy laughter. Lorenzo is also generous. Whenever he comes round, he always brings us a present – a bottle of Martini (I don't drink it, but Simon will down anything if it's free), a big box of Baci (the Italian chocolates with a romantic message inside), beautiful olives, etc. I think that shows a real generosity of spirit. He's also very intelligent and has views on everything. I like people who are culturally up to date. I think it shows an open and lively mind, as well as a willingness to engage in the world around you.

I decide that I'll wait until Simon has met someone else before contacting Lorenzo again and meeting for a drink.

Lorenzo's departure unintentionally produced a great evening; watching Simon fall apart on drink and drugs shouldn't have been funny but it was, and Simon knew it, too. Luca and I ended up having such hard, vicious, long-lasting, coke-fuelled sex that he ended up ripping the end of his cock. He put on a brave face but I could see he was nearly crying with pain. The foreskin was torn and he was clutching his penis in agony. I must admit, I've seen a few things in my time, but never a bleeding foreskin. He ignored my male menstruation jokes ('I've heard of New Men but isn't this going too far, darling?') and smoked a killer joint to knock himself out. As I laid in bed next to him, I stared at his gorgeous face, his long eyelashes, his sexy stubble, his thick, glossy dark hair, his broad shoulders and furry chest, and I suddenly felt very selfish as I considered the repercussions for me. His split cock meant no sex for God knows how long. Could I cope? Would we survive a relationship for a week without sex? Was this all this relationship was, a mutual desire for each other's bodies? We'd been together for two and a half months, which was a record for me over the last three years. Was it just sex? I asked myself a series of questions. Did I like him as a person? Did I respect him? Did he make me laugh? Would I be devastated if he left me? After a good long think and taking into account the fact that I have been pretty much on my own for the last few years, but then discounting that factor on the basis that the reason I have been on my own is that I am actually rather particular, the answer to all these questions was so overwhelmingly affirmative that I just hoped to God that he felt the same way about me.

Today, I go with Luca to the doctor, but sensibly stay in the waiting area while he sees the doctor and explains what has happened. We kill ourselves laughing over breakfast thinking of excuses. I suggest telling the doctor that his girlfriend got peckish while she was giving him a blow-job. He plays with the piercing, wanking and zip options and concocts a surprisingly plausible story involving all three. We decide that the truth (minus the coke) is probably the best option and we leave the doctor half an hour later with a sachet of some sort of saline solution (I could be making that bit up – I'm not sure what it was, definitely not salt) which he later empties into a glass (we had to buy some!) and into which he plunges his sorrowful penis. The magnifying effect of the water on his cock torments me, especially as he reminds me that the doctor has told him that he must refrain from sexual intercourse for at least two weeks. I decide not to tell Simon how we have christened the flat's new set of glasses, as he has only just about recovered from the horrifying discovery that I had used his favourite breakfast bowl as a sperm spittoon. 'I'm afraid it's not congealed milk,' I told him as I observed him picking up his treasured bowl, his expression turning from puzzlement to disgust and then fury.

As Luca kneels on my bedroom floor, his cock dunked in the glass, I say, 'I'd offer to kiss it better but that might make it worse.' He smiles weakly.

'Look, I'll tell you what,' I offer, 'how about I abstain for two weeks, too? You don't get me excited and I won't get you excited.'

'Don't be ridiculous,' he says, 'You're a woman, you've got eyes and ears. You won't be able to stop yourself getting excited with me around.'

'Right, that's it,' I say, and I rummage through my drawers until I find his favourite items from my lingerie collection and drape them over him. 'Any more arrogant comments like that and I'll really punish you by rummaging through the dirty laundry bin for my all in one.' His cock starts swelling at the thought, and as I watch in wonderment at its gross (and I mean gross LARGE) size through the water, he starts explaining that water minimises things rather than magnifying them.

'Yeah, right,' I say, dreamily, as I marvel at how his penis seems to fill the glass.

As I lay in bed, I think back to the glass-throwing episode and I recall that it was Wayne's face that I was picturing as I hurled my glass against the wall. As requested by the no-win, no-fee lawyers I had spent a day searching my mind for episodes of Wayne's sexual harassment. The thing was that although the incidents I recalled provoked memories of unease, I hadn't felt tormented by the incidents when they occurred. At the time, it was him that I felt sorry for rather than myself. I suppose I didn't take his comments and actions seriously; as I've said before. I regarded them simply as the acts of an immature and insecure man with a small penis, rather than demeaning and sinister violations. However, on mentally compiling the list of his inappropriate comments and actions, I realise that they were something I should not have had to tolerate. And the fact was that I had lost my job as a result of objecting to his comments and actions.

I have worked in offices where sexual banter was rife and in which I was a willing and active participant. I've never been someone to shy away from entering discussions about sexual preferences and practices. In fact, I think I may even have initiated such discussions. What made this situation different? I think the fact that Wayne was my boss made it different. I have never made sexual comments to or expected to hear them from a boss.

I remember one job in North-West London where I tolerated a milder version of Wayne. I was working as an in-house lawyer for Ross Taylor, an extremely dull and wealthy property developer who felt deeply inadequate due to his knowledge that were it not for the nerve and business acumen of his charismatic father, from whom he had inherited his wealth and property portfolio, he would have ended up having to do a proper day's work, just like the rest of us.

His contribution towards augmenting the family's considerable wealth was limited to saving money on paperclips and ball point pens. Chancing upon a paperclip in this office was akin to finding a five-pound note on the pavement. The paperclip would be leapt upon and then jealously guarded. Careful consideration would be given to its use lest one may later regret its frivolous disposal. Incoming post would be greedily opened with the promise of finding more paperclips. On leafing through a stationery brochure while at Search, I noted with hilarity that you could buy a thousand paperclips for about twenty pence.

Ross also had a thing about biros. There would be an annual purchase of one box of biros, which led to some desperate measures. Some members of staff actually stuck little pieces of paper with their name on around these ten pence biros, while one man exercised considerable initiative by attaching string to his biro and wearing it around his neck, thus cleverly avoiding the biro theft that was rife in the office. Ross Taylor didn't realise that his efforts at consolidating his wealth were counter to good office practice. When the phone rang, everybody would scrabble around for a pen with which to take a message, pleading with others, signing over rights to their first-born, etc. 'Just-give-me- your-pen-for-a-minute-for-fuck's-sake-yes-I-promise-straight-back-hello-are-you-still-there? They've gone.'

I have noticed that most managing directors have at least one strange hang-up about office expenditure. In one office where I worked, employees had to pay monthly subscriptions in order to use the water dispenser. In another the senior partner refused to authorise the purchase of post-it notes, which are essential for flagging important clauses in contracts. Life as a lawyer before post-it notes was incomprehensible to me. They are up there with the photocopier and the word processor. I once found a pad and managed to make it last for six months by carefully tearing small strips off each note and then carefully recycling each strip. Each time I left my office, this precious pad was cunningly hidden at the back of a desk drawer. Parsimony breeds parsimony, which is, I suppose, the intention.

Anyway, back to Ross and his sexual power games. I had to get him to sign leases, contracts, property transfers, licences and cheques (he had to do something all day apart from making strategic stationery decisions) and this meant entering his large, empty office on a daily basis. As I stood in front of his grand desk waiting for his signature, he used to share with me his philosophy of life ('You have to work hard to get ahead.' 'You didn't,' I thought, and so on), while constantly removing microscopic particles of dust from the desk. All I wanted to do was whisk the signed document from him and get back to work, or at least escape his misguided attempts at educating me. And then there were the jokes. As I can't or won't do corporate laughter, I found his pathetic attempts at humour particularly painful. I smiled instead, concentrating on ensuring that my smile stayed just the right side of a contemptuous wince.

On one occasion, he combined his horror of 'mess' with the opportunity to ask me to bend over. As usual, I was waiting for him to sign something while he was pontificating on the optimum speed to maintain while driving on the A41. Something caught his eye mid-lecture and he pointed to the carpet near where I was standing. 'There are some rubber shavings on the floor near your feet,' he said. I looked down and saw nothing. 'I can't see anything,' I said. 'You must have dropped them when you used the rubber to erase the pencil markings on the contract.' *You sad bastard.* On looking closer, I *could* see some rubber shavings. 'Sorry,' I said, 'I can't see anything.' So the sad bastard got up off his chair and picked them up himself. 'You were going to just leave them there,' he said, shaking his head with disbelief and disappointment as he emptied them into his empty bin.

I started to notice that he was delaying me longer and longer in his room, while also asking me questions of a personal nature ('What does your father/mother/sister/brother do?'). I evaded these questions on the basis that I had no intention of allowing him to either intrude on my personal life or neatly pigeon-hole me in his internal socio-demographic chart.

Things took a turn for the worse when he began to extend the repertoire of his headmaster routine, which I feared arose from nocturnal wankings over schoolroom fantasies of me. 'You look like a nervous schoolgirl standing here before me,' he said. I blushed. 'Now you look like a scared schoolgirl,' he said, smiling. I didn't respond, but simply took the signed document from his desk and left the room.

I started to stockpile items that needed signing in order to minimise the number of occasions on which I needed to enter his room. I didn't tell anyone about his schoolgirl comments as he was generally liked by everyone in the office. I was also told soon after joining that the main office was fitted with a one-way intercom through which Ross Taylor was able to tune into our conversations. I was horrified not only by this but by the fact that no-one seemed particularly bothered by it. People spoke admiringly of his generosity and his large donations to charity, while rarely complaining about their own low salaries. I was being paid about five grand less than I should have been, but due to the current difficult economic situation, I thought myself lucky to have found work, while still seething at my low salary. He enjoyed playing the role of philanthropist and news of his 'anonymous' donations always seemed to filter from his office.

Meanwhile, each time I entered his office, he continued to pursue the 'schoolgirl/headmaster' routine. When I made mistakes in the execution clauses of contracts (easily done – he was the director of so many different companies), he threatened me with detention. It really was becoming a bore. I no longer smiled at his jokes and began to make truculent comments when he issued forth with bullshit. Soon, the benign but frustrated headmaster became a cold, harsh one and I wondered whether it was all going to end with him threatening to give me the cane.

I was becoming nervous and edgy at work and it was showing. I made a couple of stupid mistakes (ironically, sending off unsigned documents) and I was called into his office. He told me that I had to 'pull my socks up' and that perhaps he had made a mistake employing a female lawyer. He told me that he had never employed a woman in a managerial position before and he was beginning to realise why. I tried to argue and tell him that that was sexist crap and maybe he had unresolved issues with women. I was waved from the room with a dismissive sneer.

Do you know what I ended up doing? I actually resigned. I let the bugger off the hook and made myself unemployed. As I lay in bed recalling the incident, I feel angry but determined. This time I am not going to let a wanker boss who abused his position and who had hang-ups with women and power get away with it. I am going to fight this sexual discrimination case all the way and I am going to win.

The Liar

I spent the next day compiling a long report on Wayne's misdemeanours. I reported the fact that he always called me darling rather than Emma. I related the times when he had kissed and cuddled me; the comments on my appearance; the remarks on what I was wearing, including the obligatory comments on the length of my skirts; the lingering of hand on knee; the jokes about stiffies and hard-ons; the speculation on his wife's toilet masturbation habits; his frequent oblique references to oral sex; the wisecracks about the size of his friend's wife's (massive) breasts; the regularity with which he played full frontal pocket billiards; and, finally, his unwelcome observation on my tits and the suggestion that I don't wear a bra, leading to my memo and, ultimately, my dismissal.

I am claiming unfair dismissal, wrongful dismissal, breach of contract, sexual harassment, sexual discrimination, non-payment of notice, non-payment of holiday pay and under-payment of commission. Did that idiot really think he could get away with this? Was he really so thick and naive that he thought he could treat me like this and never hear another word from me? Every time I drive past the Search office, I am filled with rage and pain and hurt and humiliation. I resist the urge to throw bricks through the windows of the office at night and console myself with the thought that Wayne must have received my claim by now and was, hopefully, shitting it.

A month or so after Wayne is served with my claim, I receive his defence to the court in the post, with a letter from my lawyers asking for my comments. Shakily, I open the three-page official document, uncertain of what I am about to read, but knowing instinctively that I ain't going to like it. I read it and cry. It is horrible. It is full of lies and things that are true but which have been exaggerated to a ridiculous degree. The thing is that *I* could also have lied in my claim; it really only boils down to his word against mine. I could have exaggerated the extent of unwanted physical contact and sexual suggestions. However, I did not make up a single thing, and it is not until I read his defence that I realise that it didn't even occur to me to lie.

The defence is made up of ten paragraphs. Each one contains a stonking lie. In the first he says that I only worked for the company for six months, when in fact I worked for Search for nearly eighteen months. He is referring to the fact that I worked for *him* for six months, conveniently choosing to ignore the year that I worked for Mr Fox prior to his takeover of the business.

In the second paragraph he says that he believes that the Applicant (that's me) qualified as a solicitor but never in fact practised as one. Overlooking the fact that my previous existence as a lawyer has, as far as I can see, absolutely nothing to do with this case, it is also quite untrue. I *have* practised as a lawyer. Why on earth has he put that in? I'm not sure if he's trying to make out that I am weird as I've chosen not to work as a solicitor. Maybe he's implying that I am not working as a solicitor because I am unfit to do so (false) or because I am not sufficiently professional (true). Perhaps he's hinting that I'm litigious. In any case, this throws me.

When Wayne first heard that I was a qualified solicitor (I don't go round telling people, but Tina liked the kudos of working with a professional and used to slip it into any conversation she could), he was astonished that I had gone through all the studying and training. 'What a waste!' he said. 'No,' I said, 'a waste would be to spend one's life doing something one hated.'

In the third paragraph he says that I made an unacceptably high number of personal calls. The strange thing is that in previous jobs I would have been forced to admit that this was true and would have been shitting it at the thought of defending myself against this particular assertion. However, at Search, for the first time in my employment history, I made ridiculously few personal calls. When I started at Search I thought I had found the perfect career. I was getting paid to chat to people on the phone all day: to find out what the clients and temps wanted, to flirt with office managers and to gossip with personnel officers. Apart from the fact that I was fulfilling my daily chat quota from legitimate sources, my day at Search was normally so frantic that I simply did not have time for lengthy conversations with friends and family. I was so confident on this front that I made a mental note to offer my Filofax as evidence for the tribunal to sift through and compare with the itemised office telephone bills.

In the fourth paragraph he says that he gave me both written and verbal warnings about my personal phone calls. Warnings? Have I missed something? I rack my brains for any recollection of such a warning and come up with a blank. It then occurs to me that not only is he lying, but he obviously intends to *create* a written warning and submit it in evidence. This thought really sickens me. What on earth is coming next? My legs are feeling wobbly and I collapse into a sofa as I race through the rest of his defence.

I read the fifth paragraph only to discover that I regularly took extended unauthorised leave from the office. Did I? What the hell is he talking about here, and then I realise that Bert must have told him of the afternoon a month ago when I ran up and down the length of West End Lane at three o'clock in the afternoon looking for a suitable dessert for a family dinner that evening while Wayne was at a meeting away from the office. Now I know that that is a bit naughty, but it only happened once and the way I look at it is that I mostly work through lunch, and if there was ever anything to sort out beyond five-thirty in the evening, I always stayed without a second thought. Isn't it all about give and take?

The sixth paragraph states a 'persistent abuse of privileges and office facilities'. Well, I mean, who doesn't? Are you really telling me that you have never printed off a letter on the office printer? You've never sent an e-mail that has absolutely nothing whatsoever to do with work? You've never used the fax machine? A small pad of post-it notes has never found its way into your bag? Really? Not even a biro? What about unauthorised use of the photocopier?

Wayne once caught me printing a letter to my local council tax office pleading with them to give Simon and me one more chance to pay in monthly instalments rather than face an immediate bankruptcy with an every last penny upfront situation. I'd forgotten that I had printed the letter and he lifted it from the printer with raised eyebrows and the words 'I believe this is yours'. He didn't appear quite as relaxed about this small transgression as I would have expected. When he left the room, Tina warned me not to get caught again. If she needed to type and print her own letters, she was smarter than me. She just came in half an hour earlier in the morning. Same with personal calls. She made many more calls than me, either to coo to her sons or to shout at her ex-husband. It was just that she was much more subtle than me. I operated on the unapologetic basis that I occasionally needed to make personal calls (council tax queries, smear test results, quick check up on suicidal friend). I was mostly as brief as possible (when Wayne was in the office, at least) but I never tried to hide what I was doing. I have always wanted to be able to bullshit on a personal call and make out that it is a bona fide work call, but I am crap at lying and whenever I have tried I haven't been able to wipe the embarrassed smile from my face. It is partly that I don't like lying, partly that I am not very good at lying, but it's also partly that I resent having to lie and play the corporate game. I just can't say, 'Yes, take my soul, take my time, take my youth, my energy and I shall dedicate myself wholly to you and to no-one else. I have no life apart from you. You are my life.'

I know that the employer is paying for my time but as I said I believe in give and take. At Search I worked overtime, unpaid, whenever it was necessary. I would pop out and get milk twice a week without bothering to arrange reimbursement. I'd use my own mobile at weekends to arrange emergency temp bookings for Monday morning. I'd introduce clients to the company without bothering to claim Wayne's 'New Bonus Client Introduction Reward Scheme' as I saw it as my job to catch as many new clients as possible and I was keen to build up the business. In return for my flexibility, I expected the same. And that was part of the reason that I did not operate on a sneaky, apologetic basis when it came to printing off the odd letter or making a call. This rational approach has not, it seems, been successful. I am no good at playing the work game. It's not that I don't understand the rules, it's just that I don't agree with them, and being the kind of person that I am, I can't play them.

The seventh paragraph deals with my attitude (see above). Wayne states that I was argumentative and I rowed with him, Tina and Bert. The only time I can remember arguing with Wayne was over the correct payment of my commission. Bert, well, that I don't deny, but dealing with the most incompetent book-keeper in the world in a stressful environment does takes its toll, and I didn't have the time or the inclination to conform to his limited expectations of what a woman should be. And as for Tina, I cannot think of a single argument. Our rapport was excellent, we always helped each other out, we truly worked as a team. I'd spend an afternoon with my work on hold so that I could brainstorm with her about who to send where for a permanent position, while she would spend time shuffling through her index cards to see if she could help me out with a temporary booking. And then a terrible thought fills my mind.

Has she told him that we argued in order to back him up in his claim? Has she double-crossed me? Would she? Could she? I am tempted to ring Luca to ask him to find out. I even pick up the phone, but when I get his voicemail I decide to be sensible and keep him out of it. It really isn't fair on him and I don't want to screw things up between us.

The eighth paragraph states that I often dressed 'inappropriately' for work. I take it he is referring to my mini-skirts, for which he always made a point of expressing his fondness. Like most women, I own trousers and skirts; some are long bias cut affairs, some are A-line knee-length and a couple are minis. I happen to have good legs so I like to show them off every now and then. If I had a flat, firm stomach, I'd wear crop tops, but I haven't so I don't. When Wayne used to make lascivious comments about my short skirts and my legs, I did hold an internal discussion with myself about continuing to wear the skirts. The discussion lasted for about two minutes. I did not see why I should not be able to make full use of my wardrobe on account of Wayne's immaturity, and to be honest, part of the reason for wearing short skirts is to be admired by gorgeous, sexy men, even if a by-product is fat, balding, scaly, dirty old men admiring my legs, too. Anyway, he says he gave me several verbal warnings about my unsuitable dress code. He's talking bollocks. The only comments he ever made about the way I dressed were complimentary.

The ninth paragraph tells an outright lie. He denies the comment he made to me about my tits and a bra. In fact, he says I was wearing a transparent T-shirt on that day and he told me not to wear it again. The T-shirt, for your information, was thick, white, cotton, long sleeved and round-necked. Transparent T-shirts are not my thing – certainly not at work and certainly not with a boss like Wayne. It's one thing flashing a bit of leg, quite another exposing the shape of my bosom and the size and colour of my nipples to anyone other than the person who has the pleasure of licking them. This lie does cheer me up as I can produce the white T-shirt in court and then everyone will realise that Wayne is a liar. Maybe I can also produce witnesses who can confirm that I was wearing the white T-shirt on that day.

It occurs to me that Tina is the person most likely to remember, while also being the most credible witness, but I know better than to think about putting her on the line as a witness on my behalf. Her silence since my dismissal tells me all I need to know about her willingness to support me in my claim against Wayne. I don't blame her. She'd be sacked if she gave evidence against him and she has a mortgage to pay. I vacillate in my attitude towards Tina. Sometimes I am understanding and I make a big effort to see things from her perspective. If only she'd ring me, I could tell her that I understand. But then I feel agitated and disappointed and betrayed and hurt. Why the hell hasn't she called or written me a short letter or even sent a message via Luca? The one thing I don't expect from her is to appear as a witness on my behalf.

Would I do it for her? I honestly believe that I would. You may think it's easy to say that and perhaps it is, but I have always been the type of person who speaks up for what I believe is right, and I have put myself on the line for other people in the past. If I hear someone making a racist comment, it sickens me and I will always say something. I don't think to myself that it doesn't affect me, that they're not talking about me. I like to think that I would stand up for injustice wherever I see it occurring, whether it is racism, homophobia, ageism, or sexism, and that I am prepared to put myself in the firing line to defend what I believe is right and fair.

I have come to realise that not everybody shares this attitude. I once went for a drink with a group of friends (two of whom were black and one of whom was gay), and a friend of a friend who joined us made an anti-Semitic comment about stingy Jews. As I was the only Jew in the group, I felt sick at the revelation that there are still thick, ignorant, offensive oiks at large and that this person felt it was acceptable to make such a remark. Not a single person around the table said anything. I felt thoroughly alone. Had the oik in question made an insulting comment about blacks, Asians or gays, I am sure I would have joined in the condemnation rather than thinking that their comment did not affect me personally and so there was no need to get involved.

In this case, Tina does have genuinely good reasons for staying out of the picture. I'm just telling you that I hope I would have the strength to do otherwise.

Finally, the tenth paragraph. Here he denies all and any incidents of sexual harassment and requests that the case be thrown out and that I pay his costs. The costs bit causes wild panic. Shit. What if I have to end up paying his poncy lawyers' fees as well as losing my job, my chance of a reference and thus re-employment?

After a short wail and a few tears, I call my lawyers and am immediately reassured. For a start, in employment cases there is very rarely a costs order, and this will certainly be the case here where each party bears their own costs. Apparently, Wayne's defence looks as pathetic to experienced lawyers as it does to me. I admit to occasionally using the printer, photocopier and e-mail facilities and I am told that this is not a sackable offence, and anyway, it was not stated as a reason for dismissal in Wayne's sacking memo at the time. Then they tell me that although they understand I am upset at the defence, I might as well get used to it as it is going to get a helluva lot nastier.

I find the fact that Wayne is prepared to commit perjury the most shocking thing of all. He is prepared to play dirty and has absolutely no morals about the means he employs to win his case. My God, I got him so wrong. I thought he was harmless and thick but basically trustworthy and decent. You have probably gathered by now that not only do I value honesty highly, I also find it difficult, for moral, political and social reasons, to lie. Don't get me wrong, if someone buys a new sofa, has a radical hair cut or tells me they are getting engaged to their boring boyfriend, I will lie through my teeth. I may not gush, but I will certainly sacrifice my compulsion for honesty for the sake of their feelings. But I don't know how people can cheat on their partners. All that lying would make me ill and, personally, I find it quite sickening to cheat on a person in that way. If you are not happy with your partner, leave them for God's sake (unless you are French and then, I understand, different rules apply). I also wouldn't lie on an insurance claim or even a car tax form and I wouldn't buy a hot laptop at one quarter of its shop price, despite being short of cash.

What I am saying is that I find dishonesty a major turn-off. Bare-faced lying particularly sickens me. It is one of the things that for me can immediately kill off respect in any relationship. I used to live with this woman, a friend of a friend, who I wasn't mad keen on but whose beautiful flat in a prime location I nevertheless agreed to share. She worked like a dog during the day flogging financial services and was out every night snorting coke and partying at Annabel's and Tramps with rich Arabs.

As we barely saw each other, the arrangement worked quite well until one day we bumped into each other after a week of non-encounter. After my initial shock at seeing her, I suddenly realised that she was wearing a new, expensive, cream silk blouse that my mother had bought me and which I was saving for a special occasion. She was talking to me at the time, but I heard nothing except a voice in my head expressing disbelief that this cow was wearing my blouse. Now I know that an occupational hazard of sharing living accommodation with other females, whether they be sisters or flatmates, does entail a bit of cheeky borrowing every now and then. There are limits, however, and borrowing expensive, brand new cream silk blouses crosses the boundary between a bit of cheeky borrowing and complete fucking chutzpah*. She had obviously hoped not to bump into me for another day.

'You're wearing my blouse,' I blurted out while she was mid-chatter. I was not prepared for what followed.

'This is my blouse,' she said, feigning disbelief at my claim.

'What are you talking about? My mother bought me this blouse and I've never worn it,' I said, indignantly.

'No it isn't. I bought this shirt, it's one of my favourites,' she insisted.

I knew she couldn't possibly have one as well as my mother had bought it in Italy. As I am relatively inexperienced at dealing with outright lying, I didn't know quite what to say. I wasn't prepared to stand there having a Punch and Judy Oh-Yes-It-Is-Oh-No-It-Isn't style row. I think I was embarrassed at her lying, as well as feeling flummoxed. I felt shame on her behalf – well, one of us had to, she certainly wasn't going to. She was obviously a seasoned cheat and relied on other people's good nature and social discomfiture when she told these porky pies. There was a moment of silence while I racked my memory bank for an appropriate response to such a bizarre situation. Finding none, I sharply requested that she have the blouse dry-cleaned and return it to my wardrobe within twenty-four hours. She said nothing and I found the blouse in my wardrobe a few days later, completely ruined. Turned out she had washed it in the sink with soap and hadn't even bothered to iron it. I moved out.

What I found most unpalatable about this sordid experience was not that she had borrowed a new blouse without asking me, or that she ruined it by washing it with soap, but that she told such an outright, shameless lie. It was the same with Wayne. Not only is he prepared to lie, he is also prepared

---

* *Chutzpah*: a man murders both his parents and then pleads clemency at his trial on the grounds that he is an orphan.

to perjure himself in court if need be, no doubt looking me straight in the face while doing so.

It is all very disappointing.

The Blue Cheese Incident

Luca and I are still spending a lot of time together and the more I get to know him, the more I love him. We normally see each other twice during the week and most of the time at the weekend. We've even carried on seeing each other this often despite the fact that he had to keep his legs together for two weeks. He is working like a dog at the moment and tells me that he is too tired to have sex even if he could. In fact, the sexual abstention proves to be beneficial to our relationship as we realise that we still want to see each other even if we can't consummate our lust. I am starting to see Luca as a friend rather than just a lover. He has been so supportive over the Search situation and I am truly appreciative. I am learning to trust him and it feels very good, if a little scary.

One Saturday night Simon and I go to a dark and throbbing party in Putney. Within five minutes of arriving, a guy takes a very strong fancy to Simon and pursues him around the room. He makes it perfectly clear that he has eyes for no-one else, including me, as the three of us sit chatting in a corner. I feel completely invisible. Any contribution by me to the conversation is treated by him as an irritating interruption. I hate it when guys chat up your mates as if you don't exist. I think it's rude. I point out to Martin that manners do not cease to be relevant when trying to find someone prepared to have sex with you, and then I walk off to the kitchen to find alcoholic comfort and someone interesting with whom I can converse.

Simon follows me a few minutes later.

'Sorry if I fucked things up. Are you interested in him?' I ask him.

'He's very keen, but I'm not sure. Do you think he has mad, starey eyes?' he asks.

'Yes. Really weird eyes. I've got bad vibes about him.'

'Well, I'm starving,' says Simon. 'Haven't they got any food here?'

'Apparently we missed it by about two hours,' I tell him, to make him feel guilty that we were delayed at home waiting for his magic spot cream to kick in before he was prepared to leave the flat.

Out of desperation, Simon slyly opens the fridge. There isn't much in there apart from bottles of lemonade, a jar of pickled cucumber and a large lump of blue cheese. We're the only ones in the kitchen so he obviously thinks he can get away with chucking a large piece of blue cheese into his gob. As he chomps on the cheese, Martin suddenly appears in the kitchen, says to him, 'I've been looking for you everywhere,' and before Simon can stop him or swallow the rest of the cheese, he has stuck his tongue down Simon's throat. I watch with a mixture of horror and delight as they spring apart within seconds. I leave Simon to explain to Martin why that was probably the most disgusting snog of his life, and then run round the party telling everyone what has happened. Those that are tickled by the story go into the kitchen to look at the blue cheese couple and report back to me that they are still kissing passionately.

As Simon, Martin and myself sit in the cab on the way home, I think grimly to myself that this had better just be Simon's revenge on Lorenzo. Simon and Martin are all over each other. At one point, I offer to get out the cab and walk the rest of the way home as I must be disturbing them. Martin doesn't get the sarcasm and says, 'No, Emma, don't be silly. We don't mind you here.' 'Cheers,' I say, 'that's very sweet of you.' He smiles a 'that's because I'm a nice kind of guy' smile and squeezes Simon's knee. I look at Simon to see if I can ascertain any long-term motives from his expression. However, the only motive I can establish from his face is to get home without throwing up. He looks totally pissed and does in fact throw up once we get back to the flat. Unfortunately, Martin is very caring and clears up the vomit, mops Simon's brow and carries him off, like a prized possession, to Simon's bedroom. Talk about scoring Brownie points. With any luck, Simon won't remember a thing in the morning. He'll just wake up, hung-over and confused, with those mad, starey eyes upon him and kick the creep out.

In the morning, I awake to hear someone clattering around in the kitchen. Oh good, I think, Simon is making breakfast. I wander into the kitchen, ready to plonk myself down to enjoy one of his famous fry-ups, only to find Martin dressed and getting a tray together for Simon and himself. 'I've bought some croissants,' he says, pointing to a brown paper bag on the kitchen table. I say thanks but I am disturbed by two facts. The first is that I suspect that Simon must have given Martin, a relative stranger, a key to our flat for him to go and get the croissants.

Secondly, he is clearly making himself at home and this worries me, although Simon didn't seem particularly keen last night so I may be fretting over nothing. Martin has the expression of a mule, the dress sense of a New Romantic and the charm of a tree stump. He was all over Simon like a rash last night and I found the face slurping in the taxi offensive. I may have got him all wrong, but the vibes are not good. There is definitely something I don't like about him.

This feeling is confirmed later in the afternoon when I spend half an hour in their company. Martin is very self-absorbed with little discernible humour, although of course, if you asked him, I am sure he'd tell you he had a wonderful sense of humour. Well, let's just compromise and say that we have different senses of humour. Simon doesn't seem to notice any of this. He is languishing on the sofa while Martin fusses over him with lots of kissing and tell-me-all-about-yourself, God-aren't-we-the-luckiest-people-in-the-world-to-have-met going on. Little effort is made to ingratiate himself with me. In fact, once again, I feel that my presence is using up valuable space that is needed for his ego.

I decide to ask him a couple of questions to be polite and to see whether I have misjudged him and can end up liking him instead of praying for the quick demise of this beautiful fledgling relationship. Although he answers all my questions, he asks none in return. I find out that he lives in Pimlico in what he describes as a 'completely divine flat'. He is an only child and seems to be over-indulged by his parents who bought him his flat and his jeep. Other facts ascertained include the fact that Martin is an engineer and very well paid, which I know will excite Simon who is constantly broke and had been rather hoping for a sugar daddy to come along. He's in his late-thirties and recently single, having just split up with his partner of six years. This is another worrying sign. He obviously goes in for long-term relationships. His age may also mean that he wants to settle down, particularly as Simon is nice and young.

I don't blame Simon for enjoying the attention and adoration, and I am not saying that he doesn't deserve it. He's had a shit romantic ride for a while and I know that Lorenzo broke his heart and of course he's going to respond to someone coming on so strong. I suppose I had better leave them to it and get on with my own life.

The Betrayal

Although I am still luxuriating in the freedom of unemployment, there is one major disadvantage to a life of idleness – my cash reserves are dwindling. If I don't get another job soon, I'll be living off Tesco Value Baked Beans (nine pence a tin), porridge and broth made up of boiled potato peelings and other vegetable waste. Although I am not a big spender and can happily go without things most people crave, such as nice meals out, holidays and an up to date wardrobe, I'm not terribly good at economising, either. If I see something I really like that I feel I have to have for the flat, I will actually buy it, despite promises to myself to spend nothing unless it is an essential item. It is very easy to persuade yourself that a ceramic fruit bowl is a must-have when retail therapy is your favoured means of numbing out. And when I go food shopping, I do prefer to buy the baby ready-washed spinach rather than the gritty, wash each leaf three times adult spinach. I know I could cut down on the pennies but somehow I don't manage to do it.

I also feel like a sponger. Luca has been paying for all our trips out and so have my other friends. Whenever I go out for a drink, I always hope that my companion will offer to pay, which is not a wonderful thing to be thinking when they are sitting there pouring their hearts out. I've been on the dole for four months now and although it's marvellous not to be working, I don't know how much longer I can realistically expect my friends and Luca to subsidise me. When birthdays come round, I spend a third of what I would like to spend on gifts. The thing I dislike most about the situation is having to think about every penny I spend, whether it's a bar of chocolate, a new lipstick or a trip to the cinema. I don't want to feel like the poor relation any more.

I am beginning to feel generally dissatisfied. I think Simon has sussed out my feelings towards his new mate and he has very quickly started to spend every available minute with Martin, thankfully at Martin's flat rather than at ours. However, this does mean that I miss Simon a lot. I am used to having him around during the day and in the evening, too. He's even taken his laptop round to Martin's so that he can work there instead. And they've only been seeing each other for two weeks! When I ask Simon why he spends so much time there, he explains that Martin has satellite TV, a whirlpool bath, a fridge stocked with yummy food from Marks & Spencer's and an extensive porn collection. I suppose I can't really compete with that and I don't push it, either. I'd rather Simon went to Martin's than have Martin round here running the place, a tendency he revealed during his short stay the weekend they met. I couldn't get near the kitchen all that Sunday while Martin prepared a gourmet meal for himself and Simon. They did ask me to join them, but only as an afterthought once they had already tucked in.

I don't feel I can say anything to Simon about my general feeling of abandonment. Firstly, I have no right. It's his life. Secondly, I want him to enjoy his new relationship without hindrance from me. Unconsciously, however, I am becoming more and more resentful of this unpleasant invader who has stolen one of my closest friends.

And then, amid this dissatisfaction comes a genuine bona fide reason to feel thoroughly depressed. My lawyer rings me late on Friday afternoon with some news.

'There have been some developments, Emma,' says Peter, sounding serious.

'You don't mean good ones, do you?' I say, knowing already that I am not going to welcome these 'developments'.

'Wayne has managed to get a key witness.'

'Do you mean Bert?'

'So far we haven't had a witness statement from Bert,' he says. Suddenly, I know what is coming next.

'It's Tina, right?'

'I'm afraid so. She will be appearing at the tribunal as a witness for Wayne.'

I feel choked. I can't speak.

'Hello? Emma, are you there?'

'Sorry, yes, I'm here. It's just sort of sinking in.'

'It's not as unusual as you'd think for colleagues to side with the boss.'

'But we were so close.'

'I've seen this kind of thing many times. People want to protect their own position.'

'Obviously.'

There is silence while he allows the impact of his news to sink in.

'I'm gutted, Peter, I really am.'

'I'm sorry. It must be very disappointing, but we really do need to address this in an unemotional way now. Perhaps you'd like to call me back when you feel a little better.'

I suppose that's fair enough. He's a lawyer not a counsellor.

'Before you go, do we know what she is going to say? Could she just be giving a neutral statement?' I ask him.

'Unlikely,' he says. 'Otherwise Wayne wouldn't be using her. I've already applied for a copy of her statement so I'll let you know as soon as I receive it.'

'Thanks. Thanks a lot. Speak to you soon.'

I put down the phone and sink to my knees on the floor. It hurts. I'm in pain. It feels like my own mother has turned against me. In some ways, she was like a mother to me. She used to bring me in food on a Monday morning, the beautiful leftovers of a weekend cooking frenzy, and when she baked the boys her melt in the mouth biscuits she'd bring me in a tin. I felt like one of her kids. She was supportive and affectionate, wise and sassy, and I looked up to her as a survivor who flourished on her own. And this is the woman who is now stabbing me in the back. This is why I feel so wounded. I am gutted. Literally floored. I feel as if I have been punched in the stomach.

Questions spin round my head as I sit hunched on the floor in the lounge. What can she possibly say about me? Is she going to lie as well? Is she that desperate to keep her job? Does she believe that siding with Wayne was going to give her the job security she so obviously craves? Does she not realise the snake cannot be trusted? Is she that stupid? Is she that unprincipled? Can she feel good about herself? Does she hate me? Is this her revenge for me going out with her son? How could I have got her so wrong? Have I got Luca wrong as well? How could any son of hers be decent?

No wonder I've had such bad vibes about her since leaving Search. I am so confused, hurt and distraught that I don't even bother to ring Simon or Claudia or anyone else to tell them of the latest development. I feel ashamed of myself for some reason. I feel naïve and foolish. Underneath the pain, I somehow feel that my relationship with her son is now doomed to failure. It's Luca's parents' divorce all over again – two important people in his life fighting each other with him in the middle. Not only do I not want to do this to him, I don't wish to inflict it upon myself, either. It really is a no-win situation. How can I face him when I despise his mother? This is too big to simply ignore. So far, we have been able to negotiate our way around the situation, but now, as I sit on my own in the dark of the late afternoon, I realise that I've simply been denying the reality of the situation. Simon was wrong when he said it would all blow over. He predicted that Tina would keep a low profile until the case had been settled and would then welcome me back into her life with open arms. He said I would then feel nostalgic about the good old days when I didn't have an interfering Italian mother on my hands. He always urged me to enjoy the freedom of Tina's non-involvement in my relationship with her son. And it was easier to believe this outcome than the present scenario.

I don't return Luca's phone calls for two days. Like most people, I sometimes find it easier to wimp out of a situation and I really can't face speaking to him. Who knows, maybe subconsciously I want to punish him for his mother's behaviour. I probably want him to blame her for the breakdown of his relationship. I also really don't think I can hold back from expressing my feelings towards her and I know that really isn't fair on him. He's not done anything wrong. Why should he have to witness my pain? I convince myself that I am being fair to him by not speaking to him.

On Sunday morning, the third day of non-contact, he comes round to the flat. I pretend I'm out so he leaves me a note asking what the fuck is going on and could I please get in touch with him as soon as possible. I gaze at the aggressive note for about an hour and then I chuck it in the bin. It is not just that I can't trust myself not to slag off his darling mother; I also fear I might be entering the depression zone.

I haven't been seriously depressed for about four years but I recognise all the warning signs. Before Tina's defection to the side of betrayal and perjury, I was not feeling quite as chirpy as I should have been, considering I actually had a boyfriend that I liked as well as fancied (for once, the feelings had conveniently coincided). However, I was starting to feel poor and unhappy as opposed to poor but happy. It is strange. This feeling started about the time that Simon got it together with Martin. Perhaps that was when Wayne asked Tina to appear as a witness for him. Perhaps I have been feeling queasy the whole time she has been preparing her statement. I don't know.

Over the last week, I have been getting up later and later. I've not returned a load of phone messages. It is almost as if I am preparing myself for a major disappointment, and now I fear I am about to enter my self-destructive phase. This means pushing everyone away from me so that I can feel irrevocably sorry for myself. I don't want to see or speak to Luca in this state as experience tells me he'll be the first to go. All high-risk pain threats are normally eliminated early on in my self-destructive phase.

Luca rings again during the day and by the evening I am feeling a bit guilty. He may or may not know what his mother has done, but he has not done anything other than be kind and supportive. I ring him back at about eleven in the evening, stoned. I tell him what has happened. He didn't know. He says he's coming round, whether I like it or not.

Within fifteen minutes there's a ring on the doorbell. I look a bit of a state – still in my pyjamas, unintentionally wild hairdo, smudged mascara and a grey/ashen complexion. Let's put it this way, I've looked better, but as I am in a confrontational, self-destructive and if-you-don't-support-me-two-hundred-per-cent-and-adore-me-unconditionally-forever-you-might-as-well-fuck-off-now mood, I let him in. He doesn't seem to notice how I look. He doesn't look too hot himself, actually. He has bags under his eyes, stubble and he seems a little on the dejected side. I sit down on the sofa and he kneels in front of me.

'Emma, I'm sorry about my mum,' he says. 'If it helps at all, I don't feel like speaking to her, either.'

'It's not that I don't feel like speaking to her. Actually, I would rather like to speak to her so that I can tell her what I think of her,' I say.

A frosty silence follows.

'She is my mother, you know.'

'Yeah, well, shame.'

More silence.

'Where do you see us going?' I ask.

'What do you mean?'

'Well, it's a perfectly simple question, isn't it?'

'I think I love you, if that means anything,' he says.

'Oh, right. When will you know for sure?'

'I think I know for sure now.'

'Oh.'

Silence again.

'Do you think you might love me?' he asks.

'I'm crazy about you, Luca. Yes. I do love you. I feel overwhelming feelings of love for you when we're together. There, I've said it!'

He's smiling for the first time since he came round.

'But how can we be together when I hate your mum's guts?' I say.

The smile disappears.

'I know you're angry now and I don't know what to say to that because I know I'd feel exactly the same as you, but maybe in the future, when this case against Wayne is over, we can put it behind us.'

'You mean once Wayne, with your mum's help, has fucked me over good and proper and I lose my case against Search, we can all be friends again? Don't be so bloody naïve,' I say.

'Look, maybe I can speak to her and get her to change her mind.'

'You mean you haven't already?' I ask. 'Well, thanks for all your help, mate. You can go now. Shut the door on your way out.'

'I'm not going anywhere,' he says, taking off his coat and sitting opposite me.

'Why didn't you try to persuade her not to side with Wayne? Please don't give me any of this bullshit about her not finding another job, because it's not that hard. And by the way, I'm not interested in any of the martyr crap about her surviving on her own because I heard enough of it from her when we worked together.'

'Can't we just be together, you and me, and forget about Wayne and Mum?'

'Yeah, a man's solution. Compartmentalise. Well it's not that simple for me. I hate the person you love most.'

'Don't hate yourself,' he says, smiling.

'You don't mean that,' I say, half-smiling.

'How do you know?'

'Well, five minutes ago, you weren't even sure you loved me, and now you know for sure that I am the person you love most in the world. Look, Luca, it's been fun but I don't see how it can continue at the moment.'

He gets up and sits next to me. 'Please don't say it's over, Emma. I feel like it's only just beginning between us. Let me speak to Mum and see if she will change her mind.'

'Don't bother, it's too late for that. She's already irrevocably fucked things up between me and her. Can't you understand that? How can I ever be polite to her again?'

Silence. I feel so unhappy. I know what Sylvia meant about her bell jar. Here we are sitting next to each other and yet I feel we can't connect at all. He's on one side of the jar and I'm on the other (the inside, of course), and although I know he's trying to reach me, I can't let him in. I've been too hurt by Wayne and Tina to even contemplate trusting anyone else at this stage. When he puts his arms around me, I shrug them off. He puts them around me again and I get up and walk into the kitchen. Rather annoyingly, he doesn't follow me. I put the kettle on and make myself a cup of tea and then go into my bedroom and shut the door. He's still sitting in the lounge. A few minutes later, there is a knock on my door. He pops his head round the corner.

'Any chance of one last fuck?' he asks, walking into the room and sitting on the bed next to me.

'Go fuck yourself,' I say, turning round to face the wall. I can't even swallow, the lump in my throat feels so large and painful.

'I was only joking,' he says, lying down next to me and cuddling me. I turn round.

'You think we can fuck ourselves out of this mess?'

'No, but I fancy you like mad and it could release some tension.'

I am dying for things to go back to the way they were before. I hate his mother for what she has done, but were it not for her, I wouldn't have met this guy. I start crying and then he starts crying too, and we hug each other so tightly I feel I'm going to be crushed to death. Not a bad way to go, I think.

'I'm really sorry, Luca. I'm really sorry that you've been put in this terrible situation. I must be bad for you. I don't want you to go through this shit any more.'

'I can't believe it's happening again. I always have to choose between Mum and someone else. I'm fed up with it.'

'I'm not going to ask you to choose. I'll bow out. Maybe we should take a break until the case is over and see how things stand then.'

'I don't want it to be over.'

I am quiet.

'Neither do I.'

Luca and I don't leave the flat for two days. He calls in sick on Monday and we spend the day lying on the Heath, smoking grass, drinking champagne and indulging in a lot of surreptitious mutual masturbation. We have three glorious days of suspended reality until he leaves me on Monday evening to get a good night's sleep before going back to work.

On Tuesday morning I get a copy of his mother's statement. She says I made lots of personal calls, dressed inappropriately, often used office stationery and took extended, unauthorised leave from the office. As I read the statement, I know it's over between me and Luca. Self-destruction finally wins as I post a copy of the statement to Luca with a note telling him that it's been amazing but it's over. Then I ring Claudia and ask if I can come and stay with her for a week. I don't want to be alone in my flat and Simon hasn't been seen or heard of for some time.

I discuss the situation with Claudia ad nauseam and, in return for playing origami with her ear, I help her to decorate her flat. She thinks I am mad for walking out on Luca in this way and for the first twenty-four hours tries to persuade me to call him to let him know that I am OK. However, as I turn the situation over and over in my mind, I come up with a different decision. How can Luca and I work under these circumstances? I want him to make a choice between his mother and myself, while at the same time knowing that this is completely unfair, especially in view of their close bond. How can he love two women who, from my point of view, will never speak again? I don't want to put him in that situation. I realise that every time I am with him I will be reminded of her betrayal. He will never be able to speak of his mother to me. How could we get married and have kids if I don't talk to his mother, for God's sake! Claudia says couldn't I rage for a while and then put it behind me. Some people may be able to do this, but I know that, unfortunately, I am just not one of them. I find it difficult to forgive let alone forget those that have wronged me. I am not of the turn the other cheek persuasion, more of an eye for an eye kind of person. If you fuck me over this badly, I will never ever let you back into my life. I therefore, heartbreakingly, come to the conclusion that there is no future for myself and Luca. It is over.

The End

When I get back to the flat after a week in the cocoon of Claudia's home, I find about ten messages on the machine from Luca, together with a nasty letter. He says I am not the only one suffering and he doesn't deserve to be treated like this. He has been worried about me. He didn't manage to speak to Simon until two days ago when he told him I was staying with Claudia. He's tried to be understanding but he's fed up with being pushed away and he knows his mother has done wrong and he's not speaking to her at the moment, but how can I treat him like this, and I can fuck off out of his life for good.

I feel sick; actually physically sick. He's absolutely right. He doesn't deserve to be treated the way I have been treating him. He's done nothing wrong, simply been supportive, kind and loyal, and I've repaid him by ignoring him. I must have been mad. What the hell was I thinking of? I've lost the most wonderful man I've ever met. How many times does a man like that come along? I think of all the selfish arseholes I've met, the boring bastards that had the cheek to dump me, the crap lovers, the shallow, selfish, soulless saps. And then I think of Luca. There's nothing quite like someone turning round and telling you to piss off to focus your mind on what you've lost. He's funny, charming, intelligent, interesting, kind *and* phenomenal in bed. I try to think of his bad points and can't come up with much of substance. A bit of a smart arse? Being a bit of a smart arse myself, I need one to answer back. Lazy around the flat? Nothing a cleaner and a bit of retraining couldn't deal with. Morose flatmates? He's looking for his own place. And then I think of his mother. Although there's nothing I can do about that, I realise with a sudden sickening clarity that I have allowed Tina's betrayal and Wayne's creepiness to come between myself and the man with whom I could have blissfully spent the rest of my life. Were my apparently altruistic protestations of shielding him from no-win warfare between his mother and lover simply a delusion to protect myself from him choosing filial loyalty over a new romance? It did pain me to see him torn once again between two of the most important people in his life, but ultimately my own fear of abandonment featured most prominently in my decision to flee first. Did I think I could just keep pushing him away and that he would still be there? Was I testing him? How much did I imagine he would endure before finally throwing up his hands and telling me to fuck off? With his letter in my trembling hands, I finally have my answer.

I want to ring Claudia for counselling but know that despite her genuine attempts to be sensitive, I will nonetheless sense her 'told you so' vibes. My inability to sit with my pain and feelings of despair, however, propel me into my car and, despite the fact that I should clearly not be driving, I head over to her flat in Kilburn once again. As she opens the door and hugs me, I burst into tears.

'I've fucked up badly,' I say, between sobs.

'I know,' she says. Strangely, her acknowledgement of the situation if not helps, then at least soothes.

She sits me down on the sofa and, following my instructions, rifles through my handbag until she finds the letter.

'It's not over,' she says, calmly. 'He's angry, and rightly so, but you can win him back.'

'Do you really think so?' I ask, desperate for reassurance.

'Yes. You'll look back at this together in years to come and be relieved that you worked through it and survived it. You're just going to have to swallow your pride and ring him and apologise.'

'Do you reckon he'll talk to me?' I ask, meekly.

'Yes. He really likes you otherwise this letter wouldn't be so angry and emotional. It's not too late. Once you've calmed down, give him a call and arrange to meet,' she says, in a firm but motherly tone.

We go through every possible response and cover the conversation from every angle: what I am going to say to him, what he might say to me, what I will say to what he might say to me. Once I am sufficiently confident that I can handle it, I go into her bedroom with my mobile for some privacy.

My heart is pounding madly and my hands shake as I press his number. I am totally keyed up to speak to him so when I hear the answering machine instead, I am flummoxed and immediately hang up. Strangely, we had not considered the possibility of me not actually speaking to him.

As I open the bedroom door I collide with Claudia whose ear has been pinned to the door.

'Shit. I got the answering machine.'

'Did you leave a message?'

'No.'

'Good. Thank God for that. Nothing worse than waiting for a call back. Try again in half an hour.'

'I can't sit and wait here like an idiot. I am already going mad. I'll be completely balmy in half an hour.'

'Not once you've had your medication. You can have one of my valium.'

'Are you sure?' I say, knowing how precious they are to her.

'They're for emergencies. Here, I've already got you one,' she says, handing me a pill and a glass of what I think is water but turns out to be vodka.

I try his number again in twenty minutes, thirty-five minutes and every thirty minutes thereafter but consistently get the answering machine.

'Where the hell are they?' I cry in desperation. 'I thought his flatmates were cross-stitched to the sofa and the one bloody time I want them to be in, no-one's at home. Isn't there football on the telly?' For the first time in my life, I am actually looking through a TV guide to see when the football is on.

'Don't they have Sky?' she asks.

'Shit, of course they do. There's always football on Sky.' I throw the TV guide dejectedly onto the floor.

'I can't believe Luca doesn't have a mobile,' she says.

Neither can I. It's bizarre. When Luca first told me that he didn't possess a mobile phone, I was completely dumbfounded. 'That's like not having an arm or a leg,' I said. 'How do you manage?' 'I hate them. They're irritating, intrusive and give you brain tumours.' 'But won't you feel left out when everyone has a brain tumour but you?' On one hand, I loved the fact that he didn't have a mobile. Apart from being completely original, it also meant that we were never disturbed by anyone else when we were together, unless I decided to switch mine on, which, out of respect to him and his principles, I rarely did. On the other hand, it also meant that not only were we unable to send each other saucy text messages during the day, but I was unable to reach him twenty-four hours a day, should I so wish. And now I really truly desperately did so wish. I had no idea whether he was in the country, out partying with friends and surrounded by beautiful, adoring witty media babes with uncomplicated personalities and happy childhoods, or, even worse, simply avoiding me. I didn't need Claudia to point out that this was precisely the position in which I had placed Luca only the week before by disappearing from his life without warning or explanation. I'd thought I was being a tragic but mysterious wounded soul. Instead, I now realise I was being a completely selfish bitch. After only three hours of being unable to track him down, I suddenly understand why his letter was so full of aggression. Not knowing whether I would be able to speak to him in one hour, one day or one week hit me with full force. The irony of karma always kills me.

Admittedly, I am feeling a little calmer, although as Claudia points out, this may have something to do with the accumulative effect of the valium, vodka and spliffs with which she has been plying me since my arrival. Once I realise that I am now in such a semi-comatose state that I would be unable to construct a coherent sentence, let alone successfully convince Luca that not only should he take me back, but that I am also a together, happy person that he'd love to be with, I decide to give up for the night. Claudia tucks me up and, due to the anaesthetising effects of the drugs, I have a night free of dreams and, more likely, nightmares.

When I awake at seven, my predicament features immediately and exclusively in my consciousness. A surge of nervous energy follows and prevents me from luxuriating in even a few minutes' lie-in. I have a boyfriend to win back and two hours to wait before I can harass him at work. Although we have discussed the fact that ringing a man at work in this situation is far from ideal, the need to make contact as soon as possible for reasons of sanity is the overwhelming objective. I sensibly decide that a march across Hampstead Heath is the only option (apart from consuming further drugs) and I race over to the Heath to expend some of the mad, tormenting energy before making the most momentous telephone call I can imagine. I stride up and down hills, breathless but powered, and as I reach the top of Parliament Hill and see the most stunning views of London to one side and, lush green to the other, I am suddenly filled with a resurgence of hope and optimism. Everything will work out. He loves me. I love him. We'll make it. I've been stupid. I've learned my lesson. Put simply, I am not prepared to lose him and I'll do whatever I need to do to win him back. Fuck my pride, I'll beg if that's what he wants. I've been a fool, I'll admit it, and I'll make it up to him. I'll never be unreasonable again. I'll make him packed lunches, iron his socks, floss his teeth. I'll give him blow-jobs morning, noon and night. I'll do whatever it takes. Suddenly, I feel strong and confident. It's going to be OK.

By the time I get back to the flat, a little of this optimism has dissipated, although I find taking long deep breaths of nicotine helps. At nine o'clock on the dot, I make the call. He answers. Hearing his voice takes mine away. Not only am I surprised to actually get him straightaway, I am filled with longing to see him, speak to him, cuddle him, and for everything to be the way it was.

'Hello?' he says again, sounding moody and irritable.

'Luca. This is Emma.' My voice sounds shaky, although I am still clinging to my faith in our survival as a couple.

'Now is not a good time.' He doesn't sound friendly. Not hostile, but not warm. I've never heard him like this.

'I know, but I really need to speak to you.'

'I'll have to call you later.'

'When?' I know this sounds clingy and annoying, but I can't bear the thought of sitting by the phone for the rest of my life waiting for his call. It is always the uncertainty that fucks us up the most; the torture of not knowing. If he really doesn't want me, then it will be ridiculously hard to accept, but eventually I will come to terms with it (I hope), although the mental anguish of imagining every conceivable outcome from marriage, kids, laughter and love, to a life as a bitter spinster, tormented by what I have lost, is too much for my currently fragile mind to accommodate.

'Just later. Tonight.'

'Can't we meet for lunch?' I am trying not to whine but my desperation is seeping through.

'I've already got plans,' he says, curtly and unapologetically.

'Promise you'll call tonight, then.'

'Look, I said I'd call OK? Now I've really got to go.'

While I'm saying OK, I hear the phone click. He's gone.

I comfort myself with the knowledge that Luca has always been a man of his word. He always called when he said he

The End

would, he turned up when arranged, and I cling on to this, with desperation, admittedly. Unable to face the possibility of it really being over, I spend the day convincing myself that I will manage to persuade him to give me and us a second chance. When he rings at seven, my heart soars. I hadn't dared hope that he would actually ring me as soon as he got home from work. I did not allow his earlier coldness to deter me from launching straight in with protestations of love and effusive apologies.

He isn't having any of it. He tells me straight. It's over. I wasn't the woman he thought I was. How could a relationship work when, at the first sign of trouble, I disappear off the scene, he wants to know? He says he tried really hard but he's had enough of me pushing him away and blaming him for his mother's actions. I try to argue with him. I say I didn't blame him but I didn't want him to have to choose. He's not interested. He keeps saying he's had enough. As I listen to him, I feel cold inside. Although I bleat and apologise and try to convince him that we can still work, I sense that I have already lost him. Men can always beg women to come back; for some weird reason, it never seems to work the other way round. It just irritates them and strengthens their resolve to leave you. I know nothing will move him and he acknowledges this. 'This just isn't your style, Emma,' he says, and I know he's right. The conversation ends pitifully with me asking him if there is anything I can say to change his mind when I already know the answer. 'No,' he says, and once again, 'It's over.'

The Depression

I have now successfully achieved total abandonment by everyone. Simon's practically gone. He's pretty much living permanently at Martin's place these days. Wayne's sacked me
and Tina's dumped me. I've even managed to get rid of my
boyfriend as well. I can't deal with anyone. Luca, his mother,
Wayne, Simon or Martin. I feel so low it hurts. I have no
energy. I lie in bed all day, hating myself for everything –
for fucking up relationships, for being unable to trust anyone,
for lying in bed all day, for being me and for just being alive.
Self-torment has now become my main occupation and it is
exceedingly tiring. I spend ninety per cent of my time in bed,
crawling out only very occasionally for essential functions. I
know I am suffering from a serious depression and I wish I
could just file all my feelings under this label and just think of
myself as ill. Sometimes I tell myself not to take my thoughts
seriously as they are not proper sensible thoughts but the
result of a genuine illness, albeit a mental one. But when I
stop thinking, I start hurting. The emotions take over. I am
in physical pain. Sometimes I am hungry and my stomach is
rumbling like mad, but I can't face leaving the flat. I wait for
Claudia to come round with provisions. I'm like a zombie. I
don't answer the phone. I haven't the concentration to read.
I can't be bothered with the television.

The only place I do drag myself to is the dole office,
which is hell on earth. I seem to be the only young, white,
middle-class person there and I am filled with self-disgust
that I am scrounging off the State. Despite my education,

intelligence, opportunities and lack of discrimination, I am unable to support myself. I feel alienated and worthless.

And where is my good friend and flatmate in all this misery? Very sensibly, you may say, he is nowhere to be seen. As I said, he has practically moved in with Martin, and in his joy at finding someone to whom he can devote all his time and energy, he is impervious to those around him. When he does occasionally come back to the flat, he listens to me as I monosyllabically detail the reasons why I am worthless. He makes sympathetic noises, he goes to the shop and buys me some food, and within an hour he has disappeared, not to return for another four or five days.

I feel incredibly let down. All those times I have been there for him when he has needed me, hour after hour, bored rigid at times but never letting it show. I bought him books and bottles of wine. I rented him videos. Most of all, I listened to him and sat with him during the worst times. Now I get the feeling he can't get away quick enough in case I infect him with my misery. I realise that although Simon is great fun to have around, he is also incredibly selfish, and that over the four years that I have known him he has dumped his friends each and every time he's met a bloke. As it hasn't happened for quite a while, I'd forgotten that this was what he was like, and I'm pretty sure I wasn't depressed last time it happened.

I seem to be caught in some pattern of being let down by those around me. I am not saying that *everyone* has let me down, but right now I can only think about those that have. I blame myself for this. If it were just Wayne, say, then I could comfortably relax with the unanimous verdict of wanker. However, with Tina and now Simon crossing enemy lines, I am convinced that the fault lies with me. I tell myself the following:

(a) I don't know anyone else who has been sexually harassed. Why me? It must somehow be my fault.

(b) I don't know anyone who has had as many jobs as me

(last count: 100). This seems pretty incontrovertible evidence that it is my fault that the job at Search did not last.

(c) Tina let me down. Believe it or not, I blame myself for this, too. I blame myself for exercising bad judgement and allowing myself to invest trust in someone who is clearly not a sister. I also think (and I doubt you'll follow the logic of this unless you are a qualified and experienced psychotherapist) that somehow it was my fault that she dumped me after I was sacked and is now giving evidence against me. Maybe I wasn't a good enough friend to her. Maybe I crossed the boundaries by going out with her son and not telling her for a couple of days. Maybe, and I'm talking karmic here, because I am a shit, nasty person, I attract similar people into my life. Anyway, somehow or other, I am sure that it is my fault.

(d) Ditto Simon. Why do I choose selfish, fair-weather friends? I must have a defective friend-selector mechanism in my make up. I am also upset by my selfish neediness in wanting Simon to devote some of his time and energy to me when he is currently so happy and madly in love. I feel bitter that his new relationship is just taking off while mine has crashed and burned and I feel guilty about that too as it must mean that I am a horrible person.

Although I am horrible and fucked up, I am actually a fair person. I divide my time equally between self-hate and projecting it on to others, including Wayne, Tina, Simon, Martin, everyone else who has ever let me down, and the miserable cunt in the newsagents who never says hello, goodbye or thank you, despite the fact that I have been in there every day for the last two and a half years.

Aside from my self-imposed isolation, I am painfully aware that there are very few people whose company I can tolerate in such a state. My friend David came round soon after I gave up wearing make-up. I unleashed the full scale of my misery on him, he listened with sympathy and sensitivity and I haven't heard from him since. I have other male friends, but

I am unwilling to let them see me in this state, preferring to allow them to retain their image of me as a lively, funny, party girl rather than confront their unease when I reveal the other me. My female friends can be neatly divided into two categories. The first contains those whose love and support I find hard to accept, such is my deep sense of unworthiness. I am nevertheless aware of their love and support and they are my lifeline to remembering that not all humanity is thoroughly despicable. The second category contains good friends who are nevertheless useless at times such as these and must be avoided in order to avert violence. For example, my old friend Rachel, who I adore but who I know in advance will annoy the hell out of me. She kindly rings me up with nothing but the best of intentions.

'Hi, Emma, this is Rachel. How are you?'

'Shit. Depressed. I feel very low,' I say, having neither the energy nor the inclination to lie.

'But I thought you had that lovely new boyfriend. What was his name? Lionel?'

'Certainly not. No, it was Luca, but his name is irrelevant. It's over,' I say.

'You're kidding. God, that's terrible. He was gorgeous. Roger and I really liked him. You've been really happy with him.'

'Yeah, I was. Thanks for reminding me. I don't actually want to hear how lovely he is, OK?'

'Calm down. You'll meet someone else,' she says.

'I don't want to meet anyone else, ever. I can't deal with relationships of any sort.'

'Can't you get back together?' She is clearly anxious for a happy ending.

'No. It's over for good,' I say, pleased to disappoint her.

She is unable to stomach such negativity and resorts to the practical side of things.

'What happened?' she asks.

'You know my case against my ex-boss?'

'Yeah. How is that going?'

'Well. It is going well for my ex-boss. Remember my colleague there? Tina?'

'Luca's mum?'

'Exactly. She is going to be a witness for Wayne and when I read the traitorous statement she had prepared for the case, I finished with Luca. How can I see a man whose mother I hate?'

'Hang on, I'm not too keen on Roger's mum but it didn't stop us getting married,' she says.

Look, I know she's trying to be helpful, but I don't have the patience.

'Rachel,' I start wearily, 'there's a bit of a difference between "not too keen" and your ex-colleague, your ex-friend, your boyfriend's mother and another woman giving evidence against you in a sexual discrimination case.'

She sighs. She's got the point, I think. She doesn't know what to say. She doesn't want to have to deal with my misery. She spends too much time running from her own dark thoughts to blow it all by acknowledging mine. And then it comes.

'Cheer up, Emma.' *Fuck off.*

'Why?' I ask.

'You'll feel better,' she says.

'You mean you'll feel better,' I say.

'Yes, I will. I don't want to think of you on your own there, feeling unhappy.'

'Oh, right. You want me to feel happy to make you feel better?' I ask.

'Listen, I am trying to help,' she says, puzzled that her failsafe advice to 'cheer up' has failed.

'Well, if you really want to help, please don't tell me to cheer up. It's not that easy and, if it were, don't you think I'd have tried it?'

'I suppose so,' she says, sounding despondent. I feel guilty.

'Enough of me,' I say, 'how are you?'

The conversation proceeds smoothly from here but I know I won't be picking up the phone to her until I feel a hell of a lot better.

Admonitions to 'cheer up' are not the worst of it. Some people's aversion to acknowledging their own pain is so great that they are more aggressive in their words of comfort. Claudia actually manages to drag me out one night. I look normal from the outside, a little haggard and with a greyish skin tone, but I could pass for a member of the human race without too many questions. Our mutual friend, Karen, is having a girls' night in and I am lured by promises of spliff, booze and bawdy conversation. Actually, I am lured more than anything by the spliff. I haven't been out to score as even in my mental state I am wise enough to know that the down experienced the day after smoking might render me suicidal. I haven't had a smoke for about three weeks, but the idea of going to bed comatose for a change is very appealing. Claudia thinks it's an improvement that I am venturing from my flat; she thinks I am ready to re-enter the world. I haven't mentioned my prime motivation for leaving the sanctuary of my home in case she tries to be sensible and tell me what I already know: I'm going to feel a lot worse tomorrow. I don't care. I just want to escape from reality now.

The first person I see is Lisa, who I know quite well and who also works in recruitment. She's OK, not quite my cup of tea, a bit too driven for me – always out and about. The kind of person who makes arrangements three weeks ahead, often with two arrangements a night. I don't know who she sees as I would not describe her social skills as exceptional. I suppose she sees other busy people who like to have the security of knowing on Monday morning exactly what they will be doing for the next week or so. You know before, I was talking about me not wanting the silence to think? Well, my theory is that people like Lisa can't bear to be alone, hence the compulsion to ensure that they are out every goddam night of the week. Lisa's worst nightmare would be to stay in on a Saturday night. To have to stay in and contemplate being a social failure on the one night of the week when everyone else in the world is out having a fabulous time would be simply unthinkable.

Anyway, she tells me she has heard about the case from Karen and wants to know more. Once I have started, I am off, and before I know it I have confessed to feeling severely depressed, and then I tell her that this is the first time I have been 'out' (excluding the newsagents) for nearly a month.

'You really should pull yourself together,' she says. 'You can't just sit around feeling sorry for yourself. You need to pick yourself up, get out there and make it happen.'

I am too depressed to stick up for myself and say what I want to say, so I sink into the sofa and blink back my tears.

If I were not depressed, this is what I would have had the nerve and energy to say to Lisa: 'Oh my God. You mean it's that easy? I don't have to sit as a prisoner in my flat? I can go out and party and enjoy myself? Why didn't I think of that? So when I wake up with no energy and a pain in my heart, I should bounce out of bed and get out there? Oh my God! All this time I have spent feeling utterly miserable and worthless and all I had to do was just get out there and make it happen. You're a genius. That had never occurred to me.' Once she realised that I was being sarcastic, I would go on, 'Have you ever been depressed? Or don't you let yourself? Why don't you just keep on running, hoping that if you don't sit still for a moment, you won't actually feel anything at all? If you don't accept your own sadness, why should you accept mine?' And finally, 'Would you tell someone who is physically ill, say, someone that had MS, to just get up and get out there and pull themselves together? Or are you still from the Dark Ages and believe that mental illness is all in the mind and, as such, does not really exist?'

Well, maybe next time. If I'm not depressed.

A Day in the Life of a Depressed Person

My days at the moment go like this. I often self-induce my wake up as the dreams I have are not usually about having sex with Tom Cruise but nightmares about being chased by an axe-murderer. I awake feeling disorientated for a moment, and when I realise another day is upon me: gloom. I lie there for another hour or so, immersed in misery and without the desire to officially start the day. Eventually, at around, say, 11 a.m., I am finally motivated to move by nicotine cravings and, if I am feeling particularly indulgent, a cup of tea. Once I have had a few cigarettes, I realise there is nothing that I want to do today and so I go back to bed, where I lie immobile for another four hours. I listen to the radio and occasionally weep if I hear something faintly tragic. Even a sentimental commercial can set me off. In the evening, I watch the television, speak to some 'safe' friends and then return to the sack. As you can see, physically, I am pretty much horizontal. Mentally, I am all over the place, specialising mainly in self-torment. Emotionally, I am in pain – actual physical pain.

How long will I continue to feel this way? At the moment it seems like this is the way it is always going to be. I try to think back on happier times, but all I can conclude is that happy times are actually pointless since they always seem to have a sad ending, thus soiling them forever.

Now, you're reading this and doing one of two things: (1) relating to everything I say, in which case I extend my sympathy as you are obviously also suffering from anything from low to medium level depression. You can comfort yourself that you are not severely depressed as, if you were, you would not have the concentration to sit and read this novel. *Or*, more likely, since apparently only 10 per cent of the population is depressed at any one time, (2) you are thinking that I am a depressed misery guts, in which case you will fall into one of two further categories: (i) you've been depressed before but because you are happy now you are unable to relate to how I am feeling. It's like childbirth, where you soon forget the pain of giving birth so completely that you are unable to recall it, or (ii) you've never been depressed.

The fact is that I am trapped and there ain't nothing I can do except dwell on the fact that everyone else in the world is happy, sussed and living life to the full.

I decide a visit to the doctor is in order. I don't want pills, I just want a note that will be admissible in evidence that says that as a result of my dismissal from Search I am suffering from depression, for which I expect monetary compensation. I tell my lawyer what I am doing and he says it is a good idea. I see a doctor who I have not met before. She looks very young, mid-twenties, and inexperienced. I tell her that I have been sacked and that as a result I am suffering from depression. Maybe I am looking for some type of counselling, someone who doesn't mind sitting with me while I pour out a load of unacceptable emotions and who is trained to know that telling me to 'cheer up' helps no-one but the person who says it. She doesn't, however, mention counselling but is quite insistent that I take a Prozac-style anti-depressant called Seroxat.

'It's excellent,' she says. 'We've had very good reports from patients taking it.'

'Yes, I'm sure you have. I just don't want to numb out on pills at the moment. If I get much worse and it goes on for longer than, say, three months, then I might.'

'There are very few side effects from these anti-depressants and they only take a couple of weeks to work,' she persists.

'Look, I am sure they are fine for some people. It's just that what's happened with my boss, my boyfriend and his mother has really upset me and this is how I am dealing with it. Taking pills isn't going to make it go away, it will just delay the pain until I stop taking them,' I say, feeling indignant at the doctor's insistence that I take these tablets.

Why aren't we allowed to be unhappy? I am coming to the conclusion that depression is socially unacceptable, and as I take myself home to bed, I conclude that it is the best place for me, from everyone's perspective.

Part Four

The Present

The Wanderer Returns

The depression lasts six weeks. Miraculously, it suddenly lifts and I am able to function again. Two things help. The first is a call from Sharon, personnel manager of one of Search's clients, with whom I got on particularly well. I tell her the whole Wayne story and she is furious, swearing never to use Search again. Two days later she calls me and asks whether I would like to temp for them. I name my price, substantially higher than the agency rate, and she agrees. The work is secretarial and lightweight, which is perfect for me as it gives me head space to figure out what I *really* want to do. I go for lunch with Sharon every day and we run through all the possibilities of what I might want to do with the rest of my life. I give her a brief rundown on my job history, including all of my various incarnations.

'I feel so disillusioned with the world of work. I just wish, all those years ago at seventeen, I'd given the matter more thought and received some guidance.'

Sharon is quiet, then, 'Why don't you become a careers adviser?'

'Not a bad idea,' I say, thinking about the irony of her suggestion. 'Not much money, though,' I add.

'You don't know that. You could train up, get some good qualifications, work freelance, when you want, and think of the job satisfaction!' She's getting quite excited. 'Listen, Emma, if you want money, you could always go back to law.'

We both laugh.

'With the hours they work in the City, I'd probably earn more per hour at McDonald's.'

'Think about it,' she says.

'I will.'

It's actually quite nice getting up in the morning and having somewhere to go. I like mixing with people again during the day, and the repartee with the other secretaries in the office is superb, as long as you don't mind having the piss taken out of you, which I don't as I dish it back plenty.

Every day feels like a celebration of the fact that I am no longer depressed. I am now free to leave my prison; I can go out and face the world again. I can get dressed without feeling so exhausted that I need to return to bed. I can face returning telephone calls, and I even find I can initiate a few. It really is like coming round after a serious illness.

Two weeks after starting work, I come home to find Simon sprawled on the sofa, surrounded by bags overflowing with his possessions. I can tell he's pissed and stoned.

'What's all this?' I ask.

'I'm back,' he announces.

'Oh, right,' I say, walking towards my bedroom and closing the door behind me.

A few minutes later, I hear a meek tapping at the door. I stay silent. I don't want to see or speak to him. More tapping.

'Emma, please can I come in?' he persists. I sit on my bed, mildly panicking. I have lost all trust in our friendship and fear that it is now beyond repair. Shit. What am I going to say to him?

'Come in then,' I say, grudgingly.

He sits next to me on the bed.

'I've left Martin,' he says. 'He turned into Lawrence.'

'Oh, right' I say, with the attitude of someone who's just said 'Excuse me, I think you've mistaken me for someone who gives a shit.'

'So will we be expecting an incessant phone barrage for the next two months?' I ask.

'You're not being very sympathetic, you know.'

'You mean like you've been over the last three months?'

'I thought you wanted to be left alone.'

'Don't bullshit me, Simon. I would have loved a close friend to rely on during my weeks of depression, so please don't try to make out that I pushed you away. And now you come back and think that everything is going to be OK between us, but it isn't. You let me down and I can't forget that.' I feel choked with tears but wish to avoid appearing vulnerable in front of him. 'Can you leave please' I say, before I start crying.

'No,' he says. 'We're gonna sort this out.'

He just stands there, hanging on to my bedroom door, while I lie on the bed, turned away from him, with tears rolling down my face.

After waiting for a while longer in silence, he leaves my room and quietly closes the door.

Then the front door slams. I sob into my pillow, feeling wretched at the waste of our friendship and disappointment at how it was between us and how it could have been. I am not just crying for him, but for all the times I have felt let down and disillusioned by people I considered friends. I think of Wayne, then Tina, and my best friend at junior school who invited everyone but me to her house for an end of term party.

An hour later, there's another knock on the door. Without waiting for an answer this time, Simon appears with a tray. He looks sheepish as he puts it down on my bed. He hands me a beautifully rolled five-skin spliff.

'I'm really, really sorry. I've been a selfish cunt. Will you smoke a pipe of peace with me?'

I am looking at the tray: there's an Indian takeaway, flowers, magazines, wine and a card. I pick up the card and read what he has written. *Emma, forgive me. I love you and promise I won't let you down again.* I am finding it hard to swallow and tears spring to my eyes.

'You have to apologise on your knees,' I say.

He gets down on his knees.

'Actually, I'd prefer to do it on my stomach,' he says, lying prostrate in front of me on the floor.

'One thing,' I say, reaching for the lighter. 'Do it again and you ain't never coming back.'

He looks at me uncomfortably. 'Don't push it, Emma.'

'I'm not. I mean it.' A short silence follows. 'I've spent the last few months thinking back over my work career and how I've allowed myself to be treated. You know what? I allowed myself to be treated like shit, not just by Wayne, but all the way along. And I can't believe I put up with it. One thing I've learnt over the last month or so is that it's up to me to teach people how to treat me. And I'm telling you now, I didn't appreciate you just fucking off like that. This friendship isn't a one way street; I felt let down by you when I needed your support. You've done this before, when you've met someone and just dumped your friends, only to expect everyone to be there for you when you break up. I give support to you and I expect support back from you.'

'I'll smoke to that. Now give me the spliff!'

'So what happened to Mart?'

'Oh God, he was a really bossy old bore and I didn't see why I should put up with it a minute longer, especially when I've got my own flat here. As it was *his* flat, he always got to decide what we watched on telly.'

'You mean he didn't let you watch *Neighbours*?' I say. 'He's not as bad as I thought.'

'He hates soaps and now I've totally missed out on weeks of *Emmerdale* and I don't know what the fuck's going on.'

'Listen, does it get any worse than not letting you watch *Emmerdale* and *Neighbours* as I think he sounds very tolerant. I would bin anyone immediately if I found out that that was their preferred TV choice.'

'OK. But not even *EastEnders*, Emma.'

'Oh, I take it all back. That is completely unreasonable. Do you want a plot update?'

'Yeah, but later. I need to bitch first.'

'Sure, go ahead,' I say, lazily stretching back on my bed, taking a slug of wine and inhaling deeply and painfully on the never-ending spliff.

'He likes listening to opera and is very snotty when I want to put on my Britney CD. I'm not particularly keen on his fucking opera but I listen to it, but when it comes to him doing the compromising, he's not interested. The only thing we could agree on was Babs. And we always had to be at his flat. He never wanted to come here.'

'But I thought you loved the luxury of his flat?'

'Well, I did. But he's so ridiculously house proud and precious about all his luxuries that, ultimately, I would have been more comfortable in a squat. At least I could have put my feet up without worrying whether I'd be causing thousands of pounds worth of damage. Him and that fucking coffee table. He doesn't know yet that I accidentally knocked one of the legs and dented it. He'll be more devastated about that than he was about me leaving him. Actually, if I think about it, I really do believe he cares more about the coffee table's legs than he does about mine.'

'Well, your legs aren't your best point, Simon.' His legs are so spindly that at no point between ankles and bollocks do they meet. 'I'm sure he loves your penis.'

'Only because the table doesn't have one. I'm sure he'd love that one more. It would be a designer penis, made from marble, ten inches high and part of a limited edition.'

'I take it you're not walking out on a fabulous sex life. Surely you're not doing anything silly like that?'

'What? You mean like you and Luca?'

I am too numb from the spliff and wine to feel anything more than a twinge.

'Well, that wasn't quite that straightforward,' I say, remembering the last time we made love.

'Neither is this. He even kept his CDs in alphabetical order.'

'I thought you liked anal.'

'And that's another thing. The last three weeks or so, his idea of a wild night is going to the theatre and cuddling up in bed with a copy of *Classic Car* magazine. The passion only lasted a month. I want it to last for ever. I know that's impossible but I didn't imagine that the ravaging part of the relationship would be quite so short. He's such an old fuddy duddy, boring, middle-aged git and I don't intend to sell myself quite so short at the prime of my life. The worst thing was that he was so fucking possessive. He hated going to bars and I'd stopped insisting, since every time we went anywhere gay, he was convinced that I was eyeing up other men. The only safe place to be was the flat, as long as I didn't express admiration for anyone on the telly.'

'That must have been very hard for you,' I say, knowing that Simon is incapable of watching TV without classifying men as dogs or tigers.

'Oooh, it's heaven to be home,' he says, crawling onto my bed.

'It's nice to have you back.'

It only takes four hours to catch up on the rest of our news.

The Lucky Break

I turn up at work the following day feeling fuzzy headed and tired. I'm getting too old for these mid-week binges. My mobile rings at lunchtime. It's Peter, my lawyer, to remind me that the tribunal is in a week's time. It has been deferred on request from Wayne's solicitors as the original date clashed with his divorce hearing.

'Do you know any local papers that would be interested in attending the hearing?' he asks.

My heart flutters as I list all the papers in which Search advertises for jobs. I've never been in print before, apart from my name appearing in *The Times* all those years ago when I passed my law finals.

'It's really happening, isn't it?' I ask Peter.

'Unless Wayne decides to settle, then yes. Are you OK about standing up and doing your bit?'

'I'm looking forward to it,' I say, sounding more confident than I feel.

In the afternoon, I get a call on my mobile from Mr Fox, who sold the business to Wayne. 'What's all this I hear about you suing Wayne?' he asks.

'What has he told you?' I want to know.

'He said you were making lots of personal calls and he gave you plenty of warnings but you chose to ignore them.'

'Then why are you ringing me?'

'I was upset when I found out you weren't there any more. You were good at your job and I am disappointed to hear that you abused the trust he placed in you.'

'Well I am disappointed that you have no trust in me.'

'Since you've left, profits have gone right down and he's delaying paying me my monthly instalments for the business. He's employed one of the temps to do your job. Do you remember miserable Rhona? I never rated her. Well, she's taken over. I spoke to her earlier today when I popped in there for my money. She said you have really hurt Wayne by suing him. What are you playing at?'

'Has he put you up to ringing me?' I ask.

'Don't be ridiculous. The business, which I built up over thirty years, is now going down the tubes fast and I can't quite believe that you're helping it on its way. I am appalled at the way you people are ruining a perfectly good business.'

'Actually, Dennis, I am suing him for sexual harassment and I have no intention of dropping the case so that you can cling onto your romantic memories of Search in its prime.'

There is silence on the other end of the phone. I have never been even remotely cheeky to Mr Fox before. In fact, I have never called him by his first name before. Despite the fact that he could be an annoying tosser, he was basically a decent person and I understood the rules. Treat him with respect and he would see that you were alright. I worked for him for a year without any major arguments, and I was certainly never cheated over money. I suddenly felt sentimental about his breed of old-fashioned boss. It was a pain calling him Mr Fox but I was suddenly aware of how well those boundaries worked. He never bought us ice-creams, but then he never talked about his wife's masturbation habits or commented on my legs or breasts, either.

'Hello,' I say, 'are you still there?'

'I need to think about this,' he says quietly. 'Can I call you this evening?'

'If you want, but I am not prepared to discuss the details of the case,' I say, sensibly deciding to be wary of his interest in my claim.

'I understand, Emma. I shall call you later. Are you still living at the same place?'

'Yes. Do you still have the number?'

'Surely.'

I get home to find an application form for my part-time course in career counselling. I am so excited at the thought of turning up at my old school, seeing all those fresh-faced schoolgirls and helping them to find out what they really want to do and encouraging them to actually believe they can do what they want.

I include my time at Search on the application form and marvel at how all my many jobs have served a purpose after all. I make a (private) list of all my different careers: babysitter, birthday party entertainer, shop assistant, painter and decorator, care assistant, receptionist, secretary, publishing executive, temp controller, waitress, cook, barmaid, warehouse worker, television researcher, market researcher, letting agent, PR assistant, court clerk, English language teacher, customer services representative, dental assistant, pear picker, kitchen porter, conference organiser, candle-maker and lawyer. I have worked for local newsagents and large department stores. I have worked at a large City law firm, a small West End firm and in-house at a suburban property firm and a wanky Notting Hill media agency. I have worked for publishers, surveyors, financial advisers, accountants and doctors. I've worked at the BBC, *The Guardian*, Sadlers Wells and the Natural History Museum.

I realise that it would be foolish to list all these jobs on my application form for fear of being classified insane. I do, however, refer to some of my more colourful careers on the separate A4 sheet in the 'why I want to be a career counsellor' section. I say that although these jobs proved not to be long-term career options for me, I would like to use my experience for the good of society so that others take a less circuitous and tortuous route to job satisfaction.

I finish the application form and decide to take a long bath. As I lie soaking in the bubbles, feeling thoroughly worthy, I hear the phone ringing. Simon brings it into the bathroom with a tea towel over his face (for his sake rather than mine). 'It's a man,' he whispers. 'Sounds gruff, posh and horny,' he adds as he passes me the phone.

'Dennis Fox here.'

'Oh, hello, Mr Fox' I say, trying not to splash the bath water. It doesn't feel appropriate to be speaking to your ex-boss with no clothes on, but before I can stop him, he launches in.

'I've been thinking long and hard about whether I should tell you this,' he starts.

Keeping very still, I try to imagine what on earth he could be about to tell me. Surely not a declaration of love, given his devotion to his truly saintly wife Maureen, three grown-up children and five grandchildren. 'I would like your assurance that what I am about to tell you is strictly confidential. I would like you to give me your word that this so.'

I am flattered that he is willing to take my word.

'I give you my word,' I say, with as much gravitas as I can manage while naked in the bath with a rubber duck floating by.

'Yes, I know you are an honourable girl and that is why I feel compelled to tell you what I have heard. I found you honest and fundamentally trustworthy, if a little volatile.'

'Thank you, Mr Fox' I say, eager to hear what he has to say.

'Please, call me Dennis. Well, soon after I sold the business I bumped into some old friends of mine at the golf club. I mentioned to one of the chaps there that I had sold the business to Wayne Burns and this chap laughed and called Wayne a crafty little bugger. On enquiring further, I discovered the reason why. This man knows Wayne's uncle and, apparently,

Wayne was asked to leave the family business due to some rather unsavoury habits.'

'What do you mean' I ask, sitting up, water splashing noisily around me.

'Well, I think he rather made a nuisance of himself with the young ladies there and his father had enough of it. It was all hushed up and the family paid Wayne off. With the money, he bought Search, perhaps hoping to meet more willing ladies there. I feel rather guilty about it. He did make some inappropriate remarks about meeting ladies through Search during the negotiations, but I chose to ignore them. In retrospect, this was perhaps rather foolish.'

I am more shocked that Mr Fox has confessed to doing something foolish than I am about the reason Wayne was forced to leave the family business. The fact that he has harassed other women in the past has an air of predictability about it.

'God. I don't know what to say.'

I am shrivelling up now but realise that it would be too noisy to get out of the bath so I am forced to raisin it in the water.

'I am not entirely shocked. I don't flatter myself that a middle-aged man suddenly develops lecherous habits at the sight of me.'

'Well I wouldn't know about that,' he says gruffly. 'When he told me he had been forced to sack you, the thought did cross my mind that something unfortunate night have happened, especially when Tina refused to talk to me about it.'

'Tina's giving evidence against me,' I say.

'Look, it's not appropriate for me to get involved in the details.' He never did want to get involved in inter-office relations in case anyone became emotional, a worst case scenario for Mr Fox and one to be avoided at all times.

'What do I do with this information then?' I ask.

'Well, that's up to you as long as you never mention that it came from me, as it was passed to me by a friend. And I'd rather not enter the fray, as it were. It might upset Maureen. She thought you were a super girl.'

'I understand. Can I tell my lawyers that it came from an anonymous source?'

'Certainly. Well, I'd better be going.'

'Thanks very much for letting me know.'

'Good luck.'

And with that I pull the plug.

The Worst Job in the World

Lorenzo and a female friend of his have come over for dinner. Amazingly, Lorenzo and Simon are friends again. Simon is cooking which means that we'll be eating mushroom risotto – the only thing he knows how to cook. It's delicious, as long as he remembers to buy the mushrooms. I run into the lounge excitedly, dripping in my bathrobe, to tell them the news.

'Fantastica bellissima,' says Lorenzo.

'That's amazing,' says Simon.

'Well, it is and it isn't. It's not fantastic if I can't use it,' I say. 'Legally, the information is classified as "hearsay" and we won't be able to use it in the case unless it is substantiated by someone or something.'

'We need to find the women who worked at his company,' says Simon, with determination.

'I don't even know the name of his dad's company, and I can hardly turn up and ask if I can interview all the women who work there.'

'You're being negative,' says Simon.

'No dear, simply practical. I'll ring my lawyer in the morning and see what he says. So let's drink to that!' I say, pouring the wine.

'What do you do, Laura?' I ask over dinner.

'I'm in personnel.'

'The enemy,' I say, and luckily everyone laughs.

Job advertisements for personnel officers should read 'Are you insincere, two-faced and capable of acting as the boss's henchman without wincing?' in order to attract the right person. Perhaps my view of personnel officers is coloured by my experience at Coopers, where the personnel ladies were so unctuously and gratuitously synthetic that they were practically flammable. Their favourite trick was to get you into their office for a cosy chat, milk you for information and then inform your boss. Eager as I am to spill the contents of my heart to anyone who will listen, I realised that Sue Grange did not have my best interests at heart. My gay friend at Coopers, Thomas, was not as wise and fell for the cups of tea, closed door, comfy armchair and bedside manner of Ms Grange. He confessed that he was down after the end of a relationship (at least he didn't mention that it was with a man) and that he had been put on a course of anti-depressants by the doctor, hence his somewhat lacklustre performance at work over the last month. Two weeks later, the partner for whom he worked asked him whether he was 'still on drugs'.

'Who do you work for?' asks Simon, who is looking for a job that will get him out of the house. He has decided that he wants to be with other people during the day.

'A distribution company,' she says.

This evening could be hard work.

'What do they distribute?' asks Simon.

'Car parts,' she says.

Now we realise why she wasn't very forthcoming with the information. It is a complete conversation killer.

Lorenzo comes to the rescue. 'Yeah, but she hates her job, don't you, Laura?'

'Well, I don't mind the job, it's just the bosses and working conditions I hate.' My personal challenge for the evening is to get Laura to open up. I believe that I can get anyone to talk, it's just a matter of asking the right questions. Sometimes, such as now, only one word is needed.

'Why?' I ask.

'Well, we work from eight-thirty till six with only forty

minutes for lunch. In reality, though, there is so much work that I stay until seven. We don't get any sick pay, only the statutory minimum which is fifteen pounds per week. We only get fifteen days holiday a year, which is terrible for me as I don't get to see my family in Milan very often. Everybody has to clock in and clock out – warehouse people, office staff, everyone.'

'How insulting!' I say. Now there's no stopping her.

'We're stuck in an industrial park and there's nowhere to go for lunch. There isn't even a canteen or any communal area. If you want to have a private chat with someone, you have to go to the loo. At the back of the warehouse are six tables for two hundred people to eat their lunch from. They don't even have a kettle, only an expensive drinks dispenser which makes the most disgusting drinks you can imagine.'

'What else?' I am eager to hear more of what sounds like the worst place to work in the UK. I can't believe such things go on.

'The managing directors listen to calls and tape them. I often hear a clicking on the phone during calls. I am covering someone who is away on maternity leave and they send her work to do at home. Apparently, she had to pay for her own computer and the cost of e-mail. They think they are doing her the favour by giving her maternity leave. No talking is allowed in the warehouse, so these poor bastards walk around like robots. If the boss doesn't like the look of someone, if they are black or raise health and safety questions, for example, they are sacked.'

'Do you do the sacking?' Simon asks.

'Yes,' she says, although at least she looks shamefaced. 'The racism is terrible and I don't understand it as the managing directors are Asian. If we're interviewing someone and they're black, one of the directors points to the skin on his hands, which I am supposed to interpret as being the wrong colour. It's very distracting and I just ignore him, but they do have the final say and they rarely employ any black people.'

'Why the hell do you work there?' I want to know.

'It's not easy finding work here, especially as I am Italian and my language isn't perfect. And I do like the actual job.' I am not convinced that this is a good enough reason, but the girl obviously has low self-esteem so I don't push it.

'I am getting worried, though. The warehouse is a complete hazard. The shelves are top heavy with parts, you know, panels, bonnets and radiators, and I fear that one day there will be a terrible accident. And the fire exits are blocked.'

'You should report them,' says Simon, 'anonymously. If you don't, I will.'

She seems scared. I see her looking at Simon and me. I am suing my boss and Simon is keen to inform on hers.

'The maternity cover ends in two months so can't you wait till I've left? Actually, I think once I've left, I'll do it,' she concedes.

'Good! Now, who wants coffee?' I say.

I call my lawyer first thing in the morning. His first reaction is not what I expect. 'Get the father's number for me and I'll ring him and let him know what his son has been up to.'

I am surprised at his approach. It doesn't seem very legal. I point this out to him.

'I bet you he's in awe of his father and he may be keen to settle with pressure from him. The other thing I am going to do is apply to the tribunal and see if there are any cases filed with Wayne's name. Even if the case has been settled or dropped, it will still be registered with the industrial tribunal's central register.'

'Do whatever you need to do, but let me know as soon as you hear anything.'

'You bet I will.'

Peter, at least, seems to be enjoying himself.

Ten minutes later, my mobile goes. It's Peter again.

'I've got some good news.'

'That was quick!'

'I haven't checked with the tribunal yet about Wayne's history but I have opened up this morning's post. They've withdrawn Tina's statement. This is very unusual. I would guess that she changed her mind about supporting him.'

I think of Tina and then Luca and then I tell him that I have to go and I'll call him back. I rush to the loo and sit in front of the mirror and cry. I try to sob quietly but I am so emotional at the news. It's all been such a waste, it's all been so unnecessary. Things could have been so different if only Wayne hadn't sacked me and Tina hadn't given evidence. I would still be with my darling Luca.

Not a day has gone by when I haven't thought about him, despite my efforts to push him to the back of my mind. I normally have the ability to banish undesirable people from my thoughts. This time, though, I don't have the luxury of hating him. Just his mother. I went through a phase of calling his answering machine at home during the day to hear his voice. I don't have any photos of him to pore over and in one mad fit I burned all the little love notes he'd left me. I removed every trace of him from my flat, but not, unfortunately, from my heart or mind. When we were together, it seemed like he had always been around. I couldn't remember my life before him. And yet when he was gone, it seemed as if he had never existed. We'd never hung out with my friends. Only Simon knew him and he also disappeared from my life at around the time I split up with Luca. After a week of self-indulgent wailing with close friends, I had decided that I was going to banish him from my thoughts, yet I still can't go anywhere near the part of the Heath where we hung out that last weekend. That's the problem with taking boyfriends to places you love. I went through the seeing him everywhere stage (only, of course, it wasn't him) and I went through the Gloria Gaynor routine.

The one stage I missed was the tears. I never shed a tear over him, due to the emotion-numbing depression, perhaps. But now, sitting in this nasty little loo, I cry and cry.

I hear a knock on the door. It is Sharon.

'Emma. Are you OK?' she asks.

'Not really. I'll be out in a minute,' I say, wiping the make-up from my face. I look terrible.

'Your mobile has been going,' she says.

I unlock the door.

'God, Emma, are you alright?'

'Shall we have lunch together?'

'Love to,' she says, putting her arms round me.

I feel pitiful.

I sit back at my desk and fumble for my phone in my handbag. A missed call from Peter. I call him back. He is beside himself.

'We've got the bugger,' he says.

'Fabulous,' I say, without emotion. He is undeterred.

'This isn't his first claim. He was cited in a case about a year and a half ago. The application was withdrawn a week after it was lodged, which probably means it was swiftly settled. I can't believe the idiot is prepared to fight this case. Persuading Tina Moretti to back him up was his trump card, now he hasn't even got that. And thanks to your old boss, we hold the mightiest trump card of all.'

I am starting to get excited.

'When's the tribunal? Do we tell him we know about the previous application? How much do you think I can get?'

'Next week. Not sure. I'm going for ten grand. I think there could be considerable mileage in dropping the bomb-shell news of the previous application during the tribunal hearing. Now, Emma, I have told you before that if we do proceed to a hearing, it's not going to be nice. His lawyers will cross-examine you and, not to put too fine a point on it, they will try and insinuate that you are a tart. We need some clean time to run through the possible routes along which they will try to lead you and you need to be steady and consistent in your answers. Now that Tina's statement has been withdrawn, that should help things, but he's bound to lie and twist things and you need to be prepared for matters to turn nasty.'

Guess what? I am still excited. I am looking forward to doing battle with Wayne. I am going in there all guns blazing.

'You'll have no problems with me, Peter. He ain't gonna get away with pinning anything on me.'

I've already started the courtroom drama movie lingo.

'Atta girl.'

So has he.

The Tribunal

The tribunal hearing is tomorrow and Peter can't believe that Wayne hasn't tried to settle. After obtaining his father's telephone number but failing to speak to the man himself, Peter left a matter-of-fact message on the answering machine bringing Wayne's parents up to date on their son's latest activities. Unsurprisingly, they have not called back and I don't know whether to feel sad, mad or glad at the thought of these elderly Jewish people coming home from bridge one night to find a message from a strange man with a Liverpudlian accent telling them that their son is the respondent in a sexual harassment case.

Simon is insistent that he comes with me to the tribunal.

'You just love the drama, don't you?' I ask.

'Actually, I just want to support you and be there for you in a way that I failed to do over the summer.'

'And you love the drama,' I persist.

'I wouldn't miss it for the world,' he says. 'Now, let's run through this again. What are you going to say when they ask you about your short skirts?'

'I suppose I'll ask them whether I deserve to be raped as well.'

'Come on, Emma. This is serious,' he whines.

I've borrowed a black trouser suit from Claudia and as I iron a white shirt (the only sensible piece of clothing I own), I realise that, in the excitement, I haven't thought about Luca all day. I wish I could ring him now and tell him about all the developments. He'd be really excited, I think, and then I correct myself. He probably wouldn't give a shit. He's probably pleased to be rid of this troublesome girl. He's probably sitting round Mama's table right now eating pasta with his simple, sussed, straightforward new girlfriend. They are probably all giving huge sighs of relief that their lives are no longer intertwined with mine.

A huge sob rises from within me, completely unexpected, and before I know it the tears have come again. It is such a relief to cry. These tears have been inside me all this time, fighting for escape, and I didn't even know it. As I go through half a roll of loo paper, I feel sad. But the funny thing is that it feels OK being sad. I have finally acknowledged the loss I feel.

I wake at three-hourly intervals through the night with my rehearsed answers swirling around my mind. I manage to calm down and get back to sleep each time, and when I wake at seven I feel wired rather than tired.

I've already smoked five cigarettes by the time Simon wakes up. He eats breakfast while I watch, smoking. I apply a bit of make-up, though not too much, obviously. I have to strike a careful balance between looking attractive to male members of the tribunal panel and faking a demure, virginal appearance. I go for the made-up not-made-up look. It takes longer than you'd think.

'Come on, Emma. We've got a sex discrimination hearing to win.'

'Can't you appear for me? Tell everyone I am frightened and if they need me, I'll be under my duvet.'

He starts clucking and doing an hilarious chicken impression round the flat. I give in and we set off to the tube.

We get out at Russell Square and both immediately light up on leaving the station. As we approach the tribunal, it suddenly dawns on me that I will be seeing Wayne again. I shudder at the thought.

Peter is outside the tribunal. I have never seen him before. He makes up for the bad suit, bad shoes and appalling haircut by being warm and thoroughly enthusiastic and optimistic. He's practically jumping up and down.

'*The Mail* is sending someone and so is *The Ham & High*. I warned him. I did warn him.'

'Shit, Peter. I don't know if I can handle this.'

'Too late for that now. You're going to be fine. We can't lose. I'll look after you and object if things get too personal.'

I introduce Simon, but Peter is not listening. He is staring down the street.

'Emma, quick. Is this them?'

I look at the approaching figures.

'Oh my God. It's Wayne and Bert.'

'Which ones?'

'The short, bald ones'

They walk straight past us. Wayne points at me. 'You are a foolish girl,' he says.

'Piss off,' I say.

Bert shakes his head wearily at me.

The hearing is in half an hour. I'd have taken a valium but I didn't want to fail for undue hesitation, as I had done on my first driving test. I feel a mixture of adrenalin and excitement as well as a sense of unreality; a feeling that this isn't happening to me, that I am in a soap opera. Every three minutes, a wave of fear comes over me and poor Simon has to reassure me. I can see that Peter and Simon are having a wonderful time.

Twenty minutes to go and the press arrive. Peter introduces himself to *The Ham & High* woman while *The Mail* journalist pushes straight past him. Peter is jumping up and down again and decides to torment Wayne's lawyer by politely, yet smugly, informing him that the press are here.

He comes back outside looking serious.

'They've made an offer. That Wayne's not looking at all well.'

'How much?'

'Five thousand.'

'Not enough,' I say, as Simon whistles.

'Perhaps now would be an opportune moment to let him know that we know about the previous application.'

'Go for it,' I say, chewing off my last remaining fingernail. I look at my watch. Ten minutes to go. Now Simon is jumping up and down.

'Let's go in and watch the negotiations. We can't miss it. Come on, Emma.'

'I can't.'

'You'll regret it if you miss it. Think of the fact that you were sacked. Think of Tina. Think of Luca, for God's sake. You can't miss your moment of glory. Please, please can we go and watch Wayne squirm?'

'Oh alright,' I say, allowing myself to be dragged in by the arm.

My first emotion on seeing Wayne and Bert sitting on the bench in the reception area is pity. For some strange reason, I feel sorry for them both. Peter walks towards me, feigning a cool, relaxed demeanour but unable to hide the jaunty, cocky expression on his face.

'I've been a bit of an arsehole. I've taken Wayne and his lawyer through a series of uncomfortable scenarios. I've pointed out the effect of losing this case on his divorce, the effect of the negative publicity on his recruitment agency, the public embarrassment and shame for his family, the harsh penalties he will face for being a serial sexual harasser. I also pointed out that if he thought I was being nasty now, he was going to get a shock when we got into the hearing and I listed his pathetic misdemeanours to the panel of two women and a man. Believe me, he's not a happy bunny right now.'

I decide to overlook the use of my pet-hate phrase of 'not a happy bunny' and concentrate instead on more serious issues.

'How much did they go up to?'

'Seven five.'

'I want ten.'

'I've asked for twelve.'

'His family are minted. Let's go for fifteen,' says Simon.

Two minutes to go. Peter has spoken to the clerk and explained that we are in the middle of negotiations and can our case be put back by half an hour. The clerk looks disappointed but not altogether surprised. Peter has already explained to me that eighty per cent of cases are settled in this corridor.

I can't stand to watch any more and I walk outside into the autumn sunlight. I sit down on the steps, light another cigarette and watch other people going about their lives, completely unaware of the drama going on in my life. Simon joins me, reluctantly.

'I can't believe you are sitting out here and missing all the action.'

'I don't feel victorious, just sad.'

'Please, please, can't we go back inside?'

'Look, Simon, did you come here for me or for you? If you came for you, then go inside. If you came for me, then please shut up and sit down.'

Before Simon has a chance to sit down, Peter bursts through the doors. He comes running down the steps.

'We've done it,' he shouts. 'I got you ten plus my fees.'

Finally, I am the one jumping up and down, and it is only after I get home that I realise that although I have won the case, I have lost my ideal man in the process.

The Comeback

Three Months Later

Life is good at the moment. I like the variety. I temp three
days a week. I work freelance – it's better that way. I am
my own boss. I decide when I work, when I leave, who
I work for and how much I charge. Two days a week, I
work at the architects with Sharon, who has now become
a close and supportive friend. We are totally different. She's
from Moss Side in Manchester, with accompanying accent; a
stunning, mixed race, twenty-six-year-old, six-foot beauty. She
left school at fourteen, home at sixteen and moved to London.
She tells me that most of the guys with whom she grew up are
now dead, either through drugs or gang killings, and most of
the girls had several kids each by the time they were eighteen.
Meanwhile, she is office manager at this architect's practice
and has her own flat down the road from me. We have had
completely different upbringings, come from different parts
of England, we are different ages, races and religions, yet we
connect. There is an understanding between us as women that
transcends our diverse pasts.

One day a week I work at the estate agents round the corner
with my friend Martine. She's also very different to me. A
blonde-haired, blue-eyed, cockney; a smart, sassy, tough, no
bullshit, weight-lifting, pit-bull-terrier owner. If she doesn't
like you, she'll tell you exactly why in no uncertain terms. I
was standing at the bus stop with her once and a woman cursed
her for not giving her a cigarette. Martine was off. 'What did
you fucking say? Come here and say that you fucking bitch.'
Even I was scared. Yet she is one of the most sincere people I
know, and at least you know where you stand with her. Our

connection is humour and we spend most of the day killing ourselves laughing, putting on funny voices over the phone to customers.

And that is the wonderful thing about work. I bet you thought you'd never hear me say that. But it's true. The most wonderful thing about work is the people you meet. People that you would never come across in your usual social sphere. People that add to the richness of your life. In another sense, work is also a little like a surrogate family. There are people you hate, people you love, people with whom you argue, people in whom you confide, people who make you laugh, people who irritate you, people who compete with you, people you learn from, people who surprise you. A network of social interaction to distract you from your problems while adding a few new ones.

Listen, the work itself isn't wonderful. It's mostly typing; and yet I actually like audio typing. I find it meditative. Your eyes, your brain and your hands working in perfect harmony. The secretarial work also gives me brain space to study. I am now attending Birkbeck College two days a week, studying for a diploma in career counselling. I love it. It is such a pleasure to study something in which I am actually interested. The last time I studied something that stimulated me was my A-level English. When I studied law at university and then at law school, I was unable to focus on a word the lecturers were saying. I never asked a question and I never volunteered an answer. On this course, however, I am an active and willing participant. I even enjoy writing the essays.

I bumped into Cynthia, one of the Search temps, the other day. She also does typing work in-house for them occasionally and she told me something that amused me. Apparently, the woman who replaced me as temp controller actually seems to fancy Wayne, but according to Cynthia, Wayne is too scared to do anything about it for fear of another sexual harassment case. The irony kills me. His motivation for buying the agency has finally materialised – a woman actually finds him attractive – and because of me he can't do anything about it.

It's still a pain not being able to have a lie-in whenever you want, especially as I had a bit of boozy night last night. I met up with the Coopers crew having not seen some of them for five years. As you can imagine, it's hard to keep up with everyone with whom I have ever worked. I was writing about my life at Coopers as part of a dissertation at college and I suddenly felt very nostalgic for the gang there. I had my best work lunchtimes with those guys. What are they up to? I have bi-annual phone updates with Tariq, but what the hell has happened to the others? Through a series of phone calls, Tariq and I gather the clan together. We meet in a French restaurant at eight o'clock. Our work histories are pretty diverse. Three of us strayed from law. The other two seem to be serving a life sentence.

Tariq went from immigration law to acting on behalf of trade unions against employers. Although he enjoyed this work, he was hungry for big money and moved into property development. He made a lot of money and then lost it all. He then decided to hit the world of sales, and judging by his 8 series BMW, he's done OK for himself. He alludes to a master plan but has the presence of mind to keep his dream to himself. He divorced his wife and is now living with a copper.

Tessa has also quit law and is working as an antiques dealer on behalf of some extremely wealthy Japanese clients. She loves her job, even though she has to get up at four in the morning. More dramatically, she has gone from a size twenty-four to a size eight (Weight Watchers, aerobics and liposuction), although unfortunately it doesn't seem to have helped her love life. She divorced her husband who turned out to be gay and has since had a series of disasters with dodgy geezers. She is currently single but very much on the market.

Alasdair has settled in Winchester where he works as a lawyer. He doesn't enjoy his job at all. The workload is so pressurised and the billing quotas so high that Philip, the most laid back person at Coopers, says that he doesn't even have time to chat to people in the office, let alone be nice to them. He accepts his fate on the basis of the lifestyle it affords him, and he saves his true passion, playing the guitar, for evenings and weekends. His ten-year on-off relationship is currently off, although I fully expect it to be on by the time I next see him.

Finally, Timmy. The success story. On paper. And by paper, I mean his name is on Coopers' notepaper. He made it to the giddy heights of partner. He has arrived. Only he doesn't look too happy about it. He has worked in the construction litigation department since qualifying and it shows on his face. Out of all of us, he looks the most worn. He says he hates his job but now he's got the big house in Battersea and all those mortgage payments to meet. I ask him whether he has ever thought of doing anything different. Yes, he says. About three years ago, he inherited a sizeable chunk of money. He had always dreamed of becoming a cameraman and he toyed with the idea of giving up law and going to cameraman school.

'Why didn't you?' we all want to know.

'Security,' he says. 'I know where I am at Coopers.' And then he looks sad. He's engaged to be married to another solicitor at Coopers.

It is amazing to see them all and we arrange to keep in touch. Out of all the people I have ever come across at work, I have never had more fun than with my fellow legal trainees, and the amazing thing about meeting up again was that we seemed to pick up effortlessly where we left off. Although we are deprived of the daily gossip that comes with working in a large company, reminiscing is almost as good, although definitely not as juicy. I suppose life isn't as juicy after your twenties full stop. Hopefully more stable, but less juicy.

As part of this move towards stability over the last few months, I have found my own flat to buy. Much as I have loved living with Simon through all our ups and downs, I have been seriously yearning for a flat of my own over the last few months, as well as knowing that I will need a place of my own from which to start my career counselling business. Simon's gutted; he doesn't have any savings and complains bitterly that he hasn't been sexually harassed (my deposit account having swelled considerably following Wayne's payout), until he finds a housing association flat in Putney for half the rent he's paying at present. As our time to depart the flat looms, we decide to have a flat-leaving party. Simon suggests inviting everyone who's ever been to the flat. I immediately think of Luca.

'What about Luca?'

'Are you mad? He dumped you!'

'You've got a lovely way of putting things.'

'OK, let's try this another way, what if brings his girl-friend?'

'He wouldn't.'

'You're right. That would be unlikely. Well, say you invite him and he doesn't reply, then you'll be gutted.'

'I'll give you that one. Anyway, if we invite everyone, does that mean Martin has to come.'

'He's not that bad.'

'You've changed your tune. You hated him a few months ago.'

'To be honest, I think I'd like to invite him to remind myself how happy I am to be single as opposed to living with that anal twat.'

'I want to invite Luca to remind myself of how happy I was with him. I'd love to see him again. If I move away from here, he'll never be able to contact me again.'

'You mean, should he come to his senses and realise that he has lost his perfect woman?'

'Exactly.'

'OK, invite authorised as long as you promise not to be rude to Martin.'

'What do you care if I'm rude to him?'

'True.'

So that is what we decide. Everyone is invited – friends, enemies and Luca. He doesn't reply and let me know whether he is coming. I don't tell anyone apart from Claudia and Simon that I have invited him so I don't have to share my torment at his lack of response with too many people.

It isn't until the morning of the party that I bitterly regret my decision to invite Luca and curse the fact that I didn't listen to Simon's very sensible reservations. As well as being stomach churningly nervous about actually having a party (Would everyone turn up? Would it be a success? Would people mix? Would we have enough booze? Who was actually going to do the food? Would we wreck the flat and lose our deposit? Would my bedroom turn into a dark room?), I now had to deal with the biggest worry of all: Would Luca turn up? Would he be alone? Would he want me back? As I have not heard from him, I occasionally reassure myself that it is unlikely that he will make an appearance.

When the party finally kicks off (with a vengeance), I find myself constantly monitoring my watch. As it gets later and later, I attempt to come to terms with the fact that Luca is unlikely to show up now, and somehow, despite this sad recognition, I start having a brilliant evening. Perhaps I have finally relaxed and given up. Anyway, it's hard not to have a good party when you simply follow the three fundamental party rules: great music, plenty to drink and, most importantly of all, introducing people. Unless everyone knows each other, introducing people is the crucial ingredient to hosting a fabulous party. People are too shy to go up and introduce themselves, yet meeting new people is, I'm sure, the main motivating factor for most party guests.

It is during this twenty-five-minute gap when I'm not wondering whether Luca will turn up that I see him across the
room, chatting to Simon. Suddenly, despite having drunk
pretty consistently since five o'clock in the afternoon, I completely lose my nerve and run for safety in the kitchen. Too
late. He's seen me and is heading towards me. My whole body
is wobbling now rather than just my legs.

'I'm pissed,' I say, by way of apology, as he approaches
me. It feels like the music has stopped; everyone fades into
the background.

'I'll get you some water.'

'I think I need another drink, actually.' I couldn't play it
cool even if I wanted to. 'I didn't think you were coming.'

'Neither did I until I returned to the country this evening
and found your invitation. I came straight round. I wanted to
come and pay my respects to the flat.'

'What about its occupants?'

'Sure. I've missed Simon. He's a great laugh,' he says,
smiling.

'You look gorgeous,' I say; he's had his hair cut into a
very short crop. He looks incredibly familiar, as well as a
(handsome) stranger.

'So do you.'

'Do you think so?'

'I always thought you were gorgeous.'

I don't know what to say to that.

'Can we talk somewhere?' he asks.

'If there's no-one having anal sex in my bedroom, we could
talk there.'

'That's the most bizarre invitation to a woman's bedroom
I've ever heard.' And we're laughing again.

Once we've prodded Martin awake and transferred him to
Simon's room, we sit down opposite each other on my bed.

'I've got a lot to say,' he says, looking nervous.

'I'm ready to listen.' I have dramatically sobered up.

But instead of speaking, he just sits and looks at me.

'I thought you had a lot to say?' I question him, smiling.

'I have. I just don't know where to start.'

'Well, can I just tell you that I settled with Wayne.'

'I know.'

'How?'

'The journalist from *The Mail* was a friend of mine.'

'You're joking?'

'No. My involvement with the case didn't end when we broke up. What happened with you and the case and us splitting up was a catalyst for a big shake-up in my life.'

'What do you mean?' I ask, sitting up straight.

'I was furious with my mother for what she did. I was angry with you for disappearing, and as you know, it made me question the whole relationship. But afterwards, I realised it was my mother more than anyone who jeopardised our relationship. I mean, what the hell was she thinking of giving evidence against my girlfriend, let alone her close work colleague? I started to question her whole motivation for doing what she was doing and I had to face some pretty unpleasant truths about her. I know she was worried about losing her job and then not keeping up the mortgage payments and then losing her home again, but I really don't think that is any excuse for what she did to you, as well as to us. At some level she must have known that it would put our relationship under the most terrible strain. She loves me, but it's too much. I didn't really let on to you how much I liked you. I kind of thought you realised from the way I was with you, but maybe I didn't really spell it out. But I think *she* realised how important you were becoming to me and I honestly don't think she liked it. She was jealous. She's tried to be everything to me and Mario and I just don't want that responsibility, that pressure. As things didn't work out between her and Dad, she made us the focal point of her life. Because her marriage didn't work out, she had to make me and Mario into everything. I always felt under so much pressure to be the good son for her, to make up for the fact that she had such a lousy husband. Italian mothers are pretty claustrophobic at the best of times, but she has just involved herself in every area of our lives.

'I mean, the first time I met you I came to pick up my watch, right? I didn't want her doing stuff like that for me, but she is such a strong personality, not domineering but forceful, let's say, that I just gave in and let her take over. Those bloody meals she cooked me every week. I didn't want them, but it was just easier to go along with it. I thought I should be grateful, but it was too much. I don't want that level of involvement. I want to be able to do my own thing and not be her little boy for the rest of my life. I feel sorry for Mario stuck at home still. We've started arguing about it. I am trying to encourage him to break free and do his own thing. He's studying accountancy because Mum thinks it's a good, safe, steady, secure profession, and he hates it but lacks the strength to fight back. He's fantastic at art, you know, and wanted to do graphic design, but Mum was totally against it and so now he's miserable and will end up spending the rest of his life doing a job he despises, just to keep Mum happy. It's like she's making him pay for the sins of his father, and he's so weak and dependent on her for everything, from money to having his bed made, he's pretty helpless. It really annoys me. He just wants an easy life, even if it means being unhappy.

'She's interfered in every relationship I've ever had and, luckily for her, before you came along she was still the most important woman in my life. If I want to do something which she doesn't want me to do, I always feel incredibly guilty, like I'm letting her down, and I'm fed up with it. I want to be my own person. I want to see my father without hearing what a fucking loser he is. Whatever he may have done, he is still my father. If I saw him, she always acted like it was this great betrayal and went on about "how can you want to spend time with him after what he's done to this family". But all this rebellion and anger has been so deeply buried until what happened with you. Realising that your mother doesn't always want the best for you is hard to accept, especially when you've been told your whole life that you are her *numero uno*; when your mum polishes your shoes and buys you expensive clothes even though she can't afford much for herself. It's too much. I don't want the guilt or the pressure. I confronted her with what I guessed were her motives, at least in part, for siding with Wayne against you. I pointed out that she could simply have refused to become involved, suggested he might even have respected her for it. He certainly couldn't have sacked her.'

Something dawns on me.

'Were you responsible for her withdrawing her statement?'

'Yes. We argued about it for weeks. It's been difficult and strained ever since. It's hard breaking away from parents, but that's what I am trying to do.'

I understand him, while also feeling terribly sorry for Tina. I don't know why but I do. I suppose it's because she's invested so much in her sons and it's all crumbling down. How can you face up to the fact that you don't want what makes your children happy? That must be a horrible realisation. And then I feel mildly sorry for little Mario, who will now receive a double dose of pressure.

We talk all night. I forget all about the party going on outside my room. Every now and then we are interrupted by people unaware of the heavy conversation going on, who blunder into the room, pissed, boisterous and happy.

At four o'clock, when everyone's gone home, I notice Luca is still wearing his shoes.

'You've still got your shoes on,' I say, smiling.

'I know the rules,' he replies immediately.

I sit at his feet and take them off and tell him that I'm going to hide them.

'Do you think we'll ever kiss again?'

'Definitely,' I say. 'I've been dreaming of it for the last five months.'

And he leans over and my dream becomes a heart-fluttering, skin-tingling reality.

I know I said I'd iron his socks if he came back to me, but somehow I think that's the last thing he'd want.

This time I'm not letting him go.